HEAVEN OR HELL?

By RICHARD ANDERSON

Written in English.

WITH GRATEFUL THANKS.

Chapter 1.   The beginning? Or the end?

Tuesday 09/06/09 started out like any other day for the vast majority of people. They would continue with their existence oblivious to the opportunities life has to offer, they would never know just how exciting life can be! Chris Gaskell smiled to himself, he knew without a doubt that before the end of the day there would be a small, select number of people who would never forget 09/06/09!

 As he opened all the major newspapers of the day to check that everything was in place he paused from the job at hand just long enough for a brief moment of reflection. He was always amazed, when he gave himself the luxury of thinking back, just how his life had changed beyond all recognition. He was healthy; he had a beautiful wife and a tranquil lifestyle.

 It had not always been so!

He was a padre in the army for many years and almost everyone who had met him during his time in the army commented on the ethereal nature of his demeanour. As he progressed within the army he found himself in Burma as a fitness trainer for some of the most elite fighting forces of the world! Quite how that had happened Chris was not too sure but happen it had! Chris had always been a devout man but he had had many times in his army life when he doubted his faith and he eventually confided his concerns to his Commanding Officer Ronald Henderson. Henderson listened to what Chris had to say and agreed to help him out by getting him transferred to a hospital in Burma that specialised in treating soldiers who could not cope with the traumatic details of battle and were having hypnosis therapy to help them deal with their demons!

When Chris arrived at the hospital in Burma he spent the first 3 months getting to know the soldiers at the hospital and felt a peace descend on his soul that he had not felt for a very long time! Chris was a deeply religious man and had always prided himself on his ability to listen to each side of an argument! Chris embraced the philosophy of Hypnosis and found himself facing some difficult questions about his own religious beliefs and of religion in general!! When speaking to the soldiers Chris was always surprised and saddened by the same types of questions. Where was God during the battles? Why did God allow such cruelty to take place in the name of Religion? How could God and praying to God help with the terrible guilt that these soldiers felt at killing another human being? These and many other questions like them made Chris question his own beliefs and it was during this incredibly difficult time in his life that he met Ronnie for the first time!

Chris had never really understood how, in a split second, your life could change forever! He was instantly bowled over by Ronnie's beauty as well as her truly awesome intellect! He knew, at that very moment, that his life would never be the same again!! Within a week of meeting Ronnie they had both decided to leave their jobs and lives in Burma and return to England to start a completely new life together. All this took months to arrange as Ronnie and Chris had to go through a de-briefing procedure before the Army would sanction their departure. After agreeing to the Army's demands that their skills were to be put to use by them in "Civvy Street" they were granted permission to leave the Army.

 And so it was that on that cold October morning when the Army plane landed at the Norfolk airfield that Chris and Ronnie began to formulate their plan to create a "Haven" here in England.

Chris was brought out of his reverie by the sound of Buster the Labrador barking at the postman. Buster had one of the loudest barks of any dog Chris had ever owned but he had the gentlest nature of any animal and was, therefore, Chris's favourite of all the animals at the "Retreat". (Of course he could never let Ronnie know that. She would tell him he was going soft in his old age! Maybe, just maybe he was going soft after all!)

Chris's thoughts returned to the daily papers and he checked that all the adverts were correctly positioned and there were no errors with the wording. As he did this Ronnie came into the kitchen and smiled her incredible smile that, even after all this time, made his head spin and his knees go weak. Ronnie came into the kitchen of their isolated farmhouse near the village of Soham Toney. The name of Soham Toney always made Ronnie smile. As a Burmese born woman of above average intelligence it always amused and bemused her that she had fallen in love with the farmhouse just from its name long before she had even set foot in Norfolk! She had not been disappointed on her first glimpse of the 200 year old farmhouse. It was surrounded by forest on all sides and was not visible from the road but this only added to its charm as far as Ronnie was concerned.

Ronnie poured herself a coffee from the machine, another little indulgence and ritual she had begun the first morning at the "Retreat", and glanced at the open newspapers. She sighed contentedly as she enjoyed her coffee and looked around her. The kitchen really was the heart of this house. The farmhouse was over 200 years old and the kitchen was spacious, well lit with large windows overlooking the cottage garden and the old temperamental "Aga" cooker was the bane of Ronnie's life, but she wouldn't change it for the world! Ronnie had embraced her new life with open arms from the moment she was bundled out of the army aircraft in the dead of night just over 5 years ago. She was born in 1945, in the former capital of Burma – Amarapura -, to parents who were disappointed that Veronica was another girl child. Girl children were seen to be more of a nuisance than a blessing. Ronnie never really felt that her parents loved her; they tolerated her until such time as she was old enough to go to work.

She possessed an above average intelligence which, had she not had the good fortune to get a secretarial job with the English army, might never have realised its full potential. She came to the attention of the Commanding Officer of the Intelligence Unit based at the army camp a few miles out of her home town and she was gradually allowed more and more access to sensitive material. At the same time as Ronnie was being groomed for future glory Chris was working in a secret location in Burma about 10 miles due south of Amarapura. His name was known to Ronnie because she was typing out his reports on the events happening in the area near to the River Ayeyarwady .Little did either of them realise just what would happen when they eventually came face to face with one another! It all happened so fast that at times, even now, Ronnie could not quite believe how her life had changed beyond all recognition! Ronnie had been Chris's Hypnotherapist in Burma and had, over the months, got to know him intimately. As the sessions continued they formed this incredible bond with each other and they began to discuss life together away from the Army. Ronnie finished her coffee and made a determined effort to shake of the feelings of unease that had begun to form in the dark recesses of her mind. She followed Chris out into the garden and stood quite still, took a long slow deep breath and decided that today was going to be a good day and nothing was going to change that! She knew that Chris was her soul mate because, not only did they share views on absolutely everything but they also share the same birth date!

Ronnie and Chris had never before considered fate as an option. They always felt that things could always be explained logically but even they could never fully understand the instant connection they both felt when they first met!   Ronnie continued out to the far end of the garden where her vegetable patch was and as she tended her plants her mind was focussed on the task at hand and all thoughts of Burma and the advert placed in just the right spot in all the national newspapers drifted out of her mind and she enjoyed working in the morning sunshine with no more thoughts of the next few weeks events. Elsewhere in the country a diverse group of people would start a journey that would change their lives forever!

Chapter 2. Preparations.

Chris and Ronnie worked together in the garden at "Haven's Retreat" in companionable silence. Because they were like one in their thoughts and deeds they could go for hours with no need to speak. They seemed to communicate so easily with each other without the need for mere words! All the local people who had dealings with the Gaskells shared the same opinion, that Chris and Ronnie had such a connection with each other it was sometimes very unsettling to watch! They were tolerated by people because the produce they brought into town was of exceptional quality but most people they met in the village and surrounding areas felt no need to develop a deeper friendship or acquaintance with them!
Chris and Ronnie Gaskell had no desire to become part of the local scene and actively discouraged any invitations to local events. Eventually the invites stopped and the local business people accepted that Chris and Ronnie wanted to be left alone! As the years passed Chris and Ronnie effectively "disappeared" from most people's lives, which is exactly what both the Gaskells and the army wanted! They both drove into town on a regular basis to drop off fruit and vegetables to the local businesses but apart from that they kept themselves to themselves.

The garden was a sanctuary for both Chris and Ronnie for very different reasons. For Chris it was a place of contrasts of the mind. Part of Chris was staggered by nature and what it could produce and part of his brain was confused by his knowledge of man's imperfections and his evil doings! How could nature continue when all around the world terrible things were happening and still the flowers grow, the sun shines and the world goes round and round! Chris was always won round by the garden. He had no previous experience before he came to Norfolk but when he got to the "Retreat" none of that seemed to matter! The garden seemed to thrive with or without help from Chris or Ronnie but gradually a rich relationship developed between them and now the garden was the place that drew everyone who stayed at the "Retreat".

Over the years the house and gardens enveloped Chris and Ronnie in their arms and helped them both to deal with all the experiences that happened to them in Burma. For Ronnie the garden was her escape from reality! In Burma her life had had no time for the niceties of an English garden! When she first saw "Haven's Retreat" it had been at the dead of night on a cold October evening. The next morning, however, the most magical thing happened! Ronnie drew back the curtains and was completely spellbound by the frost covered landscape in front of her eyes! She had never experienced the cold of an English winter before and in an instant she was transfixed. She had never lost the wonder and awe she had felt on that first morning and now after 5 years working on her little piece of heaven on earth she was completely at ease with the world when, slowly but surely, the doubts and insecurities she had felt that morning re-surfaced into her conscious mind to such an extent that she could not concentrate on the job in hand! She threw down her trowel in frustration and went to see where Chris was. The Army utilised both Chris and Ronnie's background whenever the Ministry of Defence had need of their services.

Thankfully this was a fairly rare occurrence nowadays as, by now, the Army had trained many more people in the techniques used in Burma and elsewhere to help army war veterans get over their battle experiences.

The money paid by the Army was substantial to say the least and it had only been this financial consideration that had made them accept soldiers from the Army into their home! Chris and Ronnie had a natural rapport and connection with each other on almost every level. Except one!

Chris really enjoyed having guests at the "Retreat". Ronnie did not share his enthusiasm! She always felt that, whilst the guests appreciated the help they needed and received there was a part of Ronnie that wanted the "Retreat" to be for their sole use only. Chris and Ronnie rarely disagreed or argued but this was the only aspect of their life that they disagreed on. However Ronnie was very aware that the "Retreat" is an expensive labour of love and as such needs constant, large, doses of cash to satisfy its voracious appetite! As Ronnie took stock of everything they had and everything that they had achieved she knew, without any doubt, that they were doing the right thing. Ronnie knew she was being irrational in her feelings of sharing the "Retreat" but she loved the place so much she really didn't want to share it with another living soul!

Chapter 3.

And so it begins...

Gordon Jarvis started the day as he always did since he lost his beloved wife Audrey 18 months ago. He woke without the help of an alarm at 6-15 am, a throwback to a lifetime of clockwatching during his career at the nuts and bolts factory in Newcastle - a distance from Alnwick where he and Audrey had lived all their lives- but both he and Audrey agreed that they did not want to leave the town and so Gordon travelled in every day (or "commuted" as it was now known!). Gordon found the idea of him "commuting" to work faintly amusing. He and Audrey both saw it for what it was. It was getting to work for god's sake – nothing more or nothing less! Gordon did not need to travel, or "commute", anywhere nowadays. He had taken early retirement when it was offered just 10 weeks after the death of his beloved Audrey. How he had regretted that ever since. He thought it would give him the freedom to adjust to his single life. How mistaken could one man be? All it had succeeded in doing was allowing him time to wander aimlessly through his days with too much time on his hands and no enthusiasm for anything. Oh! He knew that it was all part of the grieving process. His neighbours and colleagues from work told him as much on a regular basis. What nobody seemed to grasp -that only he knew -was that whilst he was grieving he was also eaten up with terrible guilt and shame that no-one would ever know about! The pain of his guilt followed him everywhere and affected every part of his life to such an extent that Gordon had considered suicide on more than one occasion. He knew he would probably not have the nerve to do it. He could not bring any more shame on to the rest of his family. His 2 children had not seen him since the funeral 18 months ago and they did not reply to his telephone calls or his letters any more.

 Gordon got out of bed with the same weariness he had felt the previous evening when he had watched god knows what on the TV until some god forsaken time in the morning. He had got into this habit and he was sick of it! He was sick of his life and he was sick to death of death and everything associated with it! Oh how he wished he knew what to do to change and get his life back! He had not died, his wife had, but he might as well have died for wasn't he living a virtual death all day every day? He went from the bedroom into the kitchen and put the kettle on almost without realising it! Routine was slowly, but surely, draining the life out of him and he was only just 60 years old!

As Gordon was deep in thought his subconscious mind was directing him to complete his daily ritual.

Put kettle on. Put toast in toaster. Read daily newspaper etc.... However 09/06/09 will forever be etched on Gordon's memory because this was the day that would change his life forever! Of course Gordon did not realise this as he sat down in his lonely kitchen with his toast and tea to read the daily newspaper. All he does remember of that fateful morning was discovering the advert for "Haven's Retreat" and wondering if he had the courage to act on what his heart was telling him he should do?

 "Haven's Retreat." A beautiful, tranquil farmhouse where you can unwind and discover inner peace! Are you lost? Are you troubled? Does life not make any sense anymore? Do you aspire to be you again? Do you need to change your life? If you answered yes to one or more of these questions then the "Retreat" could be right for you! We are a married couple who have the good fortune to live our lives as we want to live them.

If you are able to spend the summer helping us in our market garden, re-discovering yourselves and other people and can commit to our programme of Hypnotherapy and Holistic Teachings we would be delighted to have you as our house guests! You would be expected to contribute to the running expenses of our large home and would have daily duties to perform. We do not worship Satan, we do not sacrifice small children on stone altars at midnight but we do offer you the chance of peace of mind and body!" If you feel that you would benefit from joining us -then please contact Chris or Ronnie on 01842 626145."

Gordon stared at the advert for what seemed like an eternity. What was he thinking? These people must be crazy, god bothering lunatics. So why was he beginning to even think about going there? Why did he not just turn the page and forget about this strange feeling in the pit of his stomach? He, Gordon Jarvis, 60 year old retired foreman from the nuts and bolts factory in Newcastle. He- the man's man as everyone who knew him called him – was actually considering going to Norfolk for the summer to spend it with some free loving hippy types! What the hell was the matter with him? What the devil was going on?

All these thoughts, and many more besides, would not leave Gordon's mind as he went through his usual day. He wandered aimlessly around the park, he sat in the local cafe and had a coffee he didn't really want or enjoy. He chatted to his neighbours without really hearing a word they said or knowing what he replied to them! All the time as he was going through the motions of his day Gordon could not get the "Retreat" out of his mind. That evening after a meal of god knows what Gordon picked up the discarded newspaper and re-read the advert. What harm could it do? If he didn't like it he could always come home and chalk it down to experience. He had tried all day to find reasons not to give it a go. His life was a disaster. He was heading for a nervous breakdown. He could not carry this guilt around anymore!

And so, with his heart pounding and more than a little tremor in his throat, he made the call!

Chapter 4.

Prunella Okenden was 3 weeks away from her 92nd birthday and she was not happy! Oh she didn't mind her age. She was 92-so what? Prunella was unhappy because everyone around her sounded so surprised that she was still around, could still speak, think and have an opinion! Prunella had always had an opinion. Even in the days when, in polite society, woman did not have a brain nor the ability and intelligence for an opinion! Even now, after all these years how it made her blood boil! Most things made Prunella's blood boil nowadays. How had she turned into this harridan of a woman? Why was she almost a caricature of the miserable old woman? Where had her life gone? Where was her life going?

She rose from her bed and went downstairs to the breakfast room to sit and enjoy her tea as she did every morning. It was something she had done every day she had spent in this lovely old house. She tried to remember just how long she had lived here? Why did her memory let her down so often? How frustrating it was! It must be over 60 years since she came back here to the family home in disgrace! How that made her smile now! If her parents were alive now they would be terribly shocked by society today. Her Mother would have had a "fit of the vapours" to think what young girls got up to nowadays! Prunella was secretly sorry she was 92 and not 19- oh what a time she would have had! Of course it would never do to tell any of her associates these thoughts- she had her standing in the local community to think of after all!
As she poured herself a cup of Indian tea in her best Wedgwood china Prunella began to reflect back on her life, something she had been doing a lot lately, and as always the regrets about her life came to the surface first.

Prunella was born on Friday the 12th July 1912 in Hove. George V was King and Asquith was the Liberal Prime Minister. She was born 9 days after the conclusion of the inquiry into the Titanic disaster and a full week before a 19kg meteorite exploded in Arizona showering the town of Holbrook with debris! Prunella could always remember those facts but could not always remember if she had eaten that day. How could that be? She would never understand the vagaries of the mind and had given up hope of ever fully comprehending it.

 Prunella was a beautiful child with titian red hair and alabaster skin. She was never spoilt, far from it, but she was always treated well by her adoring father and much less so by her mother who always remained slightly distant and aloof from both her and her precious father. Prunella had a good start in life and she had access to the finest education available to the middle classes of the time. So why did she not take full advantage of it? She would never stop regretting that .Her life could have been so different. Prunella knew in her heart of hearts the moment her life changed forever. It was when she was just sixteen and hopelessly, naively infatuated with her teacher Miss Fredericks, the English Language tutor brought in by her school to educate the genteel ladies of Hove in the delicacies of the English language. Prunella was smitten by Helen Fredericks from the moment she saw her. Helen was tall, aristocratic in bearing and manner and, to Prunella, the epitome of style and élan! Prunella thought that she had never met anyone quiet like Helen in her life. Helen was everything Prunella aspired to be. She was well travelled, smart, and intelligent and possessed a disdain for society and its constrictions that Prunella found intoxicating! Helen Fredericks was just the most perfect human being as far as Prunella was concerned and so she accepted the invitation to join Helen, as she had asked Prunella to call her in private, to a personal tuition session in her private apartment in the teachers quarters attached to the main building of the school. Prunella went to Helen's room with a strange mixture of excitement and nerves and when Helen opened the door to her apartment within the grounds wearing a very casual and diaphanous outfit Prunella was enchanted by Helen even more than before! Diaphanous- that word which should have been so exciting and exotic turned Prunella's stomach every time she saw it in print! Suffice to say Prunella would never be the same again after what very nearly happened that afternoon in Miss Frederick's apartment. For years Prunella could not forget the awful situation she found herself in that afternoon and she was so grateful to her dear father when he agreed to send Prunella to finishing school in Geneva at the first opportunity! Miss Frederick left her post soon after that afternoon and Prunella never saw her again! Prunella went to Geneva, had a marvellous time and married a suitably inappropriate man called Günter Henckle. Gunter was the heir apparent to a brewery fortune and although he and Prunella were never going to be compatible for the long term, Gunter proved to be a true gentleman and gave Prunella a substantial settlement when their divorce finally came through!

When Prunella came home in the autumn on 1931 her life at home was never the same again! Her mother, whilst never actually saying it out loud, was aghast at the shame that Prunella very nearly brought upon the family name! Prunella's marriage was NEVER spoken about in public; the shame would have been too much for her mother's delicate sensibilities. Prunella rejoined society and to all intents and purposes her marriage had never taken place! How Prunella's new found wealth was explained Prunella never did find out! Oh what lies we do weave whence once we practice to deceive. (Or whatever that damned quote was!) Prunella's heart was never the same after that and so the years drifted on and before she knew it Prunella had assumed the role of favourite auntie or favourite free spirit , depending on your view, to the ladies and gentlemen of Hove's genteel set. My god, what a waste of a life thought Prunella as she sipped her tea. But no more! Now was the time, before it was too late, to start and enjoy the life that she- Prunella Okenden -felt she deserved!

Prunella finished her tea and opened the paper at the crossword page, as she did every morning, and began to complete the clues in her usual efficient manner. When she had completed the crossword, in a rather quick time she thought! , she turned her attention to other pages within the newspaper and her eyes alighted on the advert for "Haven's Retreat ", she glanced at it with only a limited degree of interest but then she re-read the advert and began to wonder!

So much of her life had not gone according to plan, so many times she had wished for things to be different. Why not take this opportunity, which might be her last, to finally do something worthwhile with her life after drifting aimlessly for the past however many years. And so with a real sense of impending achievement she picked up the telephone and began to dial the number!

Chapter 5.

"To be or not to be...."

Robert Underwood was 3 months short of his 40th birthday! He was an out of work actor who had promised himself and his mother that he would find himself a new career and settle down if he had not achieved any degree of success by the time he was 40! Oh! How he had regretted mentioning that to his mother that day when he went home to Chichester after a particularly lean time with work. He had had no choice but to go home. He had not paid his rent for a month, he had absolutely no food in the one bed roomed "cupboard" he called home at the time, and he was desperate! His mother had reminded him, again, that his younger brother was doing really well at his office. He was now office supervisor at the call centre near to Chichester. Robert always felt a complete failure whenever he went home even when he had had some limited success with a provincial tour of some unforgettable play .His mother never failed to deflate his already fragile self belief. Without self belief how could he hope to convince a casting director to believe in him? Today, however, was going to be different. He felt sure of it!

Robert had an audition for a part in a new "soap opera" storyline playing the part of a family doctor who would be a central figure in the demise of this particular soap's leading lady who had "asked" to be released from her contract when, as everyone in the acting profession knew, she was being sacked for sleeping with the teenage son of the executive producer of the show!!   Robert smiled to himself as he got himself ready for his audition. Oh how he hoped that this part would be the beginning for him, especially as the leading lady in question had been to drama school with him and was such a bitch to everyone he knew that people would be queuing up to take his place if he decided not to accept the part! Of course Robert would cut his right hand off to get the part, if that is what it took, but he knew that to appear too desperate for any part was the kiss of death for any actor! So Robert spent a decent amount of time preparing himself for his make or break audition. He knew that this was probably his last chance to achieve something before his birthday and before his mother would began her campaign of trying to get him a job in the call centre!

 His mother had mentioned this to him the last time he went home and she even suggested that he would enjoy it because he could talk to people about their mobile phones in lots of different accents and he could pretend to be lots of different people so wasn't that acting after all? It had taken every ounce of his willpower not to slowly strangle the life out of the wretched woman there and then!

As Robert arrived at the T.V. Studio he felt strangely calm. He was nervous, of course he was, but he knew his lines, he was the right age for the part and THEY had asked him back for a screen test! He, Robert Underwood, was going into a studio for his very first screen test! Robert felt his stomach do a somersault at this thought and so he concentrated on revising his opening scene in his head.

 Robert sat in the waiting room with 3 other actors all up for the part that was his! One of the actors he vaguely recognised from a commercial that was currently running. He might as well go home now Robert thought- they won't want a complete unknown surely! As his confidence began to ebb away he was saved from his almost overwhelming desire to dash for the door by the sound of his name being called into the studio for his screen test! Robert took a deep breath, held his head high and went in...

On the train home Robert felt that his heart would break! He had had the worst day of his professional life and he just wanted to get back to his flat, crawl into his bed and never come out again! He would never forget walking into the studio and being introduced to the director, sound men etc before being led onto the "set" for the screen test. He thought that the test would be without any of the actors from the soap as this was usual practice according to his agent when the producers wanted everything "hush hush" !Imagine his surprise, and abject horror, when onto the set strolled the very actress the studio were planning on firing! Robert knew, in an instant, that all was lost for him when the "leading lady" said in a really loud voice that she and Robert were at drama school together and wasn't it nice that, after all this time, he was getting his first real "break"!

Robert began the test as best he could but he was an absolute disaster! He forgot his lines, he walked into a wall and sent a vase flying. In short even he, Robert Underwood, would not have employed himself as the tea boy on the show! As he was ushered away from the set and was told that he had done very well and that they would be in touch as soon as they had auditioned everyone else Robert knew he would not be asked back. He knew he had blown his final chance for success but what finally convinced him that the back stabbing world of acting was not for him was when he overheard the make-up girl telling one of the hairdressers that the "leading lady" in question had been hauled into the senior executive of the studio's office, given a severe dressing down about the affair with the underage boy, and told she was hanging on to her job by the skin of her teeth and had agreed to a pay cut for the next year! In order for the "lady" in question not to appear in court the father of the boy had agreed not to press charges if he could remain in charge of the "soap" for the next 2 years and be in charge of all storylines involving the said "lady"! As he left the studio completely unnoticed the make-up girl and the hairdresser were taking bets on what would happen to her! Would she become a nun? Would she have an affair with the oldest actor on the soap – the one with the bad breath and wandering hands? Or would she be sidelined with no decent storylines at all until the public tired of her and she could be written out without too much damage to the viewing figures!

Robert shook his head at the memory of it all and looked around the almost deserted train carriage. Where had everybody gone? As he looked out of the train window to get his bearings he decided not to tell his mother of his latest disaster. He could not bear the thought of her saying "I know that that is what you wanted dear but you know that I was right and you should put all these silly ideas away and settle down!" Robert had about 15 minutes still left of his journey and he looked around for something to take his mind off his terrible day. On the seat beside him somebody had left the daily paper open at the crossword page and so , with very little enthusiasm, he finished off as much of the crossword as he could. He could not concentrate for long and so he started to look at the rest of the page and then he saw it! "Haven's Retreat" – Robert knew right there and then just exactly where he was going to spend the summer and his 4oth birthday!

Chapter 6.

Vanessa Floyd Wright woke up that morning at around 9-30am, unusually early for her, and looked around her bedroom with trepidation! Please God, don't let it have happened again! She carefully and quietly got out of bed and slowly drew the bed sheets back – no one there! As she entered her en-suite bathroom she was trying to hear if there were any sounds coming from the rest of the house. Even though she couldn't hear anything Vanessa would not settle until she was absolutely convinced she was on her own!

She could not go on like this. She was 10 days away from her 32nd birthday for god sake and she was creeping around her own home! Why? Vanessa knew why but she would not admit it to herself because if she thought about it too long she became depressed and irritable with everybody and everything in her life.

Vanessa Floyd Wright was a spoilt bitch. There she had said it to herself for the first time! She had always known this but this was the first time she had ever acknowledged it – even if it was only in her own head and not out loud to her friends and family- but it was a start of sorts wasn't it? Vanessa was beautiful, haughty and vain. These were her best traits according to the small circle of friends that Vanessa had. Not much of a character reference was it?

Vanessa continued to search her Richmond town house until she was sure she was alone. How many times had she done this recently only to discover a total stranger in her bed or in her house making coffee or toast!? Too many times for comfort Vanessa thought.

At first Vanessa had enjoyed the hedonistic lifestyle of an independently wealthy, beautiful 21 year old heiress. She was always the life and soul of every society party. She was an excellent hostess, always supplying just the right booze and drugs for her guests, and she had met some truly amazing people. Yet after 3 or 4 years of this vacuous way of living she had grown tired, very tired, of the whole social scene and needed to stretch her mind.

She possessed a lively intellect, if anyone had stopped to discover, and she was curious about the world and its people. Of **course the** people she hung out with had never thought to ask such a ridiculous question and so Vanessa allowed herself to be led even further astray with her life becoming more and more hedonistic and outrageous with every passing season. Just when Vanessa knew it had to stop she was not quite sure, but stop it must! Vanessa had had many sexual partners of both sexes and she was fairly uninhibited but she knew that there was more to life than this and so she had begun the process of change slowly and surely in her own mind. She did not have anybody to confide in and so she had decided to change her life's direction herself - but how?

She did not go to quite as many parties as she had done. She arrived later than she used to. She left earlier than she used to. She refused drugs and she did not drink nearly as much as she used to. Her "friends" found her new behaviour unsettling and so, ever so slowly, the invitations stopped arriving and suddenly Vanessa was not" the hostess with the mostest "anymore! At first Vanessa was relieved that she was not the centre of attention any more but slowly, and painfully, Vanessa became very aware that if she was not centre of attention then just exactly what was she? Vanessa did not like what she discovered. She was nothing!

She had achieved nothing; she did not have one true friend in the whole world. She might have a fortune in the bank and she still had her looks but these meant nothing to her now.

As Vanessa surveyed her tastefully decorated town house with all the latest "must have" gadgets and the newest art that money could buy she felt completely cold inside. What did any of this mean? She knew, with absolute clarity and certainty, that this was not the life for her and had never been if she was completely truthful and if she had any chance of redeeming her mind and soul then this was the time to do it. All these thoughts were racing through her mind as she made herself a "cafetiere" of coffee and lit a cigarette. Just how could she begin to turn her life around? It was then that she picked up the newspaper and began to flick through its pages....

Chapter 7.

Adam Jenkins pulled the ring on his 4th can of strong, cheap, cider and decided that he would not go in to town to sign on the dole. They could stick their poxy dole money where the sun doesn't shine! He did not need the bastard government handout. He was going places! He was going to be someone! It was 2-30 in the afternoon and he had just come back from the "offy" with his daily supplies. 12 cans of cider (on special offer no less!) 40 fags and a microwave burger! How good could life be eh!?

Adam was feeling particularly good today, not only was he going to enjoy his booze, fags and food but Tricia was coming round at 5 to help him celebrate his good fortune and they all knew just how Tricia helped people celebrate!"

Adam was just 22 years old and came from a very poor district of Bristol. He was poorly educated and had" little or no desire to change or improve his situation!" How those words were burnt into Adam's mind! How dare that cow of a social worker dismiss him like that? He was worth 10 of her - the stuck up bitch! He had stolen the notes regarding him from his social workers handbag when her back was turned! How easy that had been. You silly cow! Admittedly he had had to get a mate's sister to read it to him because he couldn't understand some of the words. How come they wrote so stupid eh! But he knew that the system had written him off as a hopeless case! But he would show them good and proper- very soon! Hadn't he just landed himself a big job with the local gang to fence some stolen electrical gear? And hadn't they promised him £200 for his trouble? £200 quid! He was practically a millionaire! All he had to do was to wait here at his flat, the guys would hand over the gear, he would sell it on and they would come back every day to see how he was getting on and to give him his wages! Fantastic!

The next day and the boys were as good as their word. His flat was stacked with all sorts of electrical gadgets and he could hardly move for boxes. Wasn't life grand! All Adam needed to do was go out and flog the gear to mates and strangers, it didn't matter who bought the stuff as long as someone did! Filled with confidence Adam set out with a smile on his face.

After a completely useless day Adam was not quite so enthusiastic when the "boys" came round to find out how he had got on! They went ballistic and for the first time Adam felt the undeniable prickle of fear run down his spine! The "boys" very generously, in their opinion, gave Adam 24 more hours to shift some serious amounts of gear or else! After another fruitless, futile day Adam was terrified to go back to his flat! They would surely kill him or at the least cut off bits of his body! Adam slept rough that night, and for the next 3 nights until he plucked up the courage to enter his flat, pack a rucksack with small electrical walkmans etc and run for the hills! He did not dare look back in case he saw one of the "boys" or their mates and he was so glad to see a bus pull in just as he went passed that before he knew what he was doing he got on the bus and asked the driver where the hell was this bus going?

The bus driver was relieved when Adam got off his bus at Bristol railway station and Adam headed off into the crowd. God that boy stunk! His bus would need to be sterilised when it got back to the depot! How he hated this job!

Adam, meanwhile, had a rucksack filled with stolen" i-pods", walkmans etc and no idea what to do with them! It was at that precise moment that fate finally smiled on 22 year old Adam Jenkins because right there in front of him was a coach that was off loading a group of foreign exchange students! Even Adam could see that this might be his only chance! And so with his heart pounding in his chest he approached the first student.

An hour later, when the final student had bought his last i-pod and had boarded the train Adam finally allowed himself to breath! He was rich! He had made £400. £4oo in an hour! Wow! As Adam collected his thoughts he began to realise something. He could never go back home! He would be killed by the "boys" or their henchmen who would have his balls for earrings! What the hell could he do? Where the hell could he go? He decided to go into the station cafe and treat himself to some grub. When had he last eaten properly? He couldn't remember. He ordered an all day breakfast with a large tea (plenty of sugar love!) and made his way to a vacant table. After he had devoured the meal he felt better. His mind felt clearer and so Adam Jenkins, 22 year old waste of space, began to decide just exactly what he was going to do with the rest of his life!

 As Adam was eating his meal a couple sat down at the next table to kill time waiting for their connecting train. As Adam was wondering what to do suddenly the girl began to laugh. "Oh my god darling have you seen this advertisement? "Haven's Retreat"! "What a pile of shit! How could anyone be taken in by this rubbish? If you are feeling lost- then contact Chris or Ronnie on 01842 626145" The young girl continued to laugh and Adam felt strangely annoyed by her! How could she be so dismissive? What did she know about life? She looked as though she had never had a day's worry in her stupid life!

After the stupid girl and her equally stupid boyfriend went Adam noticed that they had left the newspaper behind and so, with nothing better to do, Adam began to painstakingly read the advert for "Haven's Retreat". It took Adam a full 10 minutes to read the advert and even then he was not quite sure he had read it properly! All he did know was that he needed to escape and this place didn't sound so bad! He had £400 in his pocket; he was at a railway station he could catch a train, or lots of trains, to get to Norfolk if that is what it took. Where the hell was Norfolk anyway? Adam Jenkins, 22 year old waste of space, decided that he would take the greatest risk of his short life and telephone Chris and Ronnie to found out what the crack was and also find out where the hell Norfolk was? .....

Chapter 8.

Laura Machin was 19 and a half. Lauren knew that the half was important to some of her "gentlemen" she knew that when she was 20 some of her "gentlemen" would not telephone her again. She would be too old; she would not be a "little girl" anymore!

Laura Machin was a "working girl" or a "prozzie" as her Gran would have said!

Laura was a petite girl who looked younger than her years and she was only too aware that this was what made her popular with some of her "gentlemen" visitors! "Gentlemen" what a farce! How she hated the term "gentlemen" god how she hated that word!! Her "gentlemen" were seedy, dirty old men who paid her to have sex with them in a scruffy, filthy, room in a rundown terraced street in Bolton!

Laura's beloved Pa had died when she was 12 years old. He had been ill for months but Laura had not been told that his cancer was terminal and so that morning when she went off to school as normal she did not realise what was happening. As she came round the corner into her street she did not, at first, realise that the ambulance was outside her own front door. She did not know when she went into the front room shouting for her Dad that it was already too late! Her Dad was dead! Her Dad was dead!

Laura's world fell apart in that instant. She, like many other teenage girls, did not get on with her Ma. Her Ma did not understand her! Her Ma was always getting at her! Her Ma was a cow! Her Ma was a bitch! On the day her Pa died Laura and her Ma- Josie -should have given each other the strength to get through that terrible day. It did not happen! Josie fell apart. She could not be there for her only child. She could not function at all. Her Pa's sister helped her through the next few days until the day of the funeral. What a day! Laura would never forget, or forgive, any of her family for what happened at the reception afterwards!

How could people, her family, her drunken family, behave like that? Her Pa's sister shouting out in public that she had helped Laura, the ungrateful madam, over the last few days and she was entitled to something from her dead brother's estate! Laura's Pa had no estate for god's sake! What was Auntie Pauline saying? Her mother becoming hysterical and threatening to pull out Auntie Pauline's hair by the f****** roots! Laura had never heard any adult say that word. Oh she used to say it all the time about her mother to her best friend Mandy but to hear it from her own mother' mouth! Laura was bundled out of the reception and taken to Mandy's house for the evening. Laura had never felt so alone and lonely as she did on that night but she remembered thinking that tomorrow would be different and better!

It wasn't.

Josie fell apart and never recovered. She became seriously depressed and so Social Services were called in to help decide what should be done about Laura. Laura was never really consulted about what she wanted. Oh! She was told that any decisions made would be for her benefit. She would, of course, be kept fully informed about what was going on. This did not happen! She was taken into care just 6 months after the death of her beloved Pa. Auntie Pauline couldn't possibly take on a teenage girl when her own nerves were so upset at the death of her brother!

Couldn't Josie's family help out? She would have to give up work to look after Laura. Would Social Services pay her bills for her?

Laura's mum ended her own life on September 12th 2005 - their wedding anniversary! Laura was almost 15 and an orphan! Social Services looked after her body, but not her mind and soul, until she was 16 and she was then informed that she was now able to choose where she wanted to stay.

Laura just needed to escape and so as soon as she was able she caught a bus out to Bolton - it was the destination of the first bus that stopped! - And Laura's new life began!

As she looked around at the squalor surrounding her she felt nauseous! God! How the hell had she got herself into this state? She did not know a soul when she arrived in Bolton. She walked around all night and slept rough in a small park. She did not sleep; she lay awake listening to the sounds of the night. She jumped at the sound of the bushes, the sound of birds, the sound of footsteps - in fact at the sound of anything! She was just thinking that, maybe, she should go back when a woman in her forties began to ask her if she was o.k.? Did she have anything to eat or drink? The woman invited her to go with her to a house where she could get a shower and something to eat and drink. Laura was so grateful! The gratitude did not last! Within a few days she was paying back the ladies "kindness" by entertaining gentlemen in the back room of the house she now sat in!

Laura went, as she did most mornings, to the local cafe for a large mug of tea and bacon butty. At the cafe she ordered her food and sat in the quietest corner in order to avoid eye contact with the owner .She was so ashamed and disgusted with herself. She needed to change her life. How? As she pondered this her thoughts were interrupted by the waitress handing her the food and drink she had ordered. Laura took one bite of her bacon butty and put it straight down. Please don't let me be sick here at the table she thought! She waited a few moments before she gingerly took a sip of her tea. That was not too bad. Lauren knew she was attracting attention in the cafe and so she left as quickly as she could before the owner asked her to leave! She knew she looked a mess; she had not washed in days. Her hair and clothes were dirty and smelly and she was so ashamed of herself that before she knew what was happening she collapsed in the street in tears. How miserable she felt! Lauren lay on the floor for several minutes and no-one stopped to ask her if she was alright, no-one came anywhere near her at all!

As she got to her feet Laura looked around her and made a decision. She was going to change her life right now. She did not know how just yet but she felt sure that she deserved better than the miserable existence that she was enduring now. She had about 80 quid on her from her "entertaining" duties. She would be damned if that old cow would have any of it!

Laura's demeanour changed and she walked purposefully to the local library where she knew that she could read the paper in peace and quiet and she could start to get warm again! In the library it was, of course, quiet and serene and she went into the farthest corner of the library and picked up the daily paper.

Inside Laura's head the sound of her heart pounding was so loud that she was certain everyone else in the library must, surely, be able to hear it! Her breath was shallow, her palms were sweaty and she could barely focus on the page! "Haven's Retreat" could this be the answer to all her prayers. Well there was only one way to find out! ....

Chapter 9.

"Haven's Retreat" was as peaceful a place as the name suggested. The farmhouse was over 200 years old. It had enjoyed a happy life Ronnie thought and then smiled to herself. How could a house have had a happy life? Ronnie was not sure but she was certain that the house had a peaceful and serene "aura" surrounding it. That was the overriding emotion that both she and Chris experienced when they first viewed the house. It was February and cold when Ronnie first set eyes on the house but she knew that she was going to be happy here from the instant she saw the frost covered garden that first morning. She and Chris both felt the same connection but neither of them had come up with a rational explanation for this. It was almost as if the house had chosen them!

 Over the following 5 years Ronnie and Chris had spent a small fortune restoring the house to something like its former glory. It had taken all their savings plus the income from the army, which Ronnie and Chris resented but needed, and so it had been decided to open up the charms of the "Retreat" to outsiders for the first time! It was this sense of uncertainty that had caused Ronnie some sleepless nights but she had finally resolved her own misgivings and was now as fully committed to the project as Chris was.

Ronnie lost herself in the jobs she needed to do in the market garden. She was always amazed at just how much work was involved in maintaining the vegetables and flowers for the local community. She, however, took an enormous amount of pride in the vegetables the farm produced and she felt that there was nothing more satisfying than working on the land until your very bones ached with the effort and sinking into a hot bath at the end of another productive day. Simple pleasures that Ronnie had come to really appreciate. She was sure that if they had the right combination of guests then the equilibrium could be maintained and everyone could benefit from their time at the "Retreat".

The Norfolk countryside had worked its magic on Ronnie and Chris from the beginning. They both felt that this place was their spiritual home. Chris had been a padre in the army but was not the most conventional Christian you would ever meet. For one thing he was very" open- minded "to the possibilities that God did not have all the answers! Ronnie had introduced the holistic approach to their lives and Chris had adopted the approach with complete openness and enthusiasm. There were times when Ronnie thought that he was more committed to it than she was!

The morning had started well for Chris and Ronnie. The sun had shone brightly from first thing. The vegetables, herbs and flowers were looking great and life felt "good" on this very special day and so it was that when the telephone rang Ronnie was feeling positive that today was going to be the start of something special. She hoped so with all her heart!

Chapter 10.

Chris answered the telephone and heard a gentle "Geordie" voice asking him for final directions to the isolated farmhouse. Gordon was to be the very first guest at the Retreat and had sounded as nervous and apprehensive as Chris had felt!

The sun shone all that day as if it knew that there was something worth celebrating. Chris had worked hard in the garden selecting the finest fruit and vegetables available to take to the local hotel in town.

Gordon drew up to the gates, took a deep breath and continued into the farmyard. He was hot, stiff and exhausted from the journey. Suddenly a voice called out to him and as he looked around a small wiry man came towards him.

"Hi! You must be Gordon. Welcome to Haven's Retreat! Did you have a good journey? You must be whacked? Would you like to come into the house and have a cool drink?"

All these questions were asked in one hurried, breathless sentence and Gordon was pleased to note that Chris appeared to be as ill at ease as he was! Why should that please him? He knew from speaking to Chris that this was a new adventure for everyone and so Gordon began to relax a little and allow him to be ushered into the kitchen. Once there Chris introduced him to Ronnie and asked him to take a seat while he got that drink! Ronnie was a complete revelation to Gordon- she was striking looking and she was a woman! Gordon had been a little wary in case Ronnie had been a great big hairy biker bloke! Well you never know in this day and age he had told himself!

"Hello Gordon. Welcome to Haven's Retreat!"

"Thanks Hinny"

"I hope you are not too tired from your journey?" (Again that sense of awkwardness!)

"Nah Pet I'm just fine!

"Well when you have had your drink Chris and I will show you round the place and then let you settle in before the others arrive if that is o.k. with you?"

"No problem pet, whatever you say!"

Chris brought him a glass of cool fresh lemonade which went down a treat. As he sipped his drink Gordon looked around the kitchen. Why it looked just like one of them kitchens you see in them fancy magazines his Audrey was always reading about in the hairdressers! My god, will I fit in here with these posh folks Gordon wondered?

Ronnie and Chris seemed ok at least Gordon thought as he allowed the cooling drink to slip slowly down. My, that felt good! "So, how long have you folks been here hinny?"

"Pardon me?"

"Oh! Sorry, hinny, you'll get used to my funny accent in time! Hinny is a bit like "dear" or "love" where I come from!

"Oh, it's just that I've never heard that expression before. I like it! We've been here about 5 years haven't we Chris?

"That's right love."

"Your place is reet bonny lass!" Gordon was instantly taken by the surprise and delight showing on the face of Ronnie as she struggled to decipher just exactly what had just been said to her!

Eventually she replied, very tentatively, "Thank you - I think!"

As she answered Gordon became the latest member of the Veronica Gaskell appreciation society!

Chris noticed the subtle change in Gordon's face and he slowly began to relax. Perhaps this wasn't going to be such a terrible ordeal after all!

"So, Gordon, shall I show you to your room or do want to wait awhile?"

"Whatever's best for you good folk's? I don't mind either way!"

"Ronnie, you wait here and I'll show Gordon if that's o.k.? I can help him with his bags and show him around while you telephone the Hotel to see what they want for the weekend. You know how much better at increasing their order than I am!" Chris looked straight into Ronnie's eyes and laughed a full throated laugh that made Ronnie blush and push them both out of the kitchen whilst trying to keep a straight face as she did so!

Gordon was suddenly and violently taken back to the time when he and Audrey used to tease each other in that slightly sexual way! As he shook his head to dislodge the memory he was sure that Chris hadn't noticed. Even after all this time it was still so painful and close to the surface!

The room he was shown to was at the back of the house overlooking the greenhouses and the fields beyond. Chris left him to unpack and settle in and told him to treat the house like his own home and come down whenever he was ready!

After unpacking he looked around him. The room was high ceilinged, which surprised him, with traditional sash windows and a window seat. Audrey would have loved all this thought Gordon. The furniture was a happy mish-mash of styles that, somehow, worked. You could easily think that all the furniture had always been here. They obviously had good taste and an eye for detail. Even a "pleb" like him could see that thought Gordon!

As he made his way down to the kitchen Gordon began to feel calmer than he had done in months. He was sure that the next few weeks would be just what the doctor ordered – just as long as he could keep it quiet from his children! They would, no doubt, consider this yet another sign that "Dad" was "losing it", big time!

Gordon desperately needed to sort himself out so that he could at least try to explain just what went on during his darling wife's final weeks and try to make them understand why he allowed his wife to store up her strong painkillers until she had enough for her to "go to sleep with dignity" as she put it. Why he went to his wife's bedside, held her hand, cried until there were no more tears and then left his wife with all the extra pills at her side and closed the bedroom without looking back!!

As he went down the stairs he was surprised to hear a woman's voice. It was definitely not Ronnie's voice, it was a strong almost aristocratic sound that made him immediately think that it belonged to someone used to the good things in life and also used to getting her way! Gordon prided himself on being a good judge of character and within those few seconds had decided that whoever was speaking would not be his "cup of tea". Bloody snobs – he couldn't bear the upper classes. They always made him feel very defensive and so it was with some trepidation and not a little annoyance he entered the kitchen.

Prunella Okenden was holding court in the kitchen. She was regaling Chris and Ronnie regarding her "terrible "journey with some "ghastly" people on a truly "awful" train! As Gordon went in he was staggered to see a frail looking gentle lady who did not live up to his pre-conceived ideas of the landed gentry! Prunella was a pretty woman with glorious hair, a pleasant open face, and really animated eyes. What he had thought to be superiority in her voice was actually delight at her predicament! She was explaining to Chris and Ronnie with such obvious delight about her journey that Gordon immediately felt contrite and decided that he was not such a good judge of character as he thought!

"Hi Gordon, this is Mrs Prunella Okenden and she is joining us for the summer too."

"My dear man- how truly lovely to meet you!" I was just saying to - Oh sorry I've forgotten your names! How awful! – I was just saying that I have endured the most remarkable journey on the train with some truly ghastly types and I have not had such a fabulous time in years!"

Gordon was bowled over by the energy that Prunella gave out! God she must be in her eighties at least and she looked amazing. Gordon saw that both Chris and Ronnie looked bamboozled too and then Gordon caught their eyes and a smile began to form in the corner of his mouth and before he knew it he was smiling and then laughing and soon everyone in the room was helpless. Prunella kept apologising for taking over, it was something that she had always done she said, and every time she spoke she laughed even louder, and with genuine delight, that for several moments all attempts at rational conversation ceased to be an option! When everyone had regained their composure and sat down, formal introductions were totally unnecessary; they all had a cup of Ronnie's herbal tea. The tea was delicious and both Gordon and Prunella took the opportunity for quiet reflection about just exactly had brought them to this place at this time.

Prunella went with Ronnie to settle into her room and as she walked through the farmhouse she couldn't help but admire the furnishings and fittings all over the house. She was truly delighted with her room, which was at the front of the house, and she was really pleased to see that she was going to be staying here alone. She had not shared a bedroom with anybody since she had left Austria after her disastrous marriage to the unsuitable, but gorgeous, Gunter – and she was not about to start now!

Prunella took her time with unpacking her clothes and jewellery. She was proud of her jewellery and she had spent a long time deciding which pieces to bring with her and which to deposit at her bank in Hove. "You could never be too careful with staff!" Prunella had informed the Bank Manager as she insisted that only someone with authority and integrity be allowed to deal with her request!

She looked around her room and was pleased with how she had subtly re-arranged the furniture to accommodate her difficulties with moving first thing in the morning. It would not do to let the owner's think that she was not capable. (What were their names?) She did not want to let herself down. What would people think? The instant she thought this she chided herself. She was not going to start that again! She had not laughed so much, and so freely, in years. (Chris and Ronnie! That was their names. She'd remembered! Well done Prunella old girl.)Prunella suddenly realised just how hungry and tired she was and so quickly freshened up and went downstairs.

It was now just after 9 at night and it had been a long, and emotional, day for everyone and yet as they all "mucked" in to set the table and get the plates, knives, forks etc out there was a sense of companionship that no-one mentioned but everyone felt. The meal consisted of cold meat, new potatoes and salad – all washed down with either beer ("For the men obviously" commented Prunella with a wry smile at Ronnie) or wine for the ladies. As everyone tucked in the conversation flowed quite naturally.

"So Prunella, what do you think of your room?" Ronnie asked with genuine interest.

"Absolutely delightful my dear, as is the entire farmhouse. You must be so proud and pleased with it surely?"

"We are very lucky and grateful for everything." Chris replied with obvious pride as he shared a lingering look with Ronnie.

"Quite." Gordon. Tell me a little about Northumberland. Do you know I have never ventured that far up North? Are the native's friendly or do they indulge in strange Pagan rituals that you can't tell us about?" laughed Prunella in a teasing way.

"On the contrary Prunella we are quite civilised now that we have the wheel and electricity!" Gordon replied good naturedly.

Prunella, Chris and Ronnie all laughed together and they all said that they must check out this Brave New World one day!

After the meal was finished everyone helped to clear the table and then retired to the lounge where a log fire crackled invitingly.

"We don't usually need a fire at this time of the year, but as this is a special day for all of us I thought it would be nice to end our day with a few home comforts." said Ronnie quietly.

As everyone sat down with their nightcaps Chris and Ronnie breathed a sigh of relief at exactly the same moment. They were so in tune with each other that at times they seemed to be one person, a fact that did not escape the notice of both the other people in the room.

After a little more convivial conversation Prunella announced that she was absolutely "whacked" as the youth of today would say and so, if nobody minded, she would make her way up to her room. Gordon also made his excuses and left Chris and Ronnie to finish off downstairs and as they went upstairs they both felt that this had been a day full of surprises and concerns but it all seemed to go really well. What would tomorrow bring?

Chapter 11.

That evening was very different for Robert Underwood. He was busy packing his suitcase with a grim determination. On that terrible journey back to his awful flat he had decided that ANYTHING was better than going to his mother's house in Chichester and listening to her telling him she told him so and making arrangements for his lifetime of incarceration at the call centre working alongside his successful brother! He had made his choice and he was determined to go through with it! He was going to this farmhouse in Norfolk and he was going to sort himself out once and for all. He would treat it like research for a role in a movie. It would be good life experience and he could add it to his C.V.! Robert was nearly 40 years old and was no fool. He knew, in his heart of hearts, that this was the end of his acting career -such as it was – but he was also certain that he was destined for something better than the call centre. As he took a last look at his flat he sighed and shook his head slowly. Was this all he had to show for himself? He was certain that, whatever happened, he would NEVER set foot in this hell hole again. And so without a backward glance he closed the door and pushed the key through the letter box and walked to the railway station.

As he looked at the timetable for his journey he didn't even mind that his journey would take him hours and there would be many changes of station plus lots of hanging about. Robert Underwood, failed actor, felt more alive right now than he had for years! He was starting out on an adventure that would lead God knows where and, damn it, he was excited and terrified in equal measure! He had precious little money but he didn't care. Robert Underwood, new man, was ready for whatever life in Norfolk threw at him!

Robert's enthusiasm was tested to the limit when his journey was constantly delayed and it was obvious that he was not going to get to his destination before the morning. Still "Never mind" thought Robert "These things are sent to try us!" As the train finally drew into Thetford station Robert's pulse began to quicken. Why the hell did he feel so nervous? What was there to feel worried about? These and many other questions like them flooded Robert's mind and it took a supreme effort on his part not to start running blindly down the high street screaming abuse at the top of his voice! That thought made Robert laugh out loud, to the obvious disconcertion of his fellow passengers, but it also brought him to his senses. He was not under the control of his Mother anymore. He did not have to justify his actions to anybody. He was as free as a bird and he took perverse delight in knowing that his Mother and his supercilious brother did not know where he was and could do nothing about contacting him. (Robert had thrown his mobile off the train with great gusto at about 2 a.m. that morning) He hauled his rucksack onto the Number 39 'bus to his destination and allowed the beautiful countryside to ease his worries- and so it was that a fully refreshed Robert Underwood went to the public telephone box and Rang Haven's Retreat!

The telephone ringing had a different effect on all the residents of Haven's Retreat. Ronnie was the one who answered it as Chris was up early to take the vegetables into town as he did twice a week. Ronnie told Robert that she would telephone Chris on his mobile, where he should wait, and approximately how long it would be before he arrived at the farmhouse. Gordon, meanwhile, was wandering in the garden when he was startled by the telephone. He could not work out where the sound was coming from due to the lie of the land around him. At first he thought it was coming from in front of him, but there was not a building in site! Then he realised that it was coming from the kitchen and he smiled to himself. Why did the telephone ringing make him nervous?

He knew the answer to that, of course. He had thought that it was his children who had somehow found out where he was and were demanding his return so that he could face the music like a man! As the butterflies in his stomach settled Gordon decided there and then that he would not allow thoughts like that to affect him. He had made his decision and he would stand by it until such time as he was emotionally stronger to face his demons and his children!

Prunella meanwhile was lying in bed lost in her thoughts when the telephone broke into her reverie and she smiled to herself. What would her genteel friends think if they could see her now? Lying in a strange bed in a part of the country that most of her associates had never been to, with people who were not her type! What type of person was her "type" anyway? Prunella laughed heartily as she struggled out of bed. Today even the pain and discomfort of her hips and knees would not spoil this morning and so Prunella went into the bathroom and made herself presentable. Standard were standards after all!

"Morning Gordon, did you sleep o.k.?" Ronnie said.

"Never better hinny! That bed was so comfy I thought I would never get up again! "Laughed Gordon even though it was still only 7-30 in the morning and he had been up for 2 hours!

"Glad you liked it. I always take ages to feel comfy in a new bed, but maybe that's just me!" "Would you like coffee or tea Gordon?"

"Tea please, Tea is the only drink for me Ronnie. Coffee is the most awful, snooty drink, ever invented if you ask me!"

"Oh, that's telling me." giggled Ronnie.

"Sorry, hinny. You'll have to forgive my way with words .I was never formally introduced at court see!"

"Oh good, I was never schooled in the correct form of curtseying either!"

"What I thought, if it is alright with you is that we could all eat breakfast together about 9 o'clock when Chris gets back? Hope that's o.k.?"

"That's fine with me."

"Oh! Good morning Prunella! I hope the telephone didn't disturb you? It hardly ever rings so early in the morning and I know that your room is directly above it. Sorry!"

"My Dear Ronnie, think nothing of it. Is that Coffee I can smell? Divine! How I like fresh ground Coffee first thing. None of that tea drinking for me! Far too common"

"What's so funny? "Why are you both laughing? Are you two laughing at me?" As the laughter died down, and after the explanations for the outburst had been given, everyone sat around the kitchen table discussing just what to expect from the day. Ronnie kept her thoughts to herself as she was uncertain how the dynamics of the group would change when the other guests arrived. It was wonderful that Gordon and Prunella got on so famously but Ronnie was under no illusions that this would continue. She knew that a chap called Robert would be here in two hours and then who knew what would happen!

Chris and Ronnie had spent many hours discussing just what the format for the household duties would be when all the guests arrived. Chris was all for a slightly regimental approach with printed rota's for duties and responsibilities etc. Ronnie had laughed at this and ruffled Chris's hair as she patiently explained that this was not an army camp and there would be no need for drill practice!

Eventually Chris had decided that it would have a degree of formality to it but it should be allowed to evolve depending on the people who responded to the newspapers. This was just how Ronnie had wanted it! Chris, of course, would always assume that this decision had, indeed, been a joint affair!

Robert had waited at the designated place and had taken the time to look around the village. He had never realised that places like this existed except on the T.V. How ridiculous was that for a 39 year old man who desperately wanted to work in T.V! He was captivated by the place. The village seemed to have a life of its own. People wandered purposefully around the market shouting greetings, sharing raucous banter, polite conversations and everything in between. Robert was transfixed by it all. People, on the whole, seemed happy and contented. He suddenly felt jealous. Why had he never felt happy and contented? The village looked like something from one of those worthy B.B.C 2 costume dramas but in reality it had a" vibrancy" about it that Robert found contagious. As these thoughts filled his head he was startled by someone coming up to him and asking if he was Robert.

Chris had watched Robert for a few moments and knew, instinctively, that Robert was the man he was looking for. He was obviously deep in thought and troubled and so Chris had decided to wait awhile to find the right time to disturb him.

During the 20 minute drive to the farmhouse he and Robert swapped banalities with each other about the weather, the cricket, politics etc. As Chris turned the car into the farmhouse Robert gasped quietly! Chris was always pleased when anyone had the same reaction to the place as he and Ronnie had had. He knew that the house was weaving its spell on Robert and the other guests and this pleased Chris enormously. It was a new venture for everyone and who knew just what would happen next!

Chapter 12.

Robert looked around his room. It was at the rear of the house, next to the bathroom, and was as Chris explained one of the "Quirkiest" rooms in the house. It was a long "L" shaped room with a balcony which overlooked the flower garden and looked out at the forest. It was peaceful and secluded and Robert felt immediately at home. Chris and Ronnie could not have chosen a better place for him to stay. It was within the confines of the house but also slightly apart. For an actor Robert was actually very shy and tongue tied in real life and he was very aware that his social skills left a lot to be desired when he was with people he did not know. Robert Underwood took a deep breath, drew himself to his full height and with more confidence showing than he actually felt went down to have breakfast with all these new people!

"Hi Robert, Let me introduce you to everybody. Robert, this is Ronnie, my wife, and this lovely young thing is Prunella Okendon and the gentleman in the kitchen helping out is Gordon Jarvis."

"Now, what do you want to eat? I bet you are starving aren't you? Today is an exceptional day for everyone and so I hope we can start the day with a hearty meal that will set us all up for the day's events!" Everyone smiled nervously at this and Chris decided to allow everyone to relax at breakfast and enjoy their first day without any concerns. And so it was that the first day of the new adventure at "Haven's Retreat" began! It was agreed that today would be a day for introductions to the ethos of the "Retreat". Chris and Ronnie spent time with everybody individually to explain that part of each day was to be given over to contemplation and hypnotherapy. Gordon raised his eyebrows at this! He was very unsure but decided to at least give it a try before he made his mind up. Prunella felt comfortable with the whole idea and was the most vocal in her enthusiasm for the project. Robert, meanwhile, found the whole thing a little disconcerting because he had never opened up to anyone in his life, but he actually felt better than he thought about the prospect. And so it was that the first three visitors settled in to life at the "Retreat".

After lunch, which consisted of the freshest bread and tastiest cheese that all the newcomers agreed was the finest they had tasted in many a long while, Chris, Gordon and Robert went out into the farthest field to help harvest more vegetables. Chris was expecting Ronnie to work her charms on the local businessman to increase their orders and so he was going to make sure they had enough supplies. Chris felt so in touch with the garden that his enthusiasm was totally infectious and before very long both Gordon and Robert were working together to make sure they didn't let anyone down, least of all themselves. They dug, they cultivated they pruned all afternoon until both men thought their backs would break! They had never worked so hard and with such gusto in a long time and they both felt great. At 5 pm Prunella brought them cooling lemonade and home-made biscuits which all three devoured with great relish and then it was back to work for at least 2 more hours. Both Gordon and Robert wanted to continue in order for Chris and Ronnie to realise their potential. Chris had, in such a short time, really motivated them and they were as enthusiastic as Chris but without the skills and power!

Prunella and Ronnie, meanwhile, were sorting out the kitchen and house to accommodate the next set of visitors. Ronnie asked Prunella for her advice on bedrooms, meals etc. And Prunella was only too happy to oblige! Ronnie had spoken to Chris first thing that morning and it had been agreed that Prunella was to be invited to be the first client of the "Retreat". When Ronnie mentioned this during the afternoon Prunella was taken aback.

She had assumed that Chris and Ronnie were very experienced at all this sort of thing but once it had been briefly explained Prunella was only too pleased to be the first. Prunella, meanwhile, was not as confident as she appeared. She was of a different generation to everyone else here. She was a child of the "Stiff upper lip" brigade and had only ever confided to herself about the troubles in her life and look where that had got her!

As Prunella and Ronnie chatted and laughed Prunella had one of her "moments" as she would later admit and decided to announce at dinner that she was no longer Prunella Okenden 90 plus O.A.P, but "Pru" the fun loving girl of the past! At this thought Pru smiled to herself and wondered if this was to be the start of something good in her life? If it was she could not wait!

Ronnie and Pru agreed that for today only the women would do all the cooking but when the house was full everybody would be expected to help in all aspects of housework, even those who did not know one end of a kettle from another!

"Prunella? Do you want to try one of my herbal teas? I know you hate ordinary tea but these herbal ones are really refreshing!"

"Oh! What the hell! Why not?"

"Do you mind which one or will you be brave and let me choose?"

"My dear girl, I'm sure that you would not poison a frail old dear like me, not on the first morning anyway! Would you?"

"Of course not, maybe next week if you don't pull your weight! You never know!" laughed Ronnie as she put the kettle on and opened the dreaded Aga to see if the biscuits were still raw or burnt to a crisp! That bloody Aga was the bane of her life but she still loved it and would not countenance anything else in her beloved kitchen. As she opened the door the delicious aroma of ginger biscuits wafted into the hallway and Prunella was instantly drawn to the delicious aroma and, without realising, sat down at the large kitchen table and had the most expectant look on her face that Ronnie had to quickly turn away before Prunella saw her wry smile. Ronnie's food had always been special according to Chris and Ronnie felt a foolish, girly, pride when she saw the expression on Prunella's face. The kettle had boiled, the herbal tea was "stewing" and the biscuits looked fabulous even though she said so herself - and so it was that these two comparative strangers began to develop a trusting relationship that was vital if Ronnie and Chris were going to achieve everything they had set out to do.

Chapter 13.

Vanessa Floyd-White, meanwhile, had more pressing things on her mind than wondering if the biscuits were burnt or not! She was trying to negotiate the horrendous evening traffic as her mind was in such a terrible turmoil! What the hell was she doing going to Norfolk at this time of night with only a few things thrown into an overnight case? All day Vanessa had fought with her conscience and she ruefully admitted that she had lost that one particular battle with a vengeance! Try as hard as she could even Vanessa had to admit that her life was a mess, she was a mess and only she could do anything about changing things.

Knowing all this did not help Vanessa, who was a coward when it came to confrontation (even those in her own head) and so she had spent all day ignoring her "friends" phone calls and text messages. Vanessa was at a crossroads in her life, she knew that without a shadow of a doubt, but did she have the courage to do what she was thinking of doing? Having prevaricated all day Vanessa suddenly came to a decision. She was going to Norfolk, she was going to sort herself out and she was not coming back to Richmond any time soon!

Thirty seconds later Vanessa was not going to Norfolk, her life was not that bad after all and she loved her life in Richmond!

At 6 o'clock Vanessa threw a few things into her bag, checked that she had her credit card, took a brief look around her house and closed the door on her old life without a backward glance. One hour later and Vanessa's resolve was weakening slightly as she succumbed to another bout of road rage which helped to illustrate that Vanessa Floyd-Wright might be a 31 wealthy woman who had enjoyed a privileged upbringing but, my god, could she curse!! The sat- nav system in her Mercedes was a constant reminder of the distinct lack of progress Vanessa was making. However, soon the traffic eased and Vanessa was soon able to use the "cruise control" feature on the car as she headed to deepest darkest Norfolk!

As the time went on and she became more relaxed Vanessa began to wonder what she could expect at "Haven's Retreat"? Would everybody be strange? Would they be social misfits? Would they be "her sort"? At this thought Vanessa laughed out loud! Hark at her – who the hell was she to judge? The signpost said that it was 10 miles to her exit junction and so Vanessa used her "hands free" telephone to ring "Haven's Retreat" to say that she would be there soon. As the ring tone started Vanessa's stomach was in knots. She was terrified! She was alone in bloody Norfolk and she had never needed a friendly face more than she needed one right now!

As she turned into the drive and she caught her first glimpse of the house Vanessa took a deep breath, put on her best "hostess" smile and opened the car door!

Ronnie stood framed in the doorway as Vanessa walked towards her and studied her discreetly.

Ronnie was concerned that the dynamics of the group would be difficult to handle but both Chris and Ronnie had committed themselves and the house to the project and nothing was going to stop it from being the success it deserved and the financial success it just had to be if the farm was not going to bankrupt them! As Vanessa walked towards her Ronnie was making her initial appraisal of her and she was concerned! Vanessa's "aura" was not a good one. It was full of negative energy and suspicion but underlying this was a genuine need for help.

As Ronnie and Vanessa exchanged greetings and questions about the journey etc it all helped to overcome the initial embarrassment these situations sometimes caused and so it was a slightly more relaxed Vanessa that entered the kitchen at "Haven's Retreat"!

"Hello everybody my name is Vanessa and I am bloody shattered and feeling very awkward right at this moment and so I decided the best thing I could do was to grab it by the balls and face it head on. Hope everybody is o.k. with that?"

As Vanessa's gaze swept the room her heart sank. In one chair was a woman who must have been at least a hundred years old, there was a boring looking older man and a timid looking guy of about forty all looking as though someone had just farted!

"Hello my dear, I do hope you are not too exhausted after your journey? Please, take a seat next to me and have a cup of Ronnie's truly remarkable herbal teas."

Vanessa allowed herself to be propelled into the chair next to the hundred year old woman and before she knew it she was handed a cup of herbal tea and told to drink it up while it is hot!

As she sat there everyone was talking at once and all asking variations of the same questions that we all ask.

" Was the traffic in London as bad as everyone said?"

"Was she tired after her journey?"

"What did she think of the farmhouse and Norfolk?"

As all these questions were fired at her Vanessa was overwhelmed by the warmth of everyone's welcome. Well perhaps not everyone's welcome. After the introductions had been made and tea had been drunk it was time for bed and so everyone said their goodnights. Actually it was "Pru", as she insisted everyone called her from now on, and Robert who wished her a good night's sleep after her long journey and told her she would enjoy the fabulous breakfast that Chris and Ronnie provided. Gordon, meanwhile, had kept his own council with regard to Vanessa Floyd – Wright. Vanessa felt that, quite correctly as it happened, Gordon had decided he didn't like her very much and this was a completely alien thing for Vanessa to experience. During her partying phase Vanessa had always surrounded herself with "yes" men and woman who would never hint that they did not only adore Vanessa but they did not know anyone else more perfect! Vanessa was, of course, no fool and fully understood and appreciated the motivations of her feckless, vacuous associates in her other life but she found it disconcerting to note that within this small group of people there was one who had taken an instant dislike to her!

Vanessa's thoughts were troubled as she climbed the stairs to her room and she could not forget the look of total contempt on the face of Gordon as he had passed her in the hallway out of her mind and she knew that sleep would elude her that night.

Gordon climbed the stairs to his bedroom and wondered just what it was about that bloody woman that had got under his skin! He had only just met her for god's sake and he had never taken such an instant dislike to someone.

He knew that part of it was the fact that she spoke in that superior manner that the truly wealthy speak, but it was more than that Gordon was certain! He decided that tomorrow he was going to apologise for his obvious rudeness and give her the benefit of the doubt!

Chapter 14.

Friday 10th June. 6 – 30 a. m.

Fridays were special to Chris. When he was a Padre in the Army Friday had been the day when he would start to write his sermon. Friday was his day with God. Friday was the day he met Ronnie for the first time and Friday now meant that his day was so full of travelling to town to deliver grocery orders, go to the dreaded bank, do a million and one other things that always seem to conspire against him that he never normally had time to draw breath! But not today! Today Chris was going to spend his day at the farmhouse with his beloved Ronnie getting to know the houseguests and beginning the process of helping them to overcome all the things that were troubling them and stopping them living their lives to the full!

Chris felt a real sense of elation and anticipation as he slowly crept out of the bedroom and walked downstairs to put the kettle on (that was if the dreaded Aga was still lit from last night! He really must do something about that Aga, but not today).   As the kettle bubbled into life Chris spent the time in quiet, peaceful contemplation. His religious beliefs were still as strong in many ways but lately Chris had been questioning himself! Was what he wanted for the farmhouse really what God wanted? Was he doing this to play God himself with other people's lives? He truly hoped not. As these thoughts battled with each other in his head Chris walked outside and breathed in the cool clear morning air. As the scent of the forest hit his nostrils Chris felt compelled to walk into the forest to collect his thoughts but just as he was about to go through the gate a voice wished him a very good morning and hoped he had had as good a night's sleep as she had? Chris smiled ruefully to himself as he turned to face Vanessa and put on his best host's smile. His moment of quiet reflection would have to wait after all!

Vanessa looked a little different this morning Chris thought as he poured her a cup of strong black coffee (the only way she knew how to start the day according to Vanessa) she looked more rested and relaxed than she did last night. She did look as though something was really troubling her but she was in total denial. Chris and Ronnie had spent an age discussing Vanessa after they had gone to bed that night, both of them felt the "aura" around Vanessa was not a good one and so it had been decided that she would have the first opportunity that arose to have a "reiki" session with Ronnie together with a relaxing massage to help to relieve the obvious tension that was spilling out of her!

As the sun began to rise and the farm animals began to rouse - so did the rest of the guests. At 8 am everyone was seated in the kitchen and the conversations around the room were polite but still reserved which Chris expected, after all these were total strangers who were all there for similar purposes so what more could be asked of them?

The aroma of a full English breakfast filled the kitchen vying for supremacy above the smells of freshly ground coffee and Ronnie's herbal teas. Chris enjoyed this morning more than any other as this was the last time that his guests would enjoy such a carefree start to the day! If only they knew!!

As everyone finished their breakfast and a routine for kitchen duties was established (Pru was in her element) Chris took the time for a brief cuddle with Ronnie. Today was going to be a busy and challenging day for all the guests and so Chris and Ronnie had decided that this morning was going to be the perfect start to a possibly gruelling day!

"Right everyone I think it's time to begin our day don't you?" Chris said.

The silence was palpable as every looked at the floor, the clock the Aga anything but at each other!

Ronnie stepped in to soothe the waters as she explained that this first morning was going to be spent wandering around the farmhouse and its gardens, agreeing on a rota system for the smooth running of the farmhouse etc and generally getting to know a little bit more about each other! As everyone visibly relaxed Chris hid a wry smile. He always found it amusing that people considered Ronnie to be the "good cop" and he was the "bad cop"! How wrong could you be? Ronnie could be just as tough as Chris when she needed to be.

 As they began their grand tour of the garden Pru decided that it was about time that the atmosphere improved and so with a grand flourish she called for everyone's attention and began to speak.

"My Dears, I think I speak for everyone when I say that this morning is feeling awkward and uncomfortable. So what I propose we do is all try and relax because we are all here for similar reasons and we all need to realise that we are all in this together so what do you say to a group hug?" As she took in the aghast looks on everyone's faces Pru laughed out loud! "Only joking! Oh my goodness. If you could only see your faces?" As everyone smiled and looked embarrassed Pru was amazed by her nerve! Just what was happening to her?

Chris and Ronnie were delighted that Pru felt comfortable enough to speak out but they both also knew that Mrs Prunella Okenden would need careful handling if she was not going to start monopolising the group!

The rest of the morning went really well for most of the others. Gordon and Vanessa were being terribly polite towards each other but it was patently obvious to everyone that very soon the fireworks would start.

After lunch was over the group left the house to continue their duties and Chris and Ronnie reflected on the events of the morning. Gordon was so rude towards Vanessa. Vanessa was so superior towards Gordon. Just what was wrong with them both? This situation could not be allowed to continue and so it was decided that tonight would be the ideal time for Gordon and Vanessa to sort out their differences and try to work together for the sake of the whole group. Tonight could not come soon enough for Chris and Ronnie!

Chapter 15.

Adam Jenkins arrived in Thetford just after 10am and did not know what to do! He had had an exhausting journey. It had taken him bloody hours to get here. To get where? This boring dump! Just what the hell had he been thinking? This was not the sort of place for him. He could never fit in with all these oldies and yuppies. As he looked around outside the station he felt his hunger pangs strike again, where could he get a Big Mac? Where the hell was the K.F.C? Did these folks know what good food was? As he walked down the high street with his usual swagger he noticed the "natives" looking at him. What was their problem? He stopped outside a local bakery and looked in the window. What he saw was a vast array of pies, quiches, baguettes etc. Maybe this place isn't so bad after all! As Adam finished his steak pasty with obvious relish his thoughts returned to the reason he was here in the first place. Not for the only time that day did his stomach do a funny "back flip" when he recalled his time sleeping rough in Bristol, for his entire swagger" Adam had to admit to himself that he was not a brave person. In fact he was a coward when it really came to it! Of course he would never admit to that to anyone else – ever! His "cool" status was everything to Adam. As he lazily dropped his wrapper on the floor he began to look around Thetford. He was used to the rougher parts of Bristol and so was not quite sure what to make of his new surroundings! As he looked around he decided that after all the time taken to get here he might as well give this "Haven's Retreat" place a ring, just to see what the "crack" was. No commitment. Adam didn't do commitment! In truth Adam was more than a little scared. If this place was crap and full of weirdo's just what the hell would he do then? Oh well! What had he to lose?

Ten minutes later and Adam Jenkins was f –ing furious! Where the hell was the signal for his mobile phone? He could not and would not survive without his state of the art phone. (Nicked from The Carphone Warehouse in Bristol no less – one of his best jobs if he says so himself!) He had sworn at it, turned it off-everything he knew how to do- and still no bloody signal! In sheer desperation and not a little frustration he yanked open the door of the public phone box just around the corner from the station and stared! What the f*** did he do now? The only time Adam had been inside a phone box was when he was ripping it apart for the money he could pinch! As he swore and cursed he noticed an elderly lady watching him. He was just about to tell her where to go when she offered to help him! Adam was dumbstruck! The lady explained that this phone box had only been installed for a few days and wasn't it a nuisance when there was nothing wrong with the old telephone! Anyway my dear, the lady said, would you mind awfully if I showed you how it works? You see I have no telephone at home, my husband won't let me have one you know – shocking in this day and age don't you think?- so I use this phone box an awful lot! What he doesn't know about can't hurt him eh?

After she had gone Adam couldn't help but smile because, despite himself, for the first time in his life he had had a conversation with a really ancient woman that did not involve him and his mates hurling abuse at old folks and he had quite enjoyed it! Her name was Martha her husband's name was Reginald or "Reg" as he liked to be called! They had lived in Thetford their entire lives and couldn't wish to live in a nicer place! She wondered where he came from as he had a funny accent! HE had a funny accent! Had she heard herself talk! Now that was a funny accent! As Adam dialled the number he very slowly began to relax and some of the tension he had felt all through the long journey began to dissipate and so it was with a lighter heart that Adam waited outside the train station to be collected. Maybe this place was not too bad after all?

Chapter 16.

The telephone ringing ended Chris and Ronnie's discussion about Pru and her potential for monopolising the group. As Ronnie replaced the receiver and shouted to Chris that he needed to go to Thetford to pick up the new arrival the fluttering doubts in her mind and soul re-emerged! Was this going to work? My God it had to work! Ronnie was pragmatic regarding the financial need to open up their home in order for it to survive. What she was less enthusiastic about was that somehow when they had shared their home with strangers would some, or all, of the magic disappear? However this was not the time or place for considering this now and so, as she walked back into the garden to begin work, she allowed those thoughts to retreat to the back of her mind and lie in wait for her when she had some time to consider them. Whenever that might be!

Chris, meanwhile, loaded the ancient Land Rover with vegetables and flowers to take to their clients in Thetford and pondered on similar things to Ronnie. He felt more certain that things would be o.k. with the farmhouse after the first guests had gone but was still uncomfortable with the knowledge that this just might be the future if the Army did not come to their financial rescue as they had promised! Just one more batch of mind wounded soldiers to put back together as best they could and the Army had promised them enough funding to pay off their exorbitant mortgage and other loans and still have plenty in the bank to survive until their old age! Just who were these soldiers? They must be very important to the Army for them to be paying so much for Chris and Ronnie's help and silence! Don't forget the silence! As if either of them could! They knew from bitter experience just what someone breaking their silence could mean! Hadn't they seen the remains of their only true friend in Burma as her body, or what remained of her body, was dumped outside the Army barracks at Amarapura . All these thoughts crowded into Chris's head on the journey to Thetford that he was pulling into the Station car park before he knew where he was! How the hell had he got here? Had he driven the entire journey on autopilot? He really MUST concentrate or else he could kill someone with his thoughtless driving! Chris parked the Land Rover in the station car park and began to unload his wares. It was only a short walk to both of his clients and he was glad that today he had a genuine reason to disappear as quickly as he could from the clutches of Mavis behind the bar of the "Kings Head" in the high street! Mavis was a lovely woman BUT MY GOD COULD SHE TALK? Chris gathered up the vegetables and made his way slowly through the crowd of shoppers, dropped off the vegetables and flowers as promised and headed back to his vehicle. As he did so he contemplated who he would meet today. He had no idea if Adam was young, old, black, white or Martian! Ronnie just said to wait outside the main entrance to the station and so that was what he would do! As he turned the corner, deep in thought, he collided head on with a young girl waiting nervously for someone and he knocked her completely over! As he helped her up he was both appalled and embarrassed by what he had done! What was the matter with him today? CONCENTRATE! For God's sake will you? The young girl he had knocked over was sitting on the floor crying quietly to herself and she had the saddest look on her face! How troubled she seemed. What was so wrong with her life that she looked so sad and lost? As he muttered his apologies he was joined by an angry looking man in a shell suit who began to shout at him to mind the F*** where he was going. You stupid tosser! Didn't you see her? Are you blind, stupid or both?

As he helped her up the young lad also began to help her up. Chris suggested that she sat in his Land Rover for a while so that she could get her breath. The young lad said something about him being a pervert asking a total stranger to sit in his car. Chris looked aghast. Could his day get any worse?

He told the youth to mind his own business and bugger off! The youth said he would not bugger off and he would wait with the girl to make sure she was safe from the likes of him! As they got to the Land Rover both the girl and the lout went quiet! The lout had such a strange look on his face - it was a mixture of disbelief and sadness. Now what was the matter with him? The young girl also had a strange look on her face. It was a similar look of disbelief and sadness. Just what the hell was going on? Adam could not keep the sound of disappointment and concern out of his voice as he asked "Is this your Land Rover?" Are you the guy from "Haven's Retreat?" Lauren looked up with total shock written all over her face. And then it hit him! Oh my God! The lad was Adam the guest he was picking up. And he was sure that the girl was the final guest of "Haven's Retreat". What an impression he had made on both of them!

Chris Gaskell drew in a huge breath and began to explain the situation they found themselves in and to grovel to both of them for the completely false impression they must have of him. At first the atmosphere was frosty to say the least but as Chris continued to explain he thought he saw a little smile playing at the corners of the girls mouth and then she began to giggle quietly to herself and before they knew it she was laughing out loud and the lout was smiling and then laughing and then Chris saw the funny side of it and he laughed until it hurt as they all tumbled over each other to apologise for the complete misunderstanding and could they start again with formal introductions and handshakes etc. At that suggestion they all collapsed into helpless giggles and decided that perhaps that wasn't really necessary after all. As Chris loaded what little luggage the kids had brought with them he pondered on life's little foibles. He couldn't help but think that his big boss up in the sky was enjoying himself at Chris's expense. Oh well, thought Chris, Gods will is Gods will! Chris reversed the Land Rover out of the parking space, looked in his rear view mirror at his final two guests chatting away as if they had known each other for all their lives and realised that God does move in mysterious ways after all! And so it was that the guest list for the first session at "Haven's Retreat" was complete.

Let the fun begin!

Chapter 17.

As the Land Rover continued on its journey to Soham Tarney with the young one's getting more acquainted and swapping horror stories of their journey and people in general Chris was able to collect his thoughts and try to decide the best way to handle the inevitable explanations demanded by Ronnie as to just what the hell went on this morning! He decided, as he knew he would, that he would be totally upfront about it and confess his sins!(Now there was a thought he smiled to himself.) And so it was after a few awkward moments and not a few side long glances from the other guests that finally the whole incident was put into its proper prospective and the day was allowed to continue.

As all the guests sat down to a cold buffet, made for the very last time by all the woman of the household as Pru was heard to say in a very loud "stage whisper"- to be greeted by general good humour and sexist banter from Gordon, Ronnie brought the discussion around to the business in hand, i.e. "Haven's Retreat" and what it would mean to everyone in the household if they would give themselves the chance to embrace everything that she and Chris would throw at them! Chris listened with transparent admiration as Ronnie talked with obvious passion and enthusiasm about the philosophy they had for the treatments offered, the special place that the house held in their hearts and the wish that the house would come to mean something special to everyone sitting around the table. As she finished her completely unrehearsed but fabulously inspirational speech it was all Chris could do to stay seated and not leap into the air and shout "Bravo" at the top of his voice. His heart felt like it would burst with pride. He was saved from his predicament by Robert slowly getting to his feet and applauding for him. Robert's eyes were transfixed on Ronnie and as Chris looked around the large dining table he could see that everyone had been similarly affected by the speech and so it was that, one by one, they all stood and gave Ronnie a rousing cheer. Ronnie looked so beautiful at that moment - she was positively glowing – not from the praise but from an inner beauty and peace that Chris had worried had been lost forever and it was at that precise moment that Chris Gaskell, former padre in the Army and devoted husband, vowed that NOTHING would ever take Ronnie and "Haven's Retreat" from him!

After lunch the guests were allocated various tasks either in the house or in the gardens. Chris and Ronnie took the time for reflection and discussion of the weeks ahead.

They both agreed that the first priority was to analyse and try to help with the obvious animosity between Gordon and Vanessa because despite their best efforts it was obvious to everyone in the household, even the new arrivals, that there was a great deal of tension bubbling under the surface that needed to be dealt with urgently if the whole group was going to live and function together for the entire summer.

Ronnie walked slowly into the "Treatment Room" as they used to call it. It had been decided without the need for words by both Ronnie and Chris that it was no longer the "Treatment Room" but was to be known as the discussion lounge or some such non-medical sounding term. As she looked around Ronnie felt a sense of calm wash over her. This room had always had that affect on both her and Chris from the very first morning five years ago when they first walked into the room and so it was the perfect place for open discussion and as such had been beautifully furnished with just the right type of furniture and paintings etc. So that it looked inviting, safe and secret. When Ronnie had first described the room as "secret"

Chris had laughed out loud and he and Ronnie had had their first argument at Soham Tarney (But they had had a great time making up Chris remembered) but Ronnie, of course, had been proven right. Despite his protestations at the beginning the more time secret Chris spent in this room the more he had to agree with Ronnie that the room did indeed have a quality about it and was the ideal place for everyone to come to when they needed a place of sanctuary and quiet reflection. The sunshine poured into the lounge from large French windows and bathed the room in its glorious light until late evening. The large inglenook fireplace, like all the fireplaces in the farmhouse, was used regularly and most nights in the winter Chris and Ronnie were drawn to this room to enjoy each other's company and relish the time for their own quiet reflection. The furniture was the casual mis-match of periods that seemed to work all over the house, thanks to Ronnie's exquisite taste for selecting just the right thing. Chris was not blessed with the same good taste but was well aware of the "hold" the house had on people when they first arrived. As they sat down they both felt a slight unease settle on them. Chris was the first to voice his concerns.

"Ronnie, we are doing the right thing aren't we? I feel sure we are but I cannot get this niggling doubt out of my mind! "

Ronnie was so glad that Chris felt as she did. How could she ever have doubted that?"I know just how you feel my love but we are doing the right thing you know!"

As they continued to discuss the guests they both relaxed and came up with a programme of tasks etc that would enable everyone to have the opportunity to help with the running of the house as well as the chance for individual or group discussions as appropriate together with a shared responsibility for all the tasks to ensure that no-one was considered to be "in charge" (who could they possibly mean?).

Each morning would consist of breakfast together, very important Ronnie said to maintain team spirit, after which tasks would be allocated on a rota basis so that everyone was involved as much as they could be with all aspects of the farmhouse.

After lunch would be the time for discussion sessions in the lounge together with" Reiki", tai-chi, aromatherapy massages or hypnotherapy sessions as appropriate.

In the evening there would be free time for everyone to do what they needed to do. This point was discussed at length by Chris and Ronnie as this was one aspect of the treatment that they still felt uncomfortable with. What if the guests went into town began talking to locals etc, and "Haven's Retreat" became the topic of conversation in the town? Chris and Ronnie had spent months' letting their profile slowly disappear which was just what they, and especially the army, wanted!

As the afternoon sunshine swathed the room in glorious colours outside the others were going about their duties with varying degrees of enthusiasm and skill! Adam and Laura spent the afternoon giggling and poking fun at all the "crap" furniture, laughing unbelievingly when they realised that there was no TV or "sky" (thank god Adam had got his i-pod with him!) and generally doing little more than getting to know each other better.

As the afternoon continued in glorious sunshine the effect it had on the other guests was incredibly varied. Pru and Vanessa had opted to stay indoors to help Ronnie with the packing of the fruit and vegetables that Chris was due to take to the market the day after tomorrow.

The work was not particularly hard but neither of the ladies had done anything like it before and it was painfully slow -to say the least. After an hour or so of this Vanessa was feeling decidedly "stir crazy" as she put it and so it was decided that the best thing she could do was to go outside to see if she could be of any more help to the men outside. As Vanessa started to walk slowly to the far field where the men were working she had time to look around at the farmhouse and its gardens. Vanessa was a "townie" at heart and she had never spent any time in the countryside. She was unsure what to expect but she was determined to "give it a go" as Pru had said. She went through the flower garden attached to the main house and was pleasantly surprised at just how beautiful and fragrant the garden was. Her only experience with flowers was when she had ordered highly expensive and artistic arrangements from one of the latest fashionable people who were the "must have" designers that only the super trendy and super wealthy could afford to have in their homes. She had never really looked at the arrangements she had ordered for her latest soiree, she had just paid the bill and then thought no more about them. As she was lost in thought she was aware that she was not alone in the garden! As she looked over her shoulder she could not help groaning as she realised that she was sharing the garden with Gordon! Oh dear god why did it have to be that man! As Gordon and Vanessa eyed one another with undisguised contempt it occurred to Vanessa that if she was going to stay here for the summer (and she was not going to be the one who left) she needed to clear the air between them and so with a heavy heart she attempted to make polite conversation with the odious man.

"Oh hello - Gordon isn't it? What are you doing here in the garden? I thought you should be in the far field helping Chris and Robert? Is something wrong?"

Gordon looked at her with transparent disgust and was about to say something when Vanessa sensed that it was taking all his effort not to turn around and storm off.

"Gordon have I done something to offend you? Only you seemed to have taken an instant dislike to me and I would like to know why?"

Vanessa was staggered at herself. Where the hell had that come from? She had never instigated that type of question. She had always shied away from any sort of confrontation! Gordon meanwhile looked completely taken aback at the directness of her question and was looking most uncomfortable. "Look hinny I don't know what it is about you that I don't like and that's the god's honest truth. I just came here to get some cooling lemonade because it's ruddy hard work out here and we are all thirsty as hell! So before you start on me can I just say that I am prepared to give you the benefit of the doubt and perhaps we can start to get to know each other better if we are going to spend the entire summer in each other's company?"

"What the hell do you mean you will give me the benefit of the doubt? Who the hell do you think you are? You do not know the first thing about me and yet you sit in judgement of me! Let me just say if it wasn't for your attitude towards me then maybe we might just get along!"

"My attitude to you! You with your superior airs and graces! You might have more money than me but that doesn't make you a better person that me! Far from it!" "What the hell do you mean my airs and graces? You have the biggest chip on your shoulder! Who the hell are you to judge me you pathetic little man?"

As the argument continued Adam and Laura came out of the house to watch the "entertainment". They could not believe that the old geezer and the toff were going at it hammer and tongs! Adam was all for the old guy to smack the stuck up bitch in the gob! Whereas Lauren was horrified that Vanessa was being judged by how she looked and spoke rather than for whom she might be! Heaven knows she knew more than perhaps anybody here that appearances could be deceptive! She wondered if any of them would realise that she was a working girl or a "prozzie" and a pregnant one at that! As the argument raged Laura disappeared into the house to escape the awful confrontation and found herself drawn to the lounge where just a short while ago Chris and Ronnie were discussing the best way to maintain peace, harmony and equilibrium within the group!

Laura sat in the largest comfiest chair she had ever sat in and looked back at her life. She was just over 19 years old and right now she felt ancient with the stresses and strains of the past few months. She needed a fix of drugs to help her get through the rest of the summer! NO! She would never go back to that life! She had been clean for over a year now and she intended to stay that way! As she relaxed in the chair she allowed herself the privilege of a few moments reflection. How long could she keep her pregnancy secret? Just what the hell was she going to do with the rest of her life? As the sounds of the argument raging outside became louder it all became too much for Lauren and she began to weep, silently at first, but then the floodgates opened and before she knew it her body was being racked with pain as she howled and howled.

Laura was never sure just how long Pru had stood in the doorway listening to her sobs.

All she did know was when she finally began to gain control of her body and look around her that she saw Pru walking towards her with the most disconcerting expression on her face! It was as if she knew! It was as if this total stranger had looked inside her head and listened to her innermost thoughts and had not judged her harshly! Pru wrapped her arms around Laura as she started to cry again and when, finally, all her tears were spent Pru cradled her until Lauren fell into an exhausted sleep! Laura woke some 40 minutes later to discover that she had been covered with a shawl, the curtains had been drawn so no-one could see her from outside and the door to the lounge had been closed. Laura, for the first time in a very long time, felt some degree of inner peace! Maybe, just maybe, she had found someone she could confide in! She had never expected it to be the ancient old woman who spoke with such a proud voice!! Well, as Laura knew only too well, you never knew just what life could throw at you! And so it was that Laura Machin and Prunella (Pru) began a friendship that would last their entire lives! Elsewhere in the house things were taking a decidedly more awkward and uncomfortable path!

Gordon and Vanessa's argument continued to rage in the garden until Ronnie arrived. As she listened to the argument Ronnie was astounded at the vitriol and anger being poured out of both Gordon and Vanessa. In an attempt to diffuse the situation Ronnie suggested that they both returned to their rooms and spend the time alone in reflection of their actions. As they both went to their rooms Ronnie was at a loss as to what to do next. She felt like she was the headmistress and she had just sent two naughty schoolchildren to their rooms! Oh how she needed Chris to be here to help her decide what to do! As she thought this she was brought back to reality when Adam spoke. "You know something, how come it's always the young ones who seem to be the trouble makers? What about those two? What the hell was that all about? They need to sort their differences out pretty damn quick before they kill each other don't you think?"

Ronnie decided that actually Adam was right they did both need to address their issues and she was damn sure that that would happen as soon as she could arrange it!

As the evening drew in the mood in the house was one of nervous anticipation, everyone seemed to be on tenterhooks and the evening meal was quiet and subdued. After the meal both Gordon and Vanessa ignored each other but the silence was almost as unbearable as the rowing. Chris and Ronnie had had the chance to discuss the events of the afternoon and had both decided that the best way to deal with this was with a head on approach and so it was that Chris took Gordon into the workshop in the stable yard and Ronnie took Vanessa into the lounge. Robert, Pru, Laura and Adam busied themselves with the washing up and the brewing of a cup of tea, anything to distract themselves from what was going on! Just what exactly was their problem?

As Chris walked towards the workshop, with Gordon silently following, Chris was at a loss as to how to broach the subject of the animosity between Gordon and Vanessa. In the end he didn't have to worry as Gordon seemed to be in a hurry to speak.

"Look Chris can I just start by apologising for my terrible behaviour?"

"I don't think it's me you should be me you are apologising to do you?"

"If you think I'm saying sorry to that stuck up cow then think again!"

"Gordon can I be completely honest with you?"

"Course you can lad!"

"Just what exactly is troubling you? It's obviously something that goes really deep. I haven't known you very long but you don't strike me as the vindictive type. So what exactly is going on?"

Gordon's face disintegrated before Chris's eyes and the tears silently fell. Chris knew that whatever was troubling Gordon was really raw and only just under the surface. As Chris went to put his arm around Gordon to try to offer him some comfort he was surprised at the vehemence of Gordon's reaction. Gordon let out a bellow of pure anguish that for a moment Chris was stunned into silence and felt rooted to the spot.

"Chris please don't be nice to me. I couldn't stand it. I don't deserve it, I really don't!"

As they spoke Chris led Gordon to the bench in the corner of the workroom and Gordon allowed himself to be seated as the tears continued to flow.

"Gordon, I know I haven't known you long but I hope you realise that you can tell me anything in the strictest confidence?"

Chris wondered if Gordon had heard him as there was no reaction at first and then slowly Gordon turned to face Chris with such an expression of pure anguish that it took Chris's breath away!

"I don't know where to begin, but begin I must for the sake of my sanity." Gordon was silent for a long time." Vanessa isn't the problem. The problem is me." Gordon struggled to control his emotions as he looked at Chris." Vanessa is the same age as my daughter. The daughter who never wants to see me again. She looks exactly like Vanessa and I cannot cope with that.

Vanessa has that same air of arrogance and superiority that Angela, my daughter, has. When I saw her arrive I was so shocked I could hardly breathe and I thought I could handle it but I can't! "

Why doesn't Angela want to see you again Gordon?"

Gordon spent the next hour telling Chris EVERYTHING - including his part in the suicide of his beloved wife. He told Chris about the rift between his family and himself. Chris sat in silence as Gordon opened his heart. Chris was stunned by the revelations and didn't know what to do when Gordon told him of the weeks spent hording the tablets his wife needed and the subsequent grief when his family disowned him. As Gordon continued to sob Chris felt an enormous amount of compassion for this man as well as concern for his own religious beliefs. How could he listen to this confession and not be appalled that this man in front of him actively helped his wife commit suicide? Chris continued to listen but his conscience was in turmoil!

As Gordon's tears finally abated he was left drained and traumatised.

"What will you do now Chris?"

Chris didn't know what he would do. He knew what he should do – he should inform the police shouldn't he? What would the point of that be? What would it achieve? All these thoughts and many more crowded into Chris's mind that he didn't hear Gordon's anguished plea.

"Sorry Gordon what did you say?"

"Please Chris don't call the police - please? I know that as a religious man you must be appalled at what I have done, but anything you or the police do to me cannot be worse than what my mind has done to myself!"

Chris decided that he could not make this decision on the spur of the moment and so he told Gordon that, for now, he would not be doing anything and that Gordon was not to worry he was sure that whatever the outcome was it would be for the best! If only Chris believed that himself- but he knew that it had taken all of Gordon's courage to finally speak to someone about the terrible secret he had been keeping for so long. As Gordon composed himself and said that, under the circumstances, he would not be joining the others for the rest of the evening Chris decided that he would speak to Ronnie as soon as he could and between them they would decide on the next course of action. Oh my God (pardon the pun thought Chris) what a terrible end to the day! This was only the beginning of the summer. What other secrets would emerge? Chris knew that he and Ronnie could cope with just about anything but even he was not sure if they would make the right decision with regard to Gordon's dilemma! As Chris made his way back into the lounge to talk to the others he decided that he would not say anything to Ronnie until the others had retired for the night and they could talk in peace. He knew it would be a long night.

Meanwhile Ronnie and Vanessa were in the lounge. Ronnie was trying to stop Vanessa from pacing around the room and sit down so that she could try and help her to resolve her issues!

Vanessa continued to pace for a little longer but the fight seemed to be going out of her until; finally, she sat down and wept silently.

As Vanessa wept Ronnie realised that, as with Gordon, her troubles ran really deep and Ronnie also knew that whatever was the matter it would not be resolved by a quick chat with her!

"Vanessa I know that you might not want to open up to me- after all I am almost a complete stranger- but I can assure you that whatever you say to me will be treated in the strictest confidence."

Vanessa looked blankly at Ronnie and Ronnie realised that Vanessa was so withdrawn that she hadn't heard a single word she had said! Ronnie led Vanessa to the chair which looked out over the garden. Ronnie knew that this always helped her, when she was troubled; to collect her thoughts and she hoped it would have the same effect on her.

Vanessa allowed herself to be led to the chair and sat down with such an exhausted but defiant look about her that Ronnie was taken aback! Whatever was going on in her head Vanessa was still determined to keep it to herself and not break down in front of a total stranger!

As they both sat in silence looking out into the garden it was broken by Vanessa murmuring something.

"Sorry Vanessa I didn't hear what you said."

"I was just saying that I am deeply embarrassed by my outburst and it will not be happening again as I will be leaving first thing in the morning!" "Oh Vanessa please don't go. I know we don't know one another but maybe you should give me a chance to try to help you. After all isn't that the reason you came here in the first place?"

Vanessa choked back a sob and it took all her self control not break down completely in front of Ronnie. As she witnessed the inner turmoil showing on her face Ronnie hoped that she could change her mind and persuade Vanessa to stay. After nearly an hour Vanessa had still not opened up to Ronnie about why she had had such a violent reaction to Gordon's animosity and Ronnie was experienced enough to know that she could help her if only Vanessa would let her defences down and let her in!

As Vanessa left the lounge to go to her room for some quiet reflection Ronnie went back to the other guests as she realised that they had all been left on their own for an age. Ronnie heard the laughter coming from the room before she had the entered it and Ronnie knew that Pru was holding court again and regaling the others with some repartee! What a woman thought Ronnie! Thank God for her though! Ronnie said to herself. Right now Pru was just what the group needed and so Ronnie came into the kitchen and was immediately given a cup of her own herbal tea and told to drink it while it was hot and Oh! What fun we have had and you don't know what you have missed! Ronnie allowed herself a wry smile and listened to the banter with half an ear as she digested what had just gone on in the lounge. She hoped with all her heart that Vanessa would stay and between them they would be able to exorcise her demons! After 15 minutes Chris rejoined the room without Gordon and it was almost 11.30 before everyone else finally retired for the evening! As they washed up the dishes Ronnie and Chris began to discuss the evening's events and it was 1.30 in the morning before they finally hit the sack. What a day it had been! What had the rest of the summer in store for them? If only they knew

Chapter 18.

The next morning everyone was up and about early. The kitchen, as always, was the heart of the house and was buzzing with activity as all the houseguests prepared for the day ahead. No one mentioned the evening before and Chris and Ronnie ensured that the day was going to be a busy one. As everybody went out into the garden or into the workroom to start on the many and varied tasks that needed to be done daily to ensure the smooth running of the business Ronnie decided that she would talk to Vanessa at the first realistic opportunity. She could not stand by and watch Vanessa and Gordon suffer like this!

Gordon was the first to leave the house and made his solitary way to the farthest field where he had made it abundantly clear that if he was going to stay at the house he needed to be left alone! Ronnie and Chris had decided that, for now, Gordon would get his wish-but it could not be allowed to continue for too long as it would be counter -productive for everybody else.

Vanessa, meanwhile, decided not to leave as long as she was also allowed her own space! How the hell could that happen thought Ronnie?

As she pondered the difficulties ahead the other guests were also considering last night's terrible row.

Robert and Adam had been given the task of uprooting vegetables in the middle field and prepare the fruit and vegetables for market on Monday, What a way to spend a Saturday thought Adam whereas Robert had quite a spring in his step. Robert had always enjoyed working outside. When he was outside he allowed himself the luxury of fantasising about what his life would be like when he was a world famous actor!! As they walked together the conversation came around to the argument and Adam surprised Robert with his insight and perception of what went on. Robert had assumed, wrongly as it happened, that Adam would not understand the intricacies of the situation but was taken aback as Adam told him that he knew from the beginning that "those two wouldn't get on!" it was obvious that he, Gordon, had had a difficult relationship with his kids – you could tell from his attitude to younger people that he had always found it difficult to talk to them and as for her it was blindingly obvious to him and Laura that she was a spoilt madam who only ever wanted love and affection from her dad and never got it! Why the hell no-one else could see that he would never know. Him and Laura watched Jeremy Kyle on T.V every chance they could. It was fabulous to see other people with crappier lives than them! So all they needed to do was sit down and talk to each other and clear the air. He would do the Jeremy Kyle bit if they wanted. Do you think he should say "summat" to them? Robert managed to cover his laughter with a coughing fit! Adam was proving to be a revelation to Robert and he felt ashamed and embarrassed that he had been so judgemental towards Adam and so as they continued on their way to work Robert found Adam more and more fascinating as Adam "told it like it is!" which Robert found so refreshing!

Chris and Ronnie had, at first, been very unsure about the mixture of personalities within the house but an uneasy truce had developed between Vanessa and Gordon. Over the next week all the house guests fell into a routine of work together with the beginnings of friendships and the sharing of confidences. It never ceased to amaze and astound Chris and Ronnie how human nature and the innate goodness of most people came out in all the little details you could observe. Pru and Laura seemed to be getting on really well!

The truce between Vanessa and Gordon was holding out (at least for now!) and Adam and Laura had stopped giggling and whispering about the "oldies" anymore! Robert was the guest that was giving Ronnie the most to be concerned about! Oh not in any obvious way. He was extremely willing and able to help in the garden with Chris and Adam. He was a good cook (when Pru allowed him into "her kitchen") he was always ready to lend a hand with any task and yet both Chris and Ronnie were worried about him. Just what exactly troubled him? Chris and Ronnie had discussed this very thing that morning and it had been decided that Robert should be allowed the most access to the therapy rooms and the hypnotherapy sessions that all the guests had succumbed to (even Gordon had expressed a somewhat reluctant and begrudging confirmation that all this talking lark wasn't too bad after all!)

Robert Underwood was indeed a troubled man. He was caught in a maelstrom of emotions! He had been at the house for such a short time but in that time he had come to love and respect everybody in the house. He woke up before 6 every morning, he worked hard all day. He enjoyed the company of all his fellow houseguests. He was exhausted when he went to bed at night and he had never enjoyed himself so much in his entire life! So why the hell was his mind playing these awful tricks on him? For the past 2 nights he had woken with his heart pounding and his mind racing with terrible thoughts of doom and gloom. He could not get his Mother and Brother out of his mind and he was racked with guilt about not being in touch with them for so long! Oh he knew it had been only a comparatively short time since he had been in contact with his family but he had never gone for longer than a few days not speaking to his mother or brother! So why did he feel so wretched? When he was living his old life he was miserable. He hated his Mother's interference; he loathed the constant comparisons to his more successful Brother. He was constantly reminded of his failings in his career. So why the bloody hell was he feeling so wretched? He should be feeling joyous and excited and scared and all the other emotions associated with someone in love! After another fitful night's sleep Robert awoke with the knowledge that he needed answers to these questions and so he had decided that he would talk to Ronnie about having a hypnotherapy session with her as well as a counselling session with Chris.

As the sun rose and filtered softly through the curtains in his room Robert lay in bed and allowed the calmness and serenity of the early morning to wash over him! He rose from the bed and went to the window and sat for a long time in the window seat looking out at the beautiful garden lost in his thoughts and so it was that Robert Underwood went down to breakfast with a renewed vigour in his stride!

The kitchen was deserted as Robert put on a pot of coffee. As the rich aroma filled the kitchen Robert took stock of just what was important in his life and he smiled to himself as he thought of Vanessa Floyd –Whyte! He had fallen hopelessly in love with Vanessa on the day of the huge row between her and Gordon. She had looked so utterly bereft that his heart had melted there and then. Of course Robert being Robert he had not said a word to anyone in the house. His morning reverie was broken by the sound of the coffee percolator bubbling into life. Robert poured himself a generous cup and strolled out into the garden to sit in his favourite seat in the quietest corner where he could be totally alone with his thoughts.

As Robert sat at his favourite spot Chris was just coming into the kitchen and was just about to shout to Robert when something stopped him!

Chris shook off the feelings of unease and concentrated on the important things in life such as a full cup of coffee- a full stomach- and a full heart! As the smell of bacon and all the trimmings wafted through the house Chris greeted the other guests as they made their way down to the kitchen with the usual greetings and requests for food and drinks. We are such creatures of habit thought Chris as he piled plates high with delicious home cooked bread, bacon, eggs and all the trimmings.

Ronnie and Chris enjoyed this part of the day with all the guests together for a short while before they all went their differing ways for the rest of the day to return each night to chat and tell everyone else all the little things that had gone on in their days that had amused them or disappointed them or made them cross in Pru's case! Robert was blissfully unaware of the intense scrutiny he was under by both Chris and Ronnie – they were, after all, experts in their fields- and so it was that Chris and Ronnie came to the same conclusion at exactly the same moment that Robert was in love with Vanessa! His gaze never left her face for a second. He watched her every move with such joy that Chris and Ronnie were both surprised that they had not noticed anything before?

So why did he seem so pre-occupied with other less pleasant thoughts? Ronnie vowed to arrange a session with Robert at the first opportunity. The opportunity arose sooner than either of them expected because Laura and Pru came into the kitchen and declared that as today was going to be a fabulous special day, the sun was shining, the birds were singing and all was well with the world the "girls" were throwing Chris and Ronnie out of their kitchen and they would cook something "exquisite" for the evening meal.

Robert smiled to himself as he contemplated just what that feeling was like. As he was lost in his thoughts Ronnie was studying every who was in the kitchen trying to decide what was the best course of action when Pru declared in her usual quiet manner that she and Laura had decided between themselves that something was obviously troubling Robert and that if it was all right with Chris and Ronnie then she and Laura would work in the house and kitchen to allow Robert to have as much time talking as he needed! Robert's face was a picture as he struggled to maintain his composure. Was he that transparent? Was it obvious to everybody that he was in love with Vanessa? Did everybody know his innermost thoughts and the turmoil he was in? As these thoughts raced around his head he heard Pru saying that of course she did not have a clue what the matter with Robert was but they could all see that something was troubling him! At that moment Robert could have kissed Pru! Nobody could read his mind! All they could see was a man who was pre-occupied and troubled.

And so it was that Robert Underwood sat down with Chris and Ronnie and opened up his heart about all the things that were troubling him! He explained about his domineering mother, his over achieving brother, his desperate need to succeed at acting (or indeed anything he attempted!) and he shyly admitted, after some gentle and careful questioning by Ronnie, that he had fallen hopelessly in love with Vanessa -a woman he had met only a few days ago and with whom he had had only two or three conversations with! How was that possible?

After an hour of discussion and not a few tears Robert felt calmer and more in control of his life and destiny than he had ever done! He knew, of course, that this was just the beginning of his journey and he would probably have more than one or two setbacks but, nevertheless, he left the room with a spring in his step and the determination in his heart that he was going to give himself the chance to see where his life could lead!

Chapter 19.

Laura and Pru spent the first few minutes in the kitchen in total silence as they cleared all the dishes and paraphernalia associated with a full English breakfast for all the guests. As the water started to fill the large sink and made that friendly gurgling sound that Lauren loved she took a moment to reflect on how her life had changed! Just a few weeks ago she was working as a prostitute, she had no money she had no friends and she was suicidal! Laura and Pru had become friends for life ever since they had spent that time in the house and Laura had cried herself to sleep! Lauren looked around the kitchen. This was her favourite room in the entire house! Oh! all the rooms were beautiful and tastefully decorated but this room had captivated her the very first time she came into it! The "Aga" set into the huge chimney breast, the fabulously grand Welsh dresser with the mismatched but lovely china, the huge dining table that dominated the room, it was as if everything about the room seemed to fit even though none of it had been designed to! Perhaps that was its secret thought Laura. Perhaps the reason everyone seemed to gravitate to this room was because the whole atmosphere created in here was one of nurturing and safety! Laura laughed out loud as this thought struck her! Where had all that come from? She had never thought like this before. She had never used fancy words like that before! At the sound of Laura's laughter Pru turned around and gave Lauren the most beautiful smile that it took Laura's breath away! How had her life changed beyond recognition? What had she done to deserve all this?

"What is so amusing my dear? " **Pru asked.**

"Oh it's really nothing Pru I was just thinking about how life can change. How things can look so awful one minute *and so fabulous the next!"*

"Tell me about it dear! So what exactly do you mean?"

And so it was that Prunella Okenden and Laura Machin continued to find out more and more about each other. The girls talked all morning as they cleaned the kitchen, vacuumed in the hallway and generally tidied the house. Pru told her about her life as a young girl, the incident at the school with the teacher and her disastrous marriage to the gorgeous but unsuitable Gunter! Laura listened with utter fascination as Pru revealed all. Pru was truly amazing thought Laura. She hoped she would never look at old people in the same way again. She began to realize that she had been very judgemental in the past. She had always thought that all old folks had been born old and had absolutely no idea about life! If Pru was anything to go by then she was sadly mistaken! As they prepared the vegetables for the evening meal the girls worked in companionable silence. During this quiet time in the kitchen Pru was considering how best it would be to bring up the subject of Laura's pregnancy! Pru had suspected for the last two days that Lauren might be pregnant. Laura had not eaten much at breakfast; she had pushed her food around the plate which made it look as though she had eaten something, and more than once Pru was certain that she had seen Laura retch and grimace as she smelled the cooking. How could she possibly broach the subject? Pru decided that the best way to approach the delicate subject was in her usual direct no nonsense manner. Pru had grown incredibly fond and protective of Laura in the short time they had known each other.

As the kettle burbled on the dreaded "Aga" in readiness for their morning coffee break Pru sat down at the huge kitchen table and sighed a very "stagey" sigh. "Are you o.k. Pru?

Only you seem tired this morning. Have you been doing too much? Tell you what, you sit there and let me make you a lovely cup of tea! How about it eh?"

"My dear I will let you make this old thing a cup of coffee on one condition. That you sit down and talk to me. I have something I want to ask you."

Laura stiffened ever so slightly but Pru noticed and decided that this would take some careful and delicate questioning if she wasn't going to frighten Laura and let her think that she was in any way judging her! God forbid she should ever do that!

As Pru and Laura sipped their drinks there was a slightly uncomfortable feeling in the room. Pru took a deep breath and spoke.

"My dear, please do not be offended by my next question. I ask only because I have come to care about you a great deal. Are you expecting a baby?"

The question hung in the air for a long time. Laura stared fixedly into her coffee cup. Pru wondered what to do next when Laura looked up at her with moist eyes and Pru suddenly remembered just how frightened she herself had felt all those years ago when she was completely out of her depth. Laura's bottom lip quivered and she took a huge breath before she raised her chin in a slightly defiant manner and said that yes she was pregnant. What of it! What business was it of Pru's? Pru held her gaze and slowly Laura's face softened as she realised that Pru was not judging her and finding her wanting. Pru was holding her gaze with nothing more than concern and not condemnation! Laura's hand reached out across the vast table and she gently enfolded the old ladies fingers in hers and silently nodded as two large tears rolled unchecked down her cheeks. Pru held Laura's gaze and her hand for an age and when they finally broke their gaze an unwritten but solid pact had been made. Laura and Pru would be friends for life and nothing would come between them. Who would have thought that two such disparate people would have developed such an affinity in such an incredibly short time?

Laura spoke first. "How did you know? I didn't think that I showed yet! What am I going to do? Chris and Ronnie seem lovely people but I can't see them letting me stay if they find out I'm having a baby can you?"

"My dear, don't worry about that I'm sure that everything will work out just fine. What I am concerned about is your health! You are such a tiny little thing I can't help but be worried about you!"

Laura could not hold Pru's gaze. What would Pru think of her if she only knew the truth? That this "tiny little thing" was in fact a prostitute who was pregnant without any way of knowing which one of her many "gentlemen" was the father?

As Pru looked into Laura's eyes it was as if she knew more than she was letting on. Finally Pru took a huge breath, squared her shoulders and spoke. "My dear I sincerely hope you will not be too offended by this but you don't know who the father is? Do you?"

At this point Laura's resolve disintegrated and she began to explain to Pru just exactly what had happened to her in her short life.

Pru listened aghast as Laura relayed the terrible things that had happened to her in such a distant and remote way. Almost as if they had happened to someone else and not to this fragile creature sitting before her.

After some considerable time, and not a few tears, Laura and Pru were exhausted by all the raw emotions teeming out of both of them. Laura was more pleased than she thought she would be that, at last, someone knew her secret. She did not have to bear it on her own anymore. Pru, meanwhile, was struggling to keep her anger in check. My God! All men are bastards! As she thought this she realised that that, of course, was not strictly true. Her beloved Günter had proven that by securing her financial future when her divorce came through. He did not have to do that, but he did, and they had kept in touch on and off for many years (Unbeknown to her Mother!) until his death some 20 years ago.

At the thought of Gunter Pru smiled to herself. How wrong it was, that relationship, and how right it was all at the same time? If she was Laura's age now she would have had a delightful fling with the gorgeous Gunter -the passion would have been spent- and she could have enjoyed a completely different life than the one she ended up with! (Now Prudence Okenden no more selfish thoughts like that my dear. This is not about you- this is about this little mite here!)Pru very often berated herself like this and it had the usual effect on her. She was able to concentrate all her energy and time on Laura as between them they would decide on the best course of action needed. As Laura spoke it brought Pru out of her reverie.

"Sorry my dear. What did you say? I was miles away!"

"I was just apologising for getting so upset. I'm sure you don't need to listen to all my troubles!"

"Nonsense my dear! I could tell that something was not quite right but I had no idea you had been through so much! And you still only a child yourself! Still I dare say there are many more poor souls just like you out there. My God but it makes my blood boil I can tell you!"

Pru then took a deep breath. This was not the time or the place for discussing that now. Now was the time for action. Pru knew that Laura was struggling to cope with all the decisions she needed to make and so Pru was not too worried about asking the next question.

"My dear I know we have known each other a very short time but I feel like I have known you forever! Does that sound silly? You remind me so much of myself. I know my situation was completely different from yours and the dilemma is not the same but I recognise the same fear and dread that your life is spiralling out of control and you don't know what to do to stop it! I felt exactly the same as you do now but for entirely different but no less real reasons.

So, my dear, if you will let me I would like to try to help if I possibly can. Will you accept help from a geriatric old duffer like me?"

Pru's heart was beating almost out of her chest and she was sure that Laura must be able to hear it! Pru realised that this could be a turning point in both their lives. Oh! How she hoped Laura would say yes. Laura kept her gaze on the floor. She did not dare to look up in case she started to cry again because she thought that if she started crying now she would never stop! As she collected her thoughts the atmosphere in the kitchen was palpable.

Slowly Laura brought her face up to Pru's and looked her straight in the eye. Laura was scared, very scared, but she was lonely and frightened about letting anyone in to her life again. She had had so many disappointments in her short life-her beloved Father , her indifferent Mother, her grasping Aunty – all the people who should have been there for her and weren't. Did she have the courage to open up her heart again? What would she do if it got broken again? She would not be able to stand it she knew that- so what the hell should she do?

As these thoughts swept over Laura's face Pru was still holding her breath and trying to decipher all the conflicting emotions showing on her face. What would she do? What would their relationship be like if she refused her help? How could she possibly stay here in this lovely farmhouse any longer? All these thoughts crowded into Pru's mind and so she did not hear Laura's quiet reply.

"Sorry my dear what was that you said?"

"I said that I would love to accept your help if you really meant it?"

Pru let out a huge sigh and held on to Laura's hand with amazing strength as they both stared at each other and laughed and cried and laughed and cried until they could not laugh or cry any longer. It was decided that, for now, Laura's condition would remain a secret until she could organise an appointment at the local doctors to check that everything was o.k. with the baby. When that had been done they would think about how and what to tell the others. In a short time Laura had begun to think in the plural i.e. they would decide etc... How had that happened? Laura felt more at ease than she had done for weeks. She knew that she had found a true friend and soul mate in Pru. She only hoped that she would not let her down. And so they continued to prepare the evening meal in quiet a hurry. Where had all the time gone? If they were lucky and worked really hard as a team (which is how they both saw themselves) then they could have the meal ready on time and no-one would be any the wiser!

In the top field Adam and Robert were working hard. Robert was subdued after his session with Chris and Ronnie and he was grateful that Adam did not ask questions about what went on. He was not ready to bare his soul anymore today. However, he had to admit, now that he had had time for reflection he felt calmer and more determined that he was going to get through this without resorting to past behavioural patterns and running straight back to his Mother's house at the first sign of trouble. As he continued to work and the sun shone on his back Robert felt more at peace with himself and the rest of the world than he had done in a very long time. He was brought out of his daydreaming by the sound of someone whistling a happy tune. Suddenly he realised that it was he who was whistling. He could not remember the last time he had whistled! So, maybe, things were not so bad after all! If he could only pluck up the courage to talk to Vanessa then his life might get back on track! Robert knew that this would all take time but a start was a start after all.

Chapter 20.

Chris Gaskell prided himself on his ability to tackle most things head on and come to a logical decision which, in turn, led to a successful outcome to any problems he had encountered. Why then did he feel so strange? He had this terrible sense of foreboding that had troubled him all morning and try as he might he could not shake of the feeling that it had something to do with Robert! As Chris drove into Thetford he tried to shake off this feeling but to no avail. As he finished off his deliveries he realised that he had completed them all in a very quick time and he realised that he had an hour to spare before he could go into Soham Tarney to deliver to the local restaurant. They were excellent customers and as such he was always willing to deliver the very best produce that had been picked that very morning. The restaurant was willing to pay premium prices for this service with one condition. They had a delivery twice a week at 3pm when the chef came on shift. He always insisted on looking through all the vegetables and flowers to check the quality. It had become almost ritualistic between the two men. Chris and Georges the French head chef exchanged pleasantries each time they saw each other but both were under no illusions that if Georges thought the produce was not up to his exacting standards then he would tell Chris in no uncertain terms that he would be taking his business elsewhere! Chris smiled to himself as he realised that he too was as exacting in his standards. In the 3 years he had never given the Head Chef any cause for concern and he was not about to start now. However Chris was not in the right frame of mind today to have any sort of altercation and so he decided that he would bite on the bullet and go and see Mavis at the "Bull's Head" in town. Now to the casual observer this might not seem such a big deal, however, for those in the know it really was a big deal! Mavis had been the landlady at the "Bull's Head " all her married life and when Arnold had had the temerity to pass away she was not going to let anyone from the brewery tell her she was not able to run the pub herself! The brewery, very wisely, decided that of course Mavis could have the licence in her own name and of course they would not dream of assuming she was not capable of making a success of it. And so it was that Mavis Riley's name was displayed over the front door of the "Bull's Head" Soham Tarney for the entire world to see that she, Mrs Mavis Riley was officially in charge. And let no man, woman, child or beast ever forget that!

As Chris turned into the car park he decided to go in have a brief chat with Mavis or her bar staff and settle himself down in a quiet corner of the pub with a glass of ginger beer and try to work out just what this feeling of foreboding was all about. He was in luck -when he entered the pub Mavis was in full flow talking to a small group of tourists about the village and all its quirky characters. That was likely to take up all the time Chris needed- unless of course the tourists lost the will to live and made a concerted dash for freedom when Mavis's back was turned! How unchristian and uncharitable thought Chris as he sat down with his ginger beer but how true though!

Chris and Ronnie had discussed, at length, all of the houseguests and their needs and they had both agreed that up until now it was working out really well so why this strange feeling? What was concerning him about Robert? Why him and not any of the other guests? All these and more questions crowded Chris's mind as he sat in the pub.

 After 20 minutes of thinking Chris was no nearer any answers and so he walked up to the bar to chat to Mavis before heading to the restaurant. Mavis was her usual effusive self flirting outrageously with Chris as she usually did.

Mavis missed having a man in her life that much was obvious and if Chris thought about it he could see that she was still an attractive woman in her mid sixties (Of course he would never dream of telling her this- he would never get out alive!). As he said his goodbyes and promised to return as soon as he could Chris reflected that Mavis was probably lonelier than she had ever been and was frightened of old age on her own. If only she could find a nice chap and settle down thought Chris as he pushed open the back door of the restaurant and prepared to do verbal battle with the redoubtable Georges!

Chapter 21.

Adam Jenkins was twenty two years old. He had had many difficult times in his comparatively short life but right at this moment life for Adam was sweet. He looked over at Robert who had suddenly burst out whistling for no apparent reason and wondered just what was going on in his head. Adam was always wondering such thoughts and he always had had. Of course no-one in his family or any of his "friends" knew any of this. Nobody knew and nobody would ever know if he Adam Jenkins had anything to do with it! Robert was obviously troubled by something. Something from his past no doubt. Adam did not have such difficulties- he had always prided himself on his ability to not care about anyone else but himself and to not having a worry in the world! He knew he would never need to go onto the Jeremy Kyle show or the Tricia show .He could sort himself and his mates out all by himself thank you very much! As these thoughts stole into his mind Adam began to question himself perhaps for the very first time. If he was so cool and laid back why was he here in the middle of nowhere with a bunch of strangers? If he could sort himself out then why hadn't he? Why was he so scared of the lads in Bristol who were his new best friends? Adam knew the answers. He was a coward and he was out of his depth. Being cool was everything to Adam Jenkins and his posse- but why? Adam also knew that he was different from his schoolmates and his best mates on the estate. Adam had had very little formal education. He had been a disruptive child and a disruptive unruly pupil, He had been expelled from all the senior schools in Bristol and he had refused to have any home tuition from the timid little creature they sent him. He had had her in tears before the end of the first day. A succession of private tutors followed each one lasting no longer a month. (Mr Gibson had given him a run for his money though- he admitted that. He soon sorted him out though when he followed him home and threatened to tell his wife that he had been interfering with him instead of teaching him!)Adam Jenkins possessed an extraordinary level of intelligence. He was by far the brightest pupil the school had ever had- they just never noticed it and put his frustration down to bad behaviour and given him the label of trouble maker. When his reputation got around Adam became something of a local celebrity and he milked it for all he was worth! Now, however, Adam was feeling frustrated, unbelievably angry and resentful for all the" tossers" at school who just forgot about him and couldn't be bothered to find out about the real Adam Jenkins. He loved being out in the fresh air and working his body into the ground. He enjoyed the feeling of achievement he felt, (the first time that had ever happened to him) but his mind and soul were not being catered for. How he wished he could read properly! He had noticed all the books in the library up at the farmhouse and he had, more than once, sneaked into the room to look at the books and try to guess what was inside them. He had managed to read some of the titles and he thought he had seen some of the books on the TV. He never knew that they were books before they became telly programmes! However Adam thought, all this thinking was going to get him nowhere because he was NEVER going to tell a living soul that he could not read properly. What would they think of him then? They would just think that they had been right along and that council house kids from a rough area were all thick as pig s###!

 Adam decided there and then that he was going to spend a little more time with all these losers and earn a bit of money down in the village by knocking off booze and fags etc and flogging them off to all the other wastes of space in the village! How hard could it be in this god forsaken place? With this plan firmly in his mind Adam should have been feeling great and whistling just like Robert. So why wasn't he?

Chapter 22

As the early evening sunshine dappled the garden and the heady aroma of countless flowers filled the air the only sound to be heard was the singing of the birds and the "tap tap "of a woodpecker. It was such a special time of the day. The hard labour had been done, the evening held promises of a balmy night, everyone seemed more at ease and so it was that everyone came down for dinner feeling a little less fraught than they had done that morning! It was decided, by a showing of hands (the most diplomatic and democratic way don't you think said Pru) that tonight the meal should be eaten out in the garden and so the men were railroaded into moving the very large and extremely heavy table out of the kitchen and into the garden. After much huffing and puffing by the men it was agreed that it was a perfect night to dine outside and thanks to Pru for thinking of it! Pru, of course, bathed in the glory whilst the entire time saying to anyone who would listen that they mustn't keep thanking her it was only a suggestion after all! As the sun moved its leisurely way across the garden time seemed to stand still for all the residents at Haven's Retreat. The table looked fabulous and positively groaned under the weight of all the food. Those two girls had certainly worked hard all day to prepare such a feast. Where had they got their energy and inspiration from? Chris and Ronnie brought wine from the cellar and beer from the utility room from whence it had been brewing for several weeks in readiness for just such an occasion. All the guests seemed to have made that little extra effort in their appearance even Adam had left his cap off in celebration of something! One by one they came into the garden and sat quietly to reflect on their innermost thoughts. Vanessa and Gordon had not spoken to each other since that terrible day and it had caused Ronnie and Chris some concern and so it was with not a little trepidation that they, and everyone else, held their breath when Gordon asked Vanessa if she would like red or white wine? He knew that she was not a beer drinker unlike himself and so which would she prefer as he was pouring for everyone! Vanessa, to her credit, stopped for the briefest of moments before she answered that she would love a glass of red if it wasn't too much trouble. As everyone sat down to a delightful goulash together with a scrumptious salad and home- made bread the atmosphere between Vanessa and Gordon relaxed and so the evening continued with everyone laughing, joking and teasing each other until 11o'clock when Pru decided that she would retire to her bed and leave the young things to party all night if they so wished!

As Pru went to her bed the others in the party started to clear up the dinner things. Robert and Vanessa went into the kitchen to begin the marathon task of washing up all the dishes! Vanessa and Gordon decided to remove as much of the furniture back to the house as was possible. It had been decided that as it was going to be a balmy, dry, night then the huge old table would survive! Chris and Ronnie organised themselves for the next day's sessions and worked out who would do what to ensure the smooth running of the estate.

Robert started to fill up the enormous Belfast sink in the kitchen and tried not to let Vanessa see how much his hands were shaking! Why the hell had he suggested that they wash up the dishes together? What the devil was he going to talk to her about? Oh! The conversation had flowed   when everyone was around the table but now they were on their own what would he say to her? As it happened Vanessa spoke first.

"Robert can I just say something to you?"

"Er... Yes of course you can!" gulped Robert.

"I have really enjoyed myself this evening thanks to you!"

"What do you mean – thanks to me?"

"Well if it hadn't been for you I would not have had the decency to answer Gordon properly when he asked me about the wine. I remembered that you are always saying the right thing and you don't seem to judge people and I wanted to be like you!"

Gordon blushed from his toes to the top of his head and looked intently at his shoes for an absolute age! What the hell was he supposed to say to that?

"Oh! I'm sorry. I've embarrassed you haven't I? I never intended to - I'm really sorry!"

"Don't be sorry Vanessa. I was just a little taken aback. No-one has ever said such a thing to me!"

As Vanessa came towards him Robert wondered just what she was about to do! Would she give him a consoling kiss? As it happened he would never know because just at that moment Adam and Laura came crashing into the kitchen giggling like the two young things they were and asking if there was anything they could do or was it o.k. if they carried on partying? As they left the moment had passed and Vanessa and Robert got on with the washing up and spoke in general terms only. Robert was fuming inside! Those stupid people – talk about bad timing- but he consoled himself with the knowledge that he was talking to Vanessa alone in the kitchen!! As he said goodnight to Vanessa at her bedroom door it seemed the most natural thing in the world to kiss her goodnight and hug her and so he did! As he closed the door to his own room Robert was floating on air just like some idiotic schoolboy. He realised of course that he was being foolish and this did not signify the beginning of a relationship but it was the start of a friendship that could, possibly, lead to other things - if he was careful.

Vanessa meanwhile went to her room and lay on her bed as she collected her thoughts. Tonight had been something of a revelation for her. She had had a reasonably civil conversation with Gordon. He had seemed as awkward and uncomfortable as she was and he did not seem any more inclined to resume their fight as she was. She was still unnerved by the argument if she was honest with herself. However, as she carried on talking to Gordon, she realised that he seemed as troubled about it as she was! Perhaps they could never be best friends but maybe they could come to some sort of permanent truce and develop some level of respect and mutual understanding of their differences.

Robert was a different kettle of fish! As they were washing up at the kitchen sink she was inexplicably drawn to Robert in a way that she had never felt before. She fancied him! She fancied him and yet he was the exact opposite of the usual self assured men she had slept with. Perhaps that was why she fancied him! She had had terrible luck with empty headed men so perhaps she should give him a try? What the hell was going on in her head? Thank God the others barged in at that time – who knows what might have happened? Robert would probably have run a mile and she would have died of shame ever time she looked at him. She could not stand rejection. Vanessa was not used to rejection. She was always the one to walk away from a relationship!

A relationship! – what she means is a one night stand!) Well she was not going down that particular road- oh no! - She would be polite to Robert but she would not allow herself the indulgence of thinking she could have a relationship with him. Vanessa undressed and lay in her bed hoping that sleep would allow her some peace of mind. No such luck! After three hours tossing and turning Vanessa went downstairs to get a drink. As she sipped her water she strolled into the garden. The night air was still warm and enveloped Vanessa in its comfort. Vanessa spent a long time looking out over the pond. As Vanessa allowed the evening atmosphere to wrap itself around her she took stock of her life so far and she found it wanting! After more time in deep contemplation Vanessa went back to her room and fell into a deep dreamless sleep and woke more refreshed and calmer than she had in a very long time!

In the following weeks and months that one night would stay in the memory of all the people there to be treasured and relived forever.

Chapter 23.

The next morning did not get off to a very auspicious start. The dreaded "Aga" was stone cold. Ronnie was the first one down in the morning and as she entered the kitchen her heart sank! She knew instantly that there was a problem as the kitchen was cold. The "Aga" was excellent at keeping the room warm and cosy. This morning, however, was going to be different. Chris was the next downstairs and he took one look at Ronnie's face and felt her frustration about to bubble over. Without a word Chris opened the "Aga" door and rattled around trying to look as though he knew what he was doing! As the noise of Chris's efforts filtered through the rest of the house the other guests emerged into the kitchen with varieties of the same question. What was going on? What was matter with the "Aga". Adam wanted to know if he was going to miss his full English breakfast. The final guest down for breakfast was Gordon. He had taken to arriving as late as possible and staying for the shortest possible time in order to avoid Vanessa. This morning was different however as Gordon spoke to Vanessa before anybody else! The other guests noticed this but did not say anything. As Gordon began to look at the "Aga" everyone else began to muck in together to make breakfast and clear the kitchen of last night's celebrations. After more than half an hour Gordon declared that the "Aga" was "knackered!" and if Chris and Ronnie wanted him to go into town he would try to get a new valve from the hardware store and do his best to repair it? It would only be a temporary measure as they would need an original "Aga" part if the job was going to be done properly. Chris and Ronnie exchanged a quick glance before saying in unison that if Gordon could do anything to help then they were more than willing as the bloody "Aga" was the bane of their lives! And so it was decided that Gordon would take the 4x4 and go into town that morning. The rest of the guests were allocated their tasks for the day and a rota for the alternative therapies was arranged for the rest of the week.

Gordon took his time over the short drive into Soham Tarney. The last few days had had a profound effect on Gordon! Vanessa had confused him. When he had taken the time to try and get to know her he had been surprised to find that she was really quiet an interesting person after all!(God! How patronising did that sound?) He had had to admit that his so called talent for knowing people in an instant was not working. Perhaps it had never really worked after all conceded Gordon. Maybe that was why he was always at odds with people and especially his children. He had begun to realise that he could be an awkward cuss at times! To admit this, even to himself, was a big deal to Gordon. Gordon had begun to really enjoy his time at the farmhouse and he would not do anything to jeopardise his future here. He realised that he had begun to change and he needed to continue to change if he was ever going to get any piece of mind. This revelation would have really disconcerted Gordon a few short weeks ago but now Gordon felt relieved and excited about the prospect of turning his life around. Why else had he come here after all?

Before he realised it Gordon was driving through the centre of town and he pulled into the "Bull's Head" car park and switched off the engine. Chris and Ronnie had told him to go into town, find the valve and come back to the farmhouse in his own sweet time. Chris and Ronnie did not miss a trick thought Gordon. (Just as well really!) As he stepped out of the 4x4 Gordon strolled in the early morning sunshine and took his time strolling through the village. He had never enjoyed "window" shopping in the past but now he found himself gazing into all the various shops and he eventually arrived at the other end of town where he entered the hardware shop. He felt very much at home here and he enjoyed a very technical conversation with the owner of the store.

They both agreed that the "Aga" could be temporarily repaired with the valve that Gordon had just bought and Fred, the shop owner, gave Gordon the telephone number of the nearest supplier of the official parts and he even let Gordon use his telephone to ring through to see if it was in stock! Gordon was amazed by this – he had not expected such level of service and he had really hit it off with Fred. How he missed the technical chats he used to have with his workmates in Newcastle! After ordering the part and arranging a delivery date he wished Fred all the best and he promised that the next time he was in town he would call in on him to have a chat! As Gordon left the shop he realised that he had really enjoyed himself that morning.

Soham Tarney is a small village with a big heart thought Gordon as he walked with a happier gait towards his car.

As he approached the pub he decided, on a whim, to go in and grab himself a coffee! "The Bull's Head"! A traditional name for a very traditional pub thought Gordon as he pushed open the bar door. It was just after 11 o'clock and Gordon was the only customer. As he went up to the bar a woman's voice told him to just hang on a minute love and I'll be right with you! Gordon wondered where the voice was coming from as a small framed woman came up from the cellar. As she wiped her hands she apologised for not being there when he arrived but it was still early and her bar staff hadn't arrived yet but she was with him now and what did he want to drink!

Mavis was such a conflicting mixture. She was barely 5ft 6in tall with a voluptuous figure but she moved with the speed and grace of a gazelle. She had a soft, locally accented, voice but she exuded such energy and fun that Gordon found himself smiling and saying that he was not in any hurry and that she should finish what she was doing.

"Sorry love but I couldn't possibly leave a valuable customer like your good self now could I? Besides it's not every day I get a total stranger in here first thing asking me for a drink now is it? So what's your poison Mr Stranger?"

"Well first things first the name is Gordon Jarvis and I would like a cup of your finest coffee if it's not too much trouble?"

"Hello Gordon Jarvis- I'm Mavis Riley, please do not mention Coronation Street or I may have to kill you ha ha! As you can imagine I have heard every variation off that particular thing. Oh assuming of course that you watch Corrie that is? Anyway where was I? Oh yes here's me the landlady of this fine establishment for donkeys years and forgetting my manners!"

With that Mavis Riley, landlady of the "Bull's Head" Soham Tarney Norfolk, held out her hand to shake Gordon Jarvis' hand and was completely taken aback when Gordon kissed her hand with a flourish and bowed to her!

Her surprise, however, was not in the same league as Gordon's who wondered just what the bloody hell was he thinking of? What the hell possessed him to do that? As Gordon wondered where the nearest exit was Mavis smiled a beautiful smile and curtseyed! With that Gordon and Mavis fell about laughing and kept interrupting each other in their efforts to apologise and say that they did not normally do such things but each time they apologised they started to laugh louder and so it was that Pauline the barmaid entered the bar and apologised for being late only to be confronted by Mavis and a total stranger crying fit to burst. Mavis' mascara had run and she was holding her side whilst laughing and as for the man well he could hardly breathe!

Not for the first time did Pauline wonder just what she was doing here and that Mavis had finally lost the plot! As Pauline went to take her coat off Gordon stopped laughing long enough to order a coffee if it wasn't too much trouble and that he would go and sit in the window seat if that was o.k.?

Gordon was not surprised and he was secretly delighted when Mavis herself brought his coffee and so it was that Mr Gordon Jarvis, a Geordie from Newcastle, and Mrs Mavis Riley, Norfolk lass, began to talk!

On the drive back to the farmhouse Gordon was marvelling on just how things can change in one day! He had not enjoyed himself so much in years. He had found Mavis fascinating and so easy to talk to. He was also wondering what excuses he could make to Chris and Ronnie to ensure that he got into the village more often? And then it hit him! How the hell could he think like that? What was he thinking? He should never have a minute's peace in his life after what he helped his late wife to do! His good mood evaporated instantly and he cursed himself for his foolishness! As the farmhouse came into view Gordon decided that he would get Robert to go into town to collect the spare part for the "Aga" and then he would not risk bumping into Mavis again. He was a murderer and as such did not deserve to have any happiness!

Chapter 24.

As the days turned into weeks the houseguests settled into a convivial routine. The daily tasks needed to keep the house and business running did not seem to be too much of a chore. Everyone appeared to find the house and gardens as relaxing and special as did Chris and Ronnie. The weather was beautiful with long sunny days and fabulously balmy nights that saw all the houseguests chatting and opening up to each other in a way that both pleased and surprised Chris and Ronnie. The therapy sessions with everyone were continuing and even Gordon had begun to open up and he had actually admitted to Ronnie during their last session that he thought that they might actually be doing some good! Faint praise indeed from the most disbelieving and unconvinced of all the guests thought Ronnie as she entered the kitchen to be met by the delicious aroma of home baked cookies and apple pie. As Ronnie stood in the empty kitchen and inhaled the heady aroma she finally threw off her concerns that this project was not working and went to look for Chris so that she could tell him how much she loved and appreciated him. They had not had much time for each other in the last few weeks and they had both decided that very morning that it was time for them to allow the houseguests more autonomy in the decision making of the farm and its business.

Laura and Pru were a force to be reckoned with! As the days turned into weeks the bond between them grew and grew. However there was one source of discontent for Pru and that was the fact that Laura had not confided in Chris, Ronnie or any of the other guests about her pregnancy. Pru knew that this situation could not last forever. Everyone would see the developments for themselves! As she dressed this morning Pru decided that she would do her best to resolve Lauren's reluctance to go into town and register with a local G.P and sort out her ante-natal appointments. Quite how she was to do this Pru had no idea until it suddenly hit her! She could be the one who needed to see a Doctor! She would need someone to go with her and who better than her young friend Laura? Pru smiled to herself as she carefully dressed and looked at herself in the mirror. She was in her early nineties, she was aged in years but young at heart .Surely no-one would suspect her ulterior motive would they? Well there was only one way to find out and that was to give it a try!

Laura looked up as Pru entered the kitchen and smiled her beautiful smile. As Pru saw this her courage almost failed her, almost but not quite, after all it was for Laura's own good wasn't it? Pru decided that now was as good a time as any to put her devious plan into action and so she avoided looking directly at Laura. Laura chatted away ten to the dozen as she always did first thing in the morning. Pru enjoyed this time more than most because Laura's enthusiasm was infectious and her chattering allowed Pru to pull herself completely together without drawing any undue attention. Not this morning thought Mrs Prunella Okenden- this morning she would give an Oscar winning performance if that is what it took to get Lauren into town. Laura turned to look at her when Pru didn't return her comment with her usual good humour. "Are you feeling O.K Pru only you seem quieter than normal?"

"Oh I'm fine thank you might dear I didn't sleep to well and my Arthritis is playing me up but I'll be O.K soon I hope!"

"You don't look too hot if I may say so Pru!"

"Thank you my dear you really know how to make an old ladies morning don't you?" laughed Pru all the time trying to avoid looking at Laura.

"Well I think you should go and see what Ronnie has to say don't you?"

"Please Laura I don't want any fuss, really I don't. I have just been a little foolish that's all."

"What do you mean Pru? How have you been foolish?"

"I have allowed myself to run out of my Arthritis medication. I have been enjoying myself so much these last few weeks and in many ways I have never felt better but the truth is I am in a lot of discomfort and I really do need to start taking the tablets again."

"Oh Pru! Why ever didn't you say something before? You don't need to be in pain. You should get yourself a Doctor's appointment in town as soon as you can. I'll come with you if you want me to?"

Pru's heart nearly broke at that moment. She was a wicked old woman who ought to be ashamed of herself! The look of genuine concern written all over Laura's face was beautiful to see. As Pru looked away Laura misread her emotions and was concerned that her best friends was in tears and embarrassed and so she gently put her arm around the old ladies shoulder in a gesture of true friendship.

Ronnie, meanwhile, had been watching this scene from the doorway of the kitchen. As she surveyed the tableau in front of her Ronnie wondered at the mysteries of human nature. How it was possible for two different people to have such a bond she would never fully understand. The sound of the other guests making their way into the kitchen ensured that Laura, Pru and Ronnie did not have the opportunity to talk for over an hour. As the kitchen finally emptied and they started on the dishes Ronnie made the decision to broach the subject of this morning.

"Ladies, can I ask you both something? This morning you did not seem as well as you normally do Pru and Laura I hope you don't mind me saying so but I have noticed that some mornings you don't seem to be as well as you could be! Please do not take offence but can I suggest that you both go into town and register with Doctor Brayford at the surgery?"

The silence was absolutely deafening and Ronnie was beginning to wish she had never said anything when the silence was eventually broken by Pru and Lauren speaking together. "My dear I'm fine really!" "I don't know what you mean Ronnie I am feeling really well!"

As the girls tripped over themselves to answer Ronnie had the distinct impression that she was somehow missing something. What was it Shakespeare said? Methinks he doth protest too much!

In the end both women stopped talking at the same moment.

"I can give you a lift into town after lunch if you want me to? Let me know as soon as you have decided will you?"

AS Ronnie left the kitchen the two women looked at each other and smiled self consciously at each other.

"Perhaps it is not such a bad idea after all don't you think my dear? You need to sort out your ante-natal appointments and I need to organize my medication. I need them more than I care to admit to."

"Oh Pru! I am so scared! What will everyone think? Will Chris and Ronnie ask me to leave? I really couldn't bear that! "

"My dear child I do not think for a second that they will throw you out on the streets. They are lovely people who are two of the least judgemental people it has been my privilege to know! What we need to do is to both be as strong as we can for ourselves and for each other. What do you say Lauren? Are you brave enough to give it a go? I am willing to swallow my pride if you are!"

And so it was that after lunch the girls went with Ronnie to register at the local surgery. As she dropped them off Ronnie began to wonder if life would ever be the same for her and Chris. Already the farmhouse and its guests had impacted on the life of the village more than it had done for years and both Ronnie and Chris were concerned about this.

Chris, meanwhile, was working in the greenhouse with Robert and Adam. The sound of the Land Rover going out of the drive towards the village made Chris decide that today was going to be the day that he and Robert started to work on his problems relating to his mother and brother.

"Adam. Will you be O.K working on the vegetables in the far greenhouse while Robert and I go into the house for our session?"

"No probs Chris take your time. After all Robert is more in need of your help than any of us. Ain't that right Robbie?"

Chris gasped and held his breath. How would Robert react? Robert walked towards Adam with his arms outstretched and started to strangle him all the time he was laughing and calling Adam a cheeky young sod. Chris visibly relaxed and went out into the yard to take a deep breath and collect his thoughts.

The farmhouse was cool and welcoming as Chris and Robert went into the treatment room. The sun was really hot even though it was only 10.30 in the morning. The sun had not penetrated the room and it was the best time for the sessions to take place. The room overlooked the garden and when the French windows were open and the sounds and smells of the garden entered the room it always helped everyone to relax and open up. Chris decided that today he would steer the conversation towards Robert's concerns about his family etc.

 And hope that he could get him to open up a little. Robert had been the most recalcitrant of all the house guests and both Chris and Ronnie had had the distinct impression that Robert was playing a part and putting on a front. Robert was an actor after all and he was used to playing different people.

"Robert I don't usually do this but I would like to suggest a topic for discussion today if that is O.K by you?" Robert was facing away from Chris as he spoke and so Chris did not see the change of expression on Robert's face. If he had he might have had second thoughts about the direction of his questioning. As it was Chris remained blissfully unaware of the can of worms he was about to open with his very first question!

"Robert, Ronnie and I have noticed that you seem to be enjoying your time here but neither of us knows quite what you are expecting from these sessions. Is that a fair assessment do you think?"

Robert spent a long time in deep contemplation before he looked over at Chris. Their eyes locked for a few seconds and then Robert came to his decision.

"Chris - you and Ronnie have been my life savers without a doubt. I was at a crossroads in my life and I was at a complete loss as to what to do and where to go. I have never felt so at ease and so ill at ease all at the same time! Does any of this make any sense or have I completely lost the plot?"

"Robert you need to resolve some of your issues so that you can enjoy more peace of mind. You realise that yourself don't you? If we just start today then we can begin the process together and hopefully you can begin to be the real you that you have always wanted to be."

Robert looked as though he would burst into tears but through sheer willpower he swallowed hard and looked Chris in the eye.

The session continued for 90 minutes and during this time Robert discussed his concerns that it had been over four weeks since he had had any contact with his family. He was convinced that his Mother would have contacted Interpol at the very least. She would be concerned for his welfare but incandescent with rage that her son had had the temerity to defy her! What would all her friends think? These things were vitally important to Robert's Mother. Robert felt that he was caught in the middle. He had never defied his Mother EVER! Robert also began to tentatively broach the subject of Vanessa. Chris was only to aware of Robert's feelings for Vanessa (Hadn't Ronnie told him all about it this very morning with the usual comment that really men were hopeless where all that sort of thing was concerned!) and he was glad that Robert felt comfortable enough to begin discussing his concerns with another man. Robert was not a virgin but he had had very limited experience with women and his lack of self esteem had always held him back. At the end of the session the sun had moved around and now the room was changing both colour and atmosphere. As the mood lightened it was decided that Robert would make contact with his Mother when he felt that the time was right and not when he felt guilty. Robert decided that when he next went into town he would purchase an inexpensive "Pay as you go" mobile phone (He told Chris of the elation he felt when he hurled his telephone from the train) Robert also decided that he would continue to woo Vanessa in the old fashioned way that a true gentlemen wooed a lady.

As the session ended Robert went out into the garden for a stroll before lunch and then he had been given the task of digging out potatoes. Chris knew that physical exercise was just what Robert needed after all the raw emotions that had been brought to the surface.

Chris made his way into the kitchen to make himself a coffee. As the percolator gurgled into life Chris took stock of the sessions to date. All the houseguests had had several sessions with both Chris and they had all had many sessions of Hypnotherapy and "Reike ". Robert had surprised and delighted Chris. He had been really concerned for his emotional well-being but since he and Vanessa had started to get closer Robert had found a degree of inner peace, so much so that he had made contact with his mother a few times. Robert had bought a cheap mobile telephone and had had a few terse conversations with his very disapproving mother! Robert had done a lot of soul searching these last few weeks and he had come to the decision that he was his own person and whilst he did not set out to actively upset his mother or other people in general he had decided that he quite liked his new life and he would do anything to protect it!

After each session Chris and Ronnie would meet up to discuss the day's events (with the full knowledge of everyone). He and Ronnie were both pleased with the progress to date. Chris and Ronnie were equally qualified and, thankfully, were both happy doing any of the tasks involved.

Chris was brought back to earth as he heard his beautiful wife arriving back with Lauren and Pru. As he helped the girls to unpack the shopping he could not help but notice that Lauren looked different than she had when she first arrived. She looked as though she was putting weight on but Chris would have thought that with all the exercise and fresh air that she had had over the past few weeks then she should have at least stayed the same. Ronnie leant in to kiss him hello and flashed him one of her amazing smiles and she gave him one of her very meaningful stares! Chris and Ronnie had developed an intense bond with each other over the years and Chris knew instantly that something had gone on. At the first opportunity he and Ronnie would find the time to talk and discuss the day's events because Chris knew just from the look exchanged between them that something major had happened!

Chapter 25.

Adam really enjoyed his time in the garden working on his own. He had always enjoyed his own company even as a small child. His upbringing had been difficult. His parents were very young when they had Adam and were little more than children themselves. Where Adam got his intelligence and his enquiring mind he did not know. He had always had an amazing thirst for knowledge even when he was in the children's home but of course the system did not allow him any real chance of developing his interests. He was told to sit down, shut up and pay attention. He eventually stopped searching for answers and began to think that maybe he was not so intelligent after all!

As the morning progressed Adam smiled to himself. If he was lucky he could sneak into the library again and try to read one of the "millions" of books on display! Of course it would help if he could actually read more than a few words!! His lack of reading ability had never bothered Adam before so why was it bothering him now? Adam had been thinking deep thoughts like this for days now. He had never been that keen before so why did he have this desire and thirst for learning? Adam tidied away the tools carefully as he always did. He had changed in so many ways that at times he hardly recognised himself. He was secretly pleased with himself though. He enjoyed his secret little world when he went into the library and tried to enter the world of books.

As he went slowly into the house and realised that there was no-one else about he had a huge grin on his face. Fantastic! Maybe today he could start on one of the books he had noticed the last time he went into the library. He had not had the time to even open the front cover before he had heard Ronnie coming onto the landing and he had only just managed to shut the library door and walk along the corridor! Ronnie did not seem to notice that Adam was breathing hard and Adam was glad that he had got away with it this time! Why was he sneaking about though?

Adam knew the answer to this really he just did not want to admit this even to himself. He was embarrassed about his lack of reading skills and he wanted to better himself but he was also too afraid to ask for help. What would he do if they all laughed at him? He could not bear the shame and humiliation. He had never admitted to any of his "cool" friend for fear of becoming a laughing stock and being ostracised from his circle of friends. As Adam thought this he smiled to himself. Where had the word "ostracised" come from? He had heard the word before and he hoped that he was using it properly but he did not know for sure. That was what was so frustrating about the library and all those books! There was any number of different worlds out there and he didn't have much idea how to get into them.

The library was cool and restful. Just like it should be thought Adam. As his gaze swept the shelves his chest tightened with anticipation. What was in those books? What worlds were in there just waiting for him to discover and explore? Adam spent a long time caressing the covers as he searched for the one he wanted to read. Or, rather, attempt to read thought Adam sourly! He gasped a little as his eyes alighted on his chosen book.

Did he have the bottle to try and attempt to read this book? He had seen the movie when it had come out but he never held any thoughts of actually being able to read the book for himself! "Charlie and the Chocolate Factory!" Johnny Depp had been fabulous in that film. It had been worth it nearly being discovered sneaking in to the cinema to watch it with his so called mates, They had talked all over the film and they had said that it was a crap movie and Jonny Depp was s### ! It had taken all of his will power not to scream at them to shut the f### up and try watching the movie for god's sake! Of course he had not done any such thing. It would not do to annoy his "mates" they could turn nasty very quickly!

Adam went to the large reading chair in the corner and gingerly opened the book .He spent ten minutes reading the first page. Why did this Dahl bloke need to write using fancy words anyway? Adam began to relax a little as he struggled to comprehend the words. His frustration evaporated as he poured over the words and tried his best to decipher this weird code called words? He started to spell out the words he struggled with. Slowly but surely he came to the end of the first chapter and he had the biggest grin on his face. He didn't think he had ever felt so good about himself .Ever! Adam suddenly looked at his watch and was horrified to see that he had been reading in the library for over two hours! He had about fifteen minutes before his session with Chris was due to start! He had not eaten anything since breakfast. He didn't have time now but what the hell! It had been worth it hadn't it! As Adam hurried out of the library he failed to notice Ronnie coming towards the library.

What was Adam doing sneaking out of the library? Ronnie wondered. Ronnie decided to investigate further and went into the library to see what she could find. As she looked around she did not notice anything out of the ordinary. Everything seemed to be in its right place. So what was Adam doing in there?

Chapter 26.

Soham Tarney. Soham Tarney is a village as pretty and unspoilt as the name suggests thought Lauren as she, Pru and Ronnie drove to the Doctor's Surgery. Small village with small minded people wondered Lauren. As the car pulled into the car park of the local pub Laura looked over at Pru. She had been quiet during the journey and Laura wondered just what was going through the old ladies mind right now?

The Doctor's Surgery was small but efficient and the Doctor was small and efficient too thought Laura as she and Pru filled in Registration forms together. After they had completed the forms Pru went in to see the Doctor first. This gave Laura the opportunity to think about what she was going to say. How could she answer honestly all the inevitable questions? How many weeks did she think she was? Did the father know? Would the father be around for the birth and to give any support? Where was she thinking of having the baby?

Pru, meanwhile, was discovering that the Doctor was small and VERY efficient. She bombarded Pru with questions. How long had she been on this medication? Who was her Doctor at home? Did she realise the seriousness of not taking her medication? Pru began to feel like a naughty schoolgirl! As Pru listened she began to feel ashamed and angry both with herself and the Doctor. How dare she speak to her as if she was simple? She was a grown woman after all wasn't she? As this thought came into her head Pru was distracted and did not hear the Doctor's next question.

"Sorry my dear what did you say?"

"I was just saying that I think you need to continue with your medication for the time being but I think it would be advisable to see a Specialist to make certain that you are getting the best possible treatment."

"Oh! I'm not sure about that. I am only here for a comparatively short time."

"We are lucky here Mrs Okenden. We do not have the waiting lists that some of the other Health Authorities have and I am certain that we can get you an appointment for you within the next few weeks."

"Well I will certain think about it Doctor but what I am more concerned about is my friend out in the waiting room!"

"Mrs Okenden as I am sure you are aware I cannot discuss another patient's circumstances."

Pru sighed to herself -Bloody Officialdom- as she put on her coat and left the Consultation Room.

Laura's heart skipped a beat as she saw Pru coming towards her. She could not put it off any longer and so she took a deep breath, squared her shoulders and entered the lion's den!

As it happened Laura's time with the Doctor was not nearly as scary as she first thought. The Doctor was efficient and surprisingly non- judgemental. She told Laura that her only concern was for her patient and her baby. It had nothing to do with her the circumstances of the pregnancy. Laura breathed out slowly and she realised just how tense she was. Her neck muscles slowly relaxed as the examination continued. She appeared to be in "quite rude health" as the Doctor said.

Laura smiled to herself. She had always enjoyed "rude" health. Didn't her Gran always say the exact same thing to her all the time!

As Laura left the examination room she felt calmer and more at ease than she had done ever since she thought she was pregnant. Now all she had to do was decide what to do with the baby! She had not told Pru that she was thinking of giving her baby up for adoption. Laura knew that Pru would be aghast and horrified. She could just see her face betraying her disappointment and disapproval. Why did that bother her thought Laura? She did not need anybodies approval if that is what she had decided to do. So why did her stomach churn every time she thought about it?

Pru looked up as Laura came out with the Doctor. How had it gone for Laura? Was she well? Did she need any help? What was next for her? All these thoughts and questions crowded into Pru's mind and it took all her not inconsiderable determination to not say a word and just let Laura open up to her in her own time!

The journey back to the farmhouse was made in agonising silence for all the ladies. Ronnie knew that whatever had taken place in the Doctor's was nothing to do with her and yet she was both curious and concerned that both women were well. She hoped that they would feel able to tell her in their own time but she knew that she would not push the point. After all it was none of her business really!

Pru thought she would burst if she didn't speak out but how could she whilst in the car? She had promised Laura that she would keep her secret and she would until her dying day. Pru was nothing if not true to her word but the suspense was killing her!

Laura's mind was in turmoil. She had known that she was pregnant. She had always had regular periods and she felt different somehow. She knew all this before she went into the Doctor's so why did she feel faint and helpless now that the Doctor had confirmed what she already knew? Just what the hell was she going to do now? She was pregnant! She was pregnant! That thought kept whizzing around her head and she could not think straight. She knew, deep down, that she would keep her baby. She had always wanted to be a mother. Had she not dreamt about this moment ever since she had been a little girl? She had pictured herself floating down the church aisle with a beautiful flowing gown and standing next to the most handsome, considerate and gentle man. She would live in a pretty cottage in the country with roses around the door! She didn't know whether to laugh or cry as she thought this. How different could her circumstances be? She had been a drug user and a prostitute who did not have a bloody clue which of her "gentlemen" callers was the baby's father!!

Pru spent the journey looking at Laura as discreetly as she could. Just what was going through that poor child's mind? Pru desperately wanted to hug Laura and tell her that everything would be fine but she knew that she could not do that until Laura decided to tell her what had gone on in the examination room and she was hardly going to do that in the car with Ronnie listening was she?

Pru was only glad that the journey back to the farmhouse only took about 10 minutes. They would be the longest 10 minutes of Pru's life if she didn't buckle up and behave herself! Just what was she thinking? It was nothing to do with her after all. Laura would tell her in her own good time if she wanted to and she would just have to wait and see wouldn't she?

Ronnie, meanwhile, was also studying the faces of both women as she drove home. She was certain that something quite monumental had occurred but she knew when to hold back and not ask too many question. The girls would tell her if they wanted to. Wouldn't they?

Ronnie also knew that Laura had change over the last few days and Ronnie suspected that she might be pregnant but she would never ask her outright because she did not know how Laura would react. After all Ronnie was almost a stranger wasn't she? Of course Laura and Ronnie had had many sessions of Reiki and Counselling together but that did not necessarily mean that Laura would feel the need to open up to Ronnie any time soon.

As the woman sat deep in thought they must have looked odd to any passing strangers. Three women in a car sitting and staring into space!

Ronnie broke the silence by starting up the car and saying in an overly cheery voice that as they had completed their business so quickly how about if they called into the local pub and grabbed a coffee? How did everyone feel about that?

AS both of the other women took time to realise just what Ronnie had asked they seem to both mentally shake off their concerns and put on a smile and said in unison that that would be a great idea and which was the best place to go to?

The "Bull's Head "Soham Tarney was quiet as the three women entered the bar. It was still very early as the three women came in. It was only just after 11 o'clock and so they were the only customers. Mavis, the landlady, greeted Ronnie with warmth and seemed fascinated to know all about the two other ladies with her. Ronnie had had dealings with Mavis before and so she was polite but gave nothing away as she ordered coffees for everybody and would Mavis mind if they sat at the window seat?

After Mavis came with the coffees and Ronnie had deftly parried any further enquiries from her they were left alone. The coffee tasted lovely and the ladies spent some time savouring the aroma and taste. Eventually the silence was broken by other people arriving and ordering drinks. The group of ladies, who looked as though they were out for a full days shopping, sat at the other end of the bar and giggled together.

Ronnie had decided that it would be up to her to ask if everything had gone O.K. with the Doctor and she was just about to speak when all three ladies spoke at once!

"I need to tell you something Ronnie and I don't think you are going to like it!"

"Laura I know you did not want me to say anything but I cannot just sit here and say nothing!"

"Pru and Laura I know it's not my place to say anything but I hope you feel able to tell me anything that is worrying you?"

All three women started and stopped speaking at the same time with none of them fully understanding just what the others had said. Pru was the first to start laughing swiftly followed by Ronnie and finally Laura who thought she would never laugh again only 5 minutes ago!

The other ladies stopped their own giggling and looked over to the women and raised their coffee cups in what looked like a silent tribute to the sisterhood of shoppers!

Ronnie wondered if she would ever get used to the idiosyncrasies of Western woman. She had never been a lady who "lunched" and she had no desire to find out just what the fascination was!

The three women looked at each other and wondered who would be the first to open up the conversation. Pru decided that she had not got to her advanced age without being the proverbial wallflower and so she looked at Ronnie and Laura before she spoke." Laura, my dear, I know that you might need time to consider just what the Doctor said but I will tell you what she said to me if you don't mind? I have been a stupid old woman who should know better. I have been neglecting myself in the mistaken belief that I knew best! I have never felt better in years and I decided that maybe I could survive without my medication. How wrong was I? I now have to go for further tests because my Arthritis had flared up again and I will probably need to increase the strength of my pills which is the exact opposite of what I wanted! I have been struggling to get myself together in the mornings and I have been feeling poorly for a while and still I didn't do anything about it! For a supposedly intelligent woman how stupid is that?"

At the end of her monologue both Ronnie and Laura did not know quite what to say!

Ronnie was the first to speak. "Pru I haven't known you long I know but thank you for your honesty. I know how proud a woman you are and it must have taken a degree of courage to admit that you are struggling!"

"My Dear I have decided that the British stiff upper lip brigade needs their bumps feeling! Just what does it achieve? "

Laura looked at both women and came to a decision. She had no family, she had no friends and she needed friends now more than ever! Lauren took a deep breath and opened her heart to Ronnie and confessed that Pru knew about the pregnancy before today. "I hope you understand that I couldn't tell you before because I wasn't absolutely certain of yours and Chris's reaction! "

Laura held her breath for an age as she looked at Ronnie's face trying to gauge her reaction. What would she say? Would she throw her out onto the streets? Of course she wouldn't .Would she?

Ronnie looked at poor frightened Laura and her heart went out to her. What a terrible life that young girl had had. The frightened expectant look on the girl's face touched Ronnie. She had seen that same look on countless girls back home in Burma. They had not been so lucky.

Any girl who was pregnant and unmarried was ostracised from their family and society in general. Many girls had been murdered by their own families to avoid the shame and stigma of being pregnant and unmarried. Her country appalled her sometimes. All these thoughts raced through Ronnie's mind in a fraction of a second and that was all it took for Ronnie to come to the decision that she would not abandon Laura in her hour of need.

"Laura I can guess how difficult telling anyone must be but I need you to know that both Chris and I will be here for you throughout your pregnancy and beyond it if you want. You will always have place at the farmhouse for as long as you need it, Rest assured you don't need to go through this alone!"

As Laura listened to this her face began to crumble and silent tears fell from her eyes. The look of sheer gratitude was etched on Ronnie's and Pru's faces forever. As the tears coursed down her face Laura could hardly breathe. She was feeling so many mixed emotions that her mind was in a whirl. Maybe, just maybe, things could work out better than she had ever hoped for!

Mavis Riley, landlady of the "Bull's Head, was watching the scene from behind the bar. That poor girl looked so distressed and happy at the same time! Just what was going on? As she was pondering this she did not notice the bar door opening and she was startled as someone spoke to her. "Hello hinny, how are you today? You are looking as lovely as ever if you don't mind me saying so?"

Mavis looked around as Gordon spoke. Gordon lived at the farmhouse with the others. Did he know what was going on? Mavis took one last look at the scene being played out just a few feet away and made an instant decision. She would get Gordon out of the way as quickly as she knew how. She was certain Gordon did not have a clue what was going on and from the looks on the women's faces she knew that whatever it was it was something monumental!

"Hello young Gordon. My- don't you look dashing in your overalls? Can I ask you a favour?"

"My Dear woman you can ask me anything you want. Within reason of course!" Gordon could not believe it. He was flirting with Mavis again and it was only the second time he had seen her! Just what was he thinking? He had told himself that he did not deserve happiness and so why was he doing?

"I need to know if you could help me change a barrel. I do it every day but today I just can't seem to manage!" As she was speaking Mavis was grabbing hold of Gordon's arm and almost pushing him towards the cellar! What the hell was she doing?

Gordon looked a little flustered as he was ushered into the cellar. He had never changed a barrel in his entire life! He had absolutely no idea what to do!

As he went behind the bar Ronnie glanced over. Was that Gordon? No it couldn't be. Could it? Mavis came back to the bar and looked over at the women. Mavis and Ronnie's eyes met and there was the briefest nod from Mavis. Ronnie nodded and a tacit understanding developed between the two women. Ronnie would find time to thank Mavis for averting a potentially embarrassing moment. Right now her main concern was getting the girls back to the sanctuary of the farmhouse. She paid her bill and nodded at Mavis and said that she would love to spend more time here and perhaps she could chat the next time she was in the village? Mavis smiled back and said she would look forward to it.

As they got to the car it was agreed that after lunch they would make time to discuss the next step for everyone. And so it was that the three women who had only recently come to know each other started a whole new phase in their lives. A phase which would change them beyond all recognition!

Chapter 27.

Ronnie found that she did not have time to discuss the events of the morning. The day seemed to run away with her! There were not enough hours in the day! She hoped that Chris had picked up on the lingering look she had given him as she came back. They would normally pick up on all the little nuances between each other but their life was anything but normal at the moment! Chris, however, sensed that Ronnie needed to tell him something - but he could wait!

Adam came into the house just as lunch was ready. He was starving hungry! He had changed so much over the last few weeks. He had a suntan for the first time in his life. He looked healthy and he felt to himself. The rota system allowed each guest some free time. Chris and Ronnie knew just how important it was to have this time. The structure of duties and counselling sessions meant that it was absolutely essential that all the guests be allowed time for reflection. When it was your turn for the afternoon off nobody questioned you about what you were going to do. Everyone needed their own private time and it was agreed that it was so special that it went without saying that you could do what you needed to do and no questions asked! Adam finished his meal and thanked everyone for a fabulous feast. He went up to his room to shower and change. As he looked at himself in the mirror he was surprised to see that he was developing some muscle tone! Wow! He hadn't really noticed before. He had NEVER had muscles before. He couldn't help grinning at his own reflection. He looked good and for the most part he felt good. His biggest regret was his inability to read! He was so determined to succeed at this reading lark that he almost ran down the stairs and flung open the library doors. He stopped himself just in time. He slowly opened the door to the library and carefully closed it behind him. He would never let anyone know his secret. He would learn to read properly if it took him his entire life!

The library fascinated and frightened him in equal measures. All these books! Every one of them full of exciting adventures! How he longed to be transfixed by a book. He adored the movies. He loved getting lost in the plot and wondering just what was going to happen next. Maybe books would do the same for him.

Adam lovingly stroked some of the books. He especially liked the leather bound volumes. They smelt fabulous but he had tried to read one of them but he had had to give it up. The words were so different somehow. What the hell did "thee "and" thou "mean anyway? He knew which book he wanted to read. "Robinson Crusoe."

 He had seen an ancient television series about this on one of the "Freeview" channels he had had when he lived in Bristol. He had stolen the box from some house in the posh part of town. He knew that the fancy folk who lived there could afford it and so he had not felt even a small twinge of regret as he had taken it from their home together with the stereo system and as much cash as he could find. It was their own stupid fault in the first place if they left it all on display anyway. They were asking for it!

He had been fascinated by the series on the television. He felt a connection with the lonely life that Robinson Crusoe was living. He was surrounded by people all the time but he was alone in his head!

As he found the book in the place where he had hidden it he had never been so determined about anything in his life.

He carefully opened the book and sat down in the large green leather armchair with the high sides. He loved sitting there. He tucked his feet under him and knew that even if someone came into the room he could not be seen. He had thought about this many times. He would hold his breath and pray to God that he would not be discovered. He could not stand the embarrassment. He was so determined to succeed that he wondered just how he would cope if he was discovered and he was held up to ridicule. He had been taunted many times in his life by his so called friends and he had hated it so much.

Adam shook off these negative thoughts and began to read. An hour and a half later Adam had managed to read the first two chapters. He was certain that he had not read it all correctly because it did not make sense! As he closed the book and carefully placed it back in the farthest corner of the bookshelf where he knew he could find it next time her suddenly felt desperately sad. He had had such high hopes for himself and now after 90 minutes of painful reading he had managed 2 chapters and he did not really have a clue what the hell was going on in the damned book anyway!

Adam left the library and went back to his room. How could his mood change so dramatically so quickly? He lay on the bed and began to think. What was he so afraid of? It was not his fault that he couldn't read properly. He had never had the chance to prove to anyone that he had a brain. If only he knew how to read! How the hell was he going to teach himself to read?

Adam spent his afternoon off thinking about nothing else and he finally came to the conclusion that he could not teach himself to read and if he was as determined to read as he knew he was he had to ask for help. As he came to this conclusion Adam was surprised that he did not feel ashamed but elated. So what if he couldn't read! He could learn couldn't he? When he knew how to read then his whole world would change. Who would he ask? He needed to ask someone soon before his nerve left him.

He knew that he had no real choice. He could not do this on his own. He thought that he would feel stupid asking someone to teach him to read but he had had enough of feeling stupid! There was a whole new world out there that he had been missing out on and only he could do something about it!

Who could he ask? Laura was the obvious first choice. He would ask her at the first opportunity. What if she said no?

If she did he would have to deal with it. He had had to deal with far worse things in his life. Why should this be any different? As he dressed for dinner he rehearsed just exactly what he would say. He could not read but he knew how to speak didn't he? He would ask her tonight when they had eaten. They normally went out into the garden so he could have a cigarette. He would ask her then! Adam walked down the stairs straightened his shoulders and opened the door. It was going to be fine. What could possibly go wrong?

Chapter 28.

Vanessa left the meeting room feeling more refreshed and at ease with herself than she had in a very long time. She had spoken at length with both Chris and Ronnie about her "demons" as she called them! She had finally acknowledged to herself what she had been searching for all her life. All she had ever craved was approval from her parents. Or more precisely her Father. He had been an irascible man who had tolerated the intrusion of a daughter into his orderly life. He had never shown any interest in his daughter from the moment she had been born. Oh! He had provided for her creature comforts there was no denying that. Vanessa had had everything material she had ever wanted. She had, however, been starved of emotional love. Her father had always been too busy to take any interest in her! Hadn't he had to work really hard to maintain their status her Mother was always saying to the young Vanessa? Why was she not more grateful? Why did she have to make such a fuss of her Father when he had just got in from a busy day making millions? Did she not realise that her Daddy needed time to himself when he came home? He did not need an over excited child driving him to distraction! When would she ever learn? As the years went on Vanessa stopped trying to get her Daddy's attention and became more introverted so much so that even her Mother noticed! And so she was packed off to Boarding School at the first opportunity. It might have been the best that money could buy but Vanessa hated every moment spent there! She decided to rebel in the only way she knew how! She was an attractive teenager with a seriously wealthy Father who could afford to pay for peoples silence if needed! He spent a small fortune covering up his wayward daughter's indiscretions and became more and more distant as Vanessa tried harder and harder to get his attention. Even when he was going ballistic with her Vanessa did not mind. At least he was speaking to her and not ignoring her!!

After his sudden and unexpected death whilst on holiday with his young, beautiful and single secretary Vanessa was plunged into a nightmare time. Her Mother never really recovered from the scandal created by her Husband's death whilst tied to his Hotel bedroom with chains etc! Her Mother never ever mentioned the circumstances of his death to Vanessa or indeed anyone else in the family and it came as no surprise to anyone in the know when Vanessa's mother left for Australia and was remarried to an extremely wealthy younger man who made it clear that Vanessa would be allowed to visit but not to live with them in Australia. Vanessa was not troubled by this. She did not like her new "stepfather" as her Mother insisted she called him. He was only 10 years older than she was for God's sake!

Her hedonistic lifestyle begins in earnest then. She had been left a seriously wealthy young woman by her Father. Maybe he thought this might help. It didn't! And so it was that Vanessa eventually tired of this transient lifestyle and found herself in deepest darkest Norfolk!

Vanessa had even admitted, quite shyly for her, that she had feelings for Robert that she couldn't begin to explain.

The session had ended with Vanessa agreeing to try to analyse her feelings regarding Gordon and she had agreed to that being the main theme of her next session with Chris.

Chris, meanwhile, was a lot more troubled than Vanessa. He had had several sessions with Gordon since his shocking revelation regarding his wife's death and Chris was still in quandary as to what to do! He had decided after much soul searching to tell Gordon at his next session that he would not be going to the Police with what he had been told! Gordon had opened up his heart to him and he would not condemn the man to spending the rest of his life in prison! It might not come to that of course but Chris would not take that risk.

Chris had discussed all this with Ronnie and they had both agreed that this was the best way forward. So why was Chris still in a tormented state of mind? How he wished he was still in contact with Colonel Henderson from his army days. Hadn't he always helped him when he could? Still no sense in dwelling on things that couldn't be changed thought Chris as he left the room to go and see what his beautiful wife was doing. How he needed to see her right now!

Chapter 29.

As the weeks progressed all the house guests began to change. Some in subtle ways others in not so subtle ways!

Laura's condition did not allow for subtlety! She was positively blossoming during her pregnancy. When she looked back to the day when she had finally admitted to all the others that she was indeed pregnant she could not help but smile as she remembered that evening. She had been so defiant! She had decided that she would brazen out any negative comments. As it happened not one of the guests or indeed Chris and Ronnie said anything derogatory to her. They had been incredibly supportive of her form that moment! No one had asked about the Father at all. Laura smiled to herself as she remembered just how vocal Pru had been when she had announced to the entire room that that sort of question should not be asked for after all it wasn't anyone else's business after all was it? Everyone had shown her such kindness and consideration that it had helped to restore some of her faith in human nature. Not everyone in the world was out for what they could get after all!

Adam had finally plucked up the courage to admit to his illiteracy. He had been astounded when Robert had admitted to being dyslexic himself. Robert had had no hesitation in putting himself forward as Adam's tutor if Adam didn't mind that is! A rota system had been incorporated into the busy schedule for running the house and the business. Adam and Robert went into the Library most evenings and Robert was astonished at how Adam devoured all the words in the books and was still hungry for more! Adam had surprised himself that he did not feel inferior any more. He had a problem with his reading and he was dealing with it. What was wrong with that anyway?

Gordon had been teased unmercifully for the evening when he had finally admitted to everyone that he had been arranging trips to the local pub as often as he had dared! He was more at peace with himself now. He had spoken to Mavis, briefly, about his life before he came to Norfolk and he had decided that very soon he would tell Mavis the complete truth about his wife as he was tired of living like this and he would take what was coming to him like a man! Gordon could do no wrong in Ronnie's eyes as everyone said when he had finally repaired the dreaded "Aga" and it had worked perfectly ever since! Gordon was a Godsend as far as Ronnie was concerned and he had been labelled as Teachers pet by everyone!

Robert had" blossomed "the most as far as the other guests were concerned! He had taken Adam under his wing. He had shown enormous patience with the lad when Adam had been struggling at first and he had thrown more than one temper tantrum! Adam would never have admitted this out loud of course but in truth Adam knew he had been a real pain in the "a### "on more than one occasion. Robert had found his niche in life. He was a natural teacher who had the patience and personality to enable Adam to flourish under his guidance. Robert felt more alive and needed here at the farmhouse. He had even kissed Vanessa goodnight on more than one occasion and he was sure that the last time he had done so he could have sworn she kissed him back!

Vanessa had changed in a subtle way. She was no longer on the defensive quite so often. She had even taken the time to get to know Gordon more and she found that if she would only take the time to listen and not judge him then Gordon was quite a decent bloke after all! Vanessa had also found an ally in Pru. Pru had kept her distance form Vanessa on an emotional level for a long time.

Oh! She was always polite and interested in Vanessa's day etc. but she maintained her distance until one day when Pru had been in her room resting and she had heard Vanessa crying in her room. Vanessa had opened up to Pru about her confused feelings for Robert and her even more confusing animosity towards Gordon. Vanessa had been astounded when Pru had told her that it was no wonder she had been feeling so lonely and confused. She had built this defensive wall around her and if she wanted any peace of mind she needed to be strong enough to let her defences down every once in a while!

Vanessa had been astonished and outraged and humbled by this statement all at the same time! She had been doing exactly that! She went on the attack as her form of defence!! After that Vanessa had, tentatively at first, opened herself up to the group and had been pleasantly surprised when people reacted more positively to her gentler manner. She and Gordon had even found a common interest. They both loved steam trains! How ridiculous was that! Vanessa's father had been an avid enthusiast and sometimes he had taken Vanessa on trips to see various engines and she and Gordon had both been to the railway museum at York more than once. Vanessa and Gordon would probably never be true friends but they were no longer arch enemies all thanks to Pru thought Vanessa.

Miss Prunella Okenden! How bloody pretentious does that sound now thought Pru? Pru had never felt more alive and more useful - ever! She still had her aches and pains and she did not do anything like the amount of physical work that the others did but she knew she played her part in the smooth running of the house and business. Especially the house which she was fiercely protective of! She had found a soul mate in the unlikely form of Laura who was over 70 years younger than she was!! She had an enormous amount of respect for Chris and Ronnie who she knew worked so hard to keep the farmhouse going. Robert and Gordon were deferential to her. Not in a superior way and not in a patronising way! Pru would not have stood for that and both men were well aware of it too! Pru had taken all of this in her stride. She had always been independent but now knew that she had missed out on many things by not allowing herself the company of others. Well no more! She knew just exactly what she was going to do but she knew she would have to do it secretly and discreetly if she was not going to jeopardise her new found friendships!

Ronnie had also changed in subtle ways. Chris was aware of them but he doubted that anybody else in the house had noticed them. Ronnie was much more at ease than she had been at first. She had been surprised by Laura's news. Surprised but also secretly delighted. She had never had the chance to have children. In Burma she had always been a disappointment to her family and she had always been surprised and not a little relieved that they had not organised an arranged marriage for her just to get her off their hands! As a result she had put the idea of a husband and children out of her mind. When she had met Chris that had been one of the major disappointments in both their lives. Ronnie knew she could not become a surrogate mother to Lauren's child. She was far too intelligent for that fantasy world but she knew that she would relish her time with the baby.

Ronnie had begun to open up to the guests and know they all knew just what a kind hearted funny woman she was. Chris knew that they had all fallen under the same spell she had cast on him. Chris meanwhile was probably the least happy of all the residents at "Haven's Retreat". He had finally come to terms with his decision regarding Gordon. He knew it was the right thing to do. After all it was not his place to be judge and jury over another man's life. He had done many things in his Army life that he would never be proud of and he knew that everyone would face judgement son enough!

Chris's main concern was the impact that the residents at the farmhouse were having on the village. The Army had always stressed the need for secrecy and it had been agreed that the Army would always be there for them if they kept their side of the bargain. As it was it was becoming more and more difficult to stop the villagers being involved in the farmhouse. Gordon was always at the pub. Pru and Lauren visited the Doctor's Surgery on a regular basis. The people he delivered to had begun to ask where the other folks who sometimes delivered were! Chris knew he could not stop them going into the village but he was also very aware of the villagers beginning "Chinese whispers" and before long they would have decided that the farmhouse was indulging in Satanic Rites at the very least!

Chris laughed out loud at this and shook off these thoughts. He was becoming as paranoid as the villagers! The farmhouse was at its busiest right now and he needed all his concentration and energy if they were going to make this year the most profitable yet! Oh! How they needed to make a profit! If they could just get through this season they would be able to clear their mortgage with the bank and finally "Haven's Retreat" would be theirs!!

Chapter 30.

Meanwhile many miles away, in an isolated army base headquarters, things were also happening! Mr Ronald Henderson was being driven into the nearest town with a small suitcase which contained all his worldly possessions and a second class ticket for the next available train to London. As he was driven silently by the Army Corporal assigned to the duty Ronald's mind was still trying to come to terms with the events of the last month. How the hell had he got himself here? What the hell was he going to do for the rest of his life? He was 57 years old and he had no idea of what life in "civvy" street was like! He was no longer Colonel Henderson of the British Army. He was now plain Mr Henderson of no fixed abode! Ronnie had been a career soldier from the moment he was old enough to join. He had given his life to his country and now he had been retired as his department's Budget had been slashed and his workforce dispersed to various locations around the trouble spots of the world and he had been thrown onto the scrapheap! Ronnie had always worried that this would eventually happen but now that it had he was filled with a mixture of emotions. He was devastated that he would not have the routine he had had all his adult life. He was worried about just exactly what he would do with all his spare time, he had no hobbies, he had no friends outside of the army and he had nowhere to live! Ronald had never bought property preferring to live at the various barracks he had been assigned to and as such had no property to call his own! What he did have, however, was a considerable amount of savings and an excellent pension which would enable him to start a new life in comparative comfort. All of this meant nothing to Ronnie as he was dropped off at the railway with a cursory salute from the Corporal and he stood alone at the railway station entrance .At that moment Colonel Ronald Henderson decided that he knew exactly what he was going to do with the rest of his life and so it was with his shoulders back and his head high he marched onto the platform and onto the train that would take him to London and then on to Norfolk to see his old colleagues from Burma. They had a lot of catching up to do and when he had finished talking to Chris and Ronnie their lives would never be the same again either! And it would serve the army right when the whole house of cards came crashing down around its ears!

 And so it was that Mr Ronald Henderson, ex military man, reverted back to Colonel Ronald Henderson Commander of Communications and Surveillance - Burma! As the train left the station Colonel Henderson sat alone in his first class compartment – he had upgraded to first class as he needed time to think- his mind went back to the last time he had spoken to Chris and he remembered all the lies he had told Chris about how his old work was progressing and how proud he would have been had he still been a serving officer! All those lies! For all those years! As the train pulled away and went into a dark tunnel this perfectly reflected the mood and mindset of Colonel Ronnie Henderson and he decided that he would stay in London for one night and then hire a car and drive straight to Norfolk. He would not waste a second of time wondering if he was doing the right thing. The army had discarded him in an instant; he was "surplus to requirements" as they put it! He who had given his whole life to the army! Well he would show them! They could not do this to him and expect to get away with it!

 He had been trained to focus his mind on a task given to him by his Commanding Officers and not to question the morals of what he had been asked to do and he had done it without any qualms and so he had become immune to the suffering inflicted on captured soldiers put under his care. As his thoughts turned darker and darker Colonel Ronald Henderson's mind went into an evil corner from which there was no escape and no turning back!

Chapter 31.

Thursday 11th August 2009. 8 am.

Colonel Henderson was ready for his journey to Norfolk. He had been up for 2 hours and he had put on his best uniform. He knew that he looked impressive in it and that was his intention. He had spent the evening at the Club enjoying the company of other soldiers. He would always be a soldier. He had never wanted to do anything else in his life and he had devoted his entire life to the Army and what had they done? They had dumped him unceremoniously and he was still smarting inside. He knew the logic behind it. After all he had also had to do the same thing to many other soldiers hadn't he?

As he packed his suitcase with the same meticulous manner he had always done things and as he checked his image in the mirror he liked what he saw. A distinguished looking soldier in his best dress uniform. He knew that people treated soldiers differently when they dressed to impress and Colonel Henderson knew the importance of giving the right impression if he was going to get away with what he proposed to do! He had no authority in the Army now but he hoped that the "Old Boy Network" that he had always found unpleasant would come good. He needed the help of some of the "Old Boy's" if he was going to gain access to the Record Offices and "borrow" one file for a short time! He would not, of course, be telling them that he had no intention of giving it back!

At 9 o'clock precisely Colonel Henderson marched into the "Club" and was shown into the inner sanctum of the Senior Member's Bar. As he looked around Colonel Henderson's mind went back down to the darkest recesses of his psyche. He was still seething with rage at his dismissal from the Army. He needed to show them that they could not expect to get away with treating him in this derisory manner. They would pay for it all right!

As he waited in a large leather armchair he took stock around him. He should have been allowed entrance to this Club! He deserved it!! Colonel Henderson shook off these negative thoughts. He needed to stay focussed today of all days! As the man he needed to see made his way towards him he stood up saluted his "victim" and began his journey towards finding just what he needed to ensure that the Army would remember Colonel Henderson for a long time to come!

At 2 p.m Colonel Ronald Henderson went to the Official Records Office with the full permission of the Army at his disposal! After more than 2 hours Colonel Henderson had everything he needed. How simple it had been after all. The Army prided itself on its unrivalled security! What a load of "bo#####s" thought Henderson as he folded the files he needed into the false bottom of his attaché case.

As he left the building he did not look left or right but focussed on keeping up the appearance of a full time soldier going about his legitimate business. Inside his head, however, it was a different thing altogether. He could not believe how easy it had been! The old fool did not suspect a thing! He had no idea just what he had allowed to happen.

When he did find out it would be far too late to do anything about it! How he did not laugh out loud he did not know. As he sat in his hire car he took deep breaths and focussed his mind on the task ahead. He started the engine, organised the satellite navigation system, and headed towards "Haven's Retreat"

Chapter 32.

August 12th 2009. 7pm.

Today had been a gloriously sunny day. The cloudless sky had ensured that the temperature had been high all day and the evening was a balmy one. All the houseguests had converged outside to eat at the huge kitchen table which seemed to have taken permanent residence outside for the last few weeks! Everyone loved eating outside on evenings like this and the table looked fabulous with all the food and drink waiting to be consumed by the very hungry guests. Chris and Ronnie particularly enjoyed these times as it gave everybody chance to relax and unwind after their long day out in the field or in the village. The houseguests had become more than clients, guests or however else you could describe them. They had formed a "family" of sorts and as such it was fascinating for Chris and Ronnie to sit back and covertly watch the interaction between everybody.

Pru and Laura were, as usual, impossible to separate. The bond between them was palpable. Everyone could see the special friendship that had developed between them and it was lovely to behold.

Vanessa and Gordon had, perhaps, been the most surprising revelation for Chris and Ronnie! As they gathered around the table Gordon was helping Vanessa into her seat and Vanessa was actually thanking him! They would probably never be true friends but it gladdened Ronnie's heart in particular that the awful animosity that had blighted the early days appeared to be behind them.

Robert was his usual affable self and Chris wondered if this was the real Robert after all and not the Robert who tried so hard to please everyone? He was obviously besotted with Vanessa and it was charming to observe how he was courting her in the old fashioned way.

Vanessa had changed into a caring and thoughtful person during her time at the farmhouse and both Chris and Ronnie knew that this was partly to do with their sessions together but it was also due, in no small part, to the attention she was receiving from Robert. She was blossoming before their eyes and everyone else in the house had seen her transformation and they were all delighted for them both! Of course as is the case with the British thought Ronnie no-one had actually said anything about the romance to either Vanessa or Robert. "That would never do my dear!" as Pru would undoubtedly say mused Ronnie!

Gordon meanwhile was now escorting Pru to her seat. She, of course, was making a big show of not needing his help thank you whilst all the time she was evidently loving every minute of the attention! What a woman thought Ronnie not for the first time. Pru looked positively radiant tonight. She had continued to take her medication as prescribed and she had seen another specialist about her "old bones" and as a result she had been prescribed a different type of medication which, by her own account, she should have had years ago if only those fools at her last doctors had bothered to enter the twenty first century!!

The laughter and bonhomie was proof, if proof were needed that the work being done here at the farmhouse was worth it. As Pru sat down at her usual place, at the head of the table no less, (Where else could I possibly go an old woman of my status and upbringing she had laughingly stated a few weeks ago), the only person left to arrive at the table was Adam.

"Where the dickens is that boy? Said Pru" I bet I know where he has been all afternoon. In the library don't you think everyone?" As everyone laughed and joined in the light hearted banter Adam arrived at the table.

"Sorry I'm late folks I just lost track of time! What's so funny eh?"

"Nothing Adam! We were just laying bets as to where you might have been all afternoon that's all. We are all so pleased for you that you so obviously enjoy your reading and I have to say Robert that I admire both you and Adam for your determination in getting Adam to where he is today!"

As Gordon finished his little speech there was a moment's silence as everyone could not quite believe their ears. Gordon was not known for making any sort of speech let alone one with such obvious passion.

"What are you lot looking at? Look I know you all thought I was just a miserable old bugger who needed to get a life when I first arrived here and you were all absolutely right. I was a miserable old bugger back then. What's with the raised eyebrows Mrs Okenden? -joked Gordon. Anyway as I was saying I think that it is marvellous that Adam had the courage to admit to his lack of reading ability. I don't think I would have had the courage at his age to do that. So well done lad and here's to many happy years enjoying the pleasure of books! And now whilst I still have a shred of dignity left and before my nerve gives in I have an announcement to make!

As Gordon looked at all the expectant faces in front of him he could not quite believe how his life had turned around in just three months. He had finally written to his family telling them just exactly how he felt. He had tried to explain what had happened to his beautiful wife and how he had agonised over what was the best thing to do for her. He had explained his reasons for leaving home and coming to the Retreat and he hoped that one day his children would find it in their hearts to at least begun to think about forgiving him for what he had done! He had also told both his children what he thought of their own behaviour since the funeral and he had asked them to look closely at themselves before condemning him outright. He had left a forwarding address at the post office in Thetford. He had not trusted his children with telling them his exact location. He would not put it past them, if he caught them at a bad time, to come down here and have it out with him in front of everyone!

Several weeks had gone by and Gordon had resigned himself to the fact that his children still did not want anything to do with him anymore when he received a letter from his daughter! In it she had written that she was glad he was alright because she and her brother had been worried sick. How could he just leave like that and not tell them where he was going? They had called the police and he was officially listed as a missing person!

Angela also went on to say that it would take time for them to get back to some sort of relationship but she and Gordon's son Michael had decided that they would be willing to at least try to see their father's point of view. Angela also told Gordon that he was going to be a Grandfather in November and so she hoped that they could at least start the long painful process of getting to know each other again. Gordon had cried for over an hour sitting in the Land Rover outside Thetford Post Office. He had eventually driven off as he was attracting a lot of unwanted attention sitting there in broad daylight blubbering like a big soft Jessie!

As all eyes turned to look at him Gordon took a deep breath and briefly outlined the details of the letter before announcing, with the biggest grin on his face, that he was going to be a Grandfather in November and he wanted to share his good news with his new found friends!

Everyone spoke at once and they all congratulated him on his news and they all bombarded him with questions. "

"When was he going back?"

"How did he feel about being a Grandfather?"

All these questions and more took up the rest of the evening for Gordon.

Meanwhile Adam also announced that he had been into Thetford to and he had applied to go on an English Language and Literature Course starting in September. He had also looked into accommodation around the College and they had promised to get back to him as soon as they could. Adam had spoken to Chris and Ronnie prior to this and he had hoped that he could stay on until his digs had been sorted but he would also realise that if they wanted him to leave he would do so straight away. Chris and Ronnie had told him that he could stay as long as he needed to and he didn't have to go at all if he didn't want to! It had taken all of his strength not to cry in front of Chris and Ronnie at that point but he told them that he would take up their generous offer for as long as he needed to but he had decided that he would never go back to Bristol EVER and he had also decided that Norfolk folk were not too bad after all! He had thanked them for the opportunities they had given him but now it was time to begin the rest of his life. He was going to College and the world was his oyster!!

As the evening drew to a close Pru decided to call it a night. She also had an announcement to make but that could wait just a few more days until everything was in place and there could be no going back!

Robert escorted Pru up to her room and when he came down he hoped his face was not quite as red at it felt! Pru, in her usual inimitable way, had asked him outright just what his intentions were towards Vanessa. "Call me old-fashioned my dear boy but you must strike whilst the iron is hot don't you think? It is obvious that you both feel the same about each other so why waste any more time dithering about? Surely tonight would be the best time to express your true feelings. We have all had a beautiful evening. The stars are out- the night is warm and the mood is just perfect so don't dilly dally young man if you know what's good for you!"

And with that Mrs Prunella Okenden had swept into her room leaving a shell shocked Robert in her wake!

As Robert went downstairs his mind was in turmoil! Pru was absolutely right of course. Tonight was the perfect time to tell Vanessa exactly how he felt. Did he have the courage though? Robert decided there and then that if he didn't speak out tonight he would probably never speak out and he could not bear the thought of losing the chance to be with Vanessa for the rest of his life. He also wondered what his Mother would say! He realised that he had not thought about his Mother for ages and he knew without a doubt that she would be horrified that she might lose him altogether to another woman! He also realised the extent that his Mother had run his life for him all these years.

He hoped that it was out of maternal love but he also suspected that his Mother needed to control him more than was good for him. He resolved to take a chance with Vanessa and to hell with what his Mother thought. It was his life after all and if she didn't like it she could lump it!!

Laura, meanwhile, had sat quietly absorbing all the events of the evening. She was really pleased for Gordon and Adam but she was worried about her own circumstances. Everyone had been incredibly supportive when they discovered her pregnancy and no-one had asked any awkward questions. She also knew that the time was coming when she would have to leave "Haven's Retreat" and start her life as a single mother with no money and no qualifications! What the hell was she going to do then? She had no idea what to do and she would not burden Pru or anyone else with her problems. She was pregnant- she would have the baby and she would cope somehow!

As she helped to clear the table she resolved to call at the Social Services office at Thetford and see if she could get her name down on the Council list for a flat or a little house. She would never go back to "home" and so she must make the most of her situation here in Norfolk. Oh God! Where would they put her? She hoped it would not be on some dreadful estate full of druggies and "Prozzies". She really didn't think she could cope with that. Oh well she would cross that bridge when she got to it!

The evening had turned cooler by this time and it was decided that they would all retire back into the house for the rest of the evening.

10.30pm.

Chris and Ronnie were the only two people still in the kitchen. Robert and Vanessa had taken themselves off for a stroll in the moonlight! Adam had gone to his room to read. Gordon had taken the Land Rover to Soham Tarney for the last half hour at the pub. "Just to see how things were with the Landlady. She is short staffed at the moment and he wondered if she might need some help with last orders and clearing up afterwards!" Laure had been a little subdued as she had said goodnight and Ronnie wondered just what was troubling her and she had resolved to have a word with her as soon as she was able to.

As the coffee percolated on the "Aga" Ronnie smiled at Chris and they both felt that tonight had been very special for everyone. They would take their coffee into the lounge and sit quietly as they both unwound. They enjoyed the guests being in the house but they relished this time of night when they could be together as a couple and not have all the distractions associated with running the farmhouse intruding on their time together. They had just sat down to enjoy a few moments quiet reflection when they heard a car coming down the drive! Gordon couldn't be back yet surely? He had only left a few minutes ago! Who the hell was coming down their drive at his time of night? Chris heaved himself out of his favourite chair and grimaced at Ronnie as they both went to the front door to find out who it was arriving so late!

Chris and Ronnie exchanged worried glances at each other as Colonel Ronald Henderson got out of his car and came towards them with the strangest expression on his face. What the hell was going on? What was he doing here at this time of night? As they waited for Colonel Henderson to speak Chris and Ronnie had no idea of the catastrophic things that were about to happen to all of the people at "Haven's Retreat."

Chapter 33.

Ronald Henderson ex Army Colonel was exhausted. He had travelled from London to Norfolk without stopping, except for fuel and food. He had not driven for so long in a lifetime. He had been assigned a driver years ago when he had first gained his rank of Colonel and he had forgotten how exhausting driving was. He was shattered by the events of the last few weeks but his mind would not let him rest until he had told Padre Chris Gaskell everything he knew about the work that was going on in the modern army in his name! He did not notice the glances of concern flowing between Chris and Ronnie he was so pre-occupied with his own thoughts and demons. As he entered the farmhouse he was completely unaware of his surroundings. If he had been asked to describe any aspect of the farmhouse he would have found it an impossible task. He was so focussed on the task at hand he did not hear Chris asking him if he was hungry or thirsty. "Sorry old chap. What did you say?" Oh! No I couldn't eat or drink a thing thank you! I need to talk to you immediately. Sorry it's so late but I got here as quickly as I could. Do you have a snifter of brandy perhaps?" Chris and Ronnie were at a complete loss as to why Colonel Ronnie Henderson had turned up here tonight. Chris handed Henderson a generous measure of brandy and was startled when Henderson drank it down in one go!

"Padre, I know it's late and you must be wondering what the hell I'm doing here arriving unannounced at this time of night but I could not rest until I got here and told you the truth about the work that is being done on our soldiers in the name of progress ! The Army has let us down in an unimaginable way!

Chris and Ronnie did not know what to do. They led Colonel Henderson to the sofa and waited. Colonel Ronald Henderson spent a not inconsiderable time in obvious torment before he began.

"I know you must be wondering just what the hell is going on? "

Chris and Ronnie looked nervously at each other.

"I have recently come into possession of some information that will devastate you!"

Colonel Henderson was still in enough control of his thoughts to realise that now what not the time to elaborate on just exactly how he acquired this information. That could wait until later.

"I know that the work you both did in Burma was highly sensitive to say the least. What you don't know, and could never have known, is just precisely what the Army was doing with the research and practices you helped to initiate."

Chris and Ronnie were now very concerned. Colonel Henderson seemed to be almost talking to himself. So it was that Colonel Ronald Henderson, ex Army man, began to explain about the changes made to the work done by them both in Burma. The methods developed by them both to help battle scarred soldiers deal with all the atrocities that they had seen in warfare had been altered to allow soldiers to be "brainwashed" into becoming torturers, unfeeling killing machines who would be sent on dangerous missions with the strict orders to ensure that no prisoners were to be left alive after their interrogations! Henderson went on to describe how the methods devised had been altered to enable the memory of the awful acts committed in the name of the British Army to be wiped clean from the subconscious mind of the poor unfortunate soldiers seconded to this heinous task!

Chris and Ronnie listened for an hour as Henderson told them that ALL their work had been a cover up for the long term goal of recruiting soldiers to become unfeeling, emotionless, killing machines! The hypnosis sessions had been changed to erase the memory of the torture and evil deeds perpetrated by these fighting men! As the full horror of just exactly was going on in Burma and other countries of the world began to sink in Chris became withdrawn and Ronnie was just in complete denial! How had their work been turned around so badly? They had been instructed to help these poor unfortunate souls with all the terrible things they had seen and witnessed firsthand!

Chris asked for proof of these outrageous allegations and when Henderson produced the stolen files with the damning evidence as final proof Chris broke down.

"In the name of God, how could they do this? How could they turn what we were doing into this abominable thing? "

Ronnie had hardly said a word during the last hour. She would not believe it! She could not believe it! Then the doubts crept in. What was it that her colleague had said to her the night before her mutilated body was found on the doorstep of the house she was living in? "Ronnie, be careful how far you take this please!" She had dismissed this without a second thought. What precisely had she meant? She would never know now would she?

"Colonel Henderson can I ask you a direct and simple question?"

Ronnie's voice was calm and collected – a dangerous thing thought Chris.

"How long have you known or suspected this?"

Colonel Ronald Henderson did not answer at first. Instead he looked straight through Chris and Ronnie as though he was in another place and time.

"Ronnie, I have known you for years and I have always been as honest with you as the Army would allow me to be. I had had my suspicions for years. I did not have proof. You must understand. I was a career soldier. I knew never to question my superior officers. Please try to understand will you?"

Ronnie remained silent. She was not about to let about to let Henderson off the hook so easily!

Ronnie asked again. "How long have you known or suspected this?"

Henderson shuddered violently before he next spoke.

"I have known for the last 5 years or so!"

Chris spoke next with a quiet but determined voice.

"So you have known, for as long as we have been here, that all the soldiers we have looked after have been sent to us to begin the process of erasing their memories before sending them back to the Army and allowing them to kill indiscriminately without a second's remorse or regret?"

Ronnie let out a strangled sob. This could not be true surely? The Army would not do such a terrible thing. To alter a person's mind to such an extent that they became incapable of feeling any sort of normal emotion! Would they?

Colonel Ronald Henderson was tired. He was tired of the Army. He was tired of his life. He was ashamed of his part in the collusion. He had nothing left to lose.

"Chris and Ronnie I know that you must despise me and the Army for the way your work has been changed to such a terrible degree. I have no other defence except that as a soldier it was my duty to obey orders."

Chris did not know what to think. His world had just come crashing down around his ears. He had spent years helping to develop the hypnosis session. He had sat with soldiers who had seen such atrocities in the name of freedom and democracy. He had devised a series of sessions to help these poor unfortunate men to get back to some sort of normality when they left the Army and went back to "civvy" street.

The Army had betrayed both him and Ronnie. They had effectively bought their silence by allowing them to leave the Army and set up here with the only proviso being that they would help some of the most traumatised soldiers towards recovery. Had they unwittingly sent these poor boys back to the Army with sufficient improvement in their mental stability for the Army to send them back into battle?

Chris was no fool. He knew that warfare was a terrible thing that never really achieved any of its goals but he truly believed in the power and good of his work! He would never, could never, sanction using his techniques in such a way!!

The evidence was overwhelming. The file that Henderson had brought with him contained information about specific soldiers and specific battles that he had been part of. He knew without a shadow of a doubt that Henderson was telling the awful truth.

Chris never fully understood what happened next. All he remembers is all the houseguests suddenly appearing out of nowhere and both Robert and Adam holding him back as he screamed at Henderson.

What happened was that Chris attacked Henderson with his bare hands. He was strangling the life out of the man when he was yanked away by the other men.

The room was a mess. Tables were overturned, the lamp was smashed, he had cut himself on the broken brandy glass and everyone was either shouting or crying for him to stop for God's sake!

God! Where the hell had he been all this time? What was he thinking? Allowing people to do this to each other. Chris wondered if he would ever regain his faith after this.

Henderson was being helped to a chair by Vanessa. She looked shocked and appalled by what she had just witnessed. Lauren was crying and swaying in the farthest corner. Pru was comforting her whilst avoiding his gaze. Ronnie was standing absolutely still in the centre of the room seemingly oblivious to everything going on around her.

As he shook off the hold that Robert and Adam had on him Padre Chris Gaskell staggered out of the room and into the night. He swore that he would kill anyone who came after him and if they didn't believe him then just wait and see what would happen to them if they were foolish enough to try!

The houseguests did not what had gone on but they knew it must have been catastrophic from the look of both Chris and Ronnie. Vanessa bathed the superficial cut to the man's hand and left him sitting in a daze in the large armchair. Laura was taken back to her room by a fragile looking Pru and the others set about repairing some of the damage done to the room. Ronnie had not uttered a sound during all of this until she began to shake, slowly at first, and then she went into a sort of convulsion and began to howl and cry and scream incoherently until she collapsed on the floor.

Robert wondered if he should go after Chris but Adam and Vanessa said that the best thing they could do right now was to get Ronnie and the stranger to their rooms. Vanessa gave Ronnie one of her sleeping pills and put her to bed. Ronnie did not appear to register any of this happening to her and fell into an immediate sleep. The stranger was led to the only spare room where a bed was quickly made up for him. He had not spoken either and Robert was not sure he knew exactly where he was or what had just happened.

Everyone eventually went back to their rooms but no-one slept again that night. The morning came and it was going to be another gloriously sunny day. The mood in the house was not in the least sunny. What did the rest of the day have in store for everyone?

Only time would tell!

Chapter 34.

The morning sun dappled the grass around Chris. He had wandered into the forest and sat down beside one of the oldest trees in the forest. He had always liked to sit here in quiet reflection and he realised that he must have come automatically here when he had left the house. He did not have any recollection of getting here. He had sat devoid of feelings for several hours trying to come to terms with what he had been told. He sat staring straight ahead and did not notice the sun making wonderful patterns on the grass or the sounds of the birds in the trees. All he was aware of was this deep chasm that had appeared where his heart used to be. He knew that he had to go back to the farmhouse. He wanted with all his heart to run and keep running until his heart gave up and he died there and then. He could not face dealing with what he knew would be the terrible outcome of finding out just what the Army had been doing. Chris knew, of course, that he would not run and run. He knew that he needed to be with Ronnie. He knew that if they helped each other they would, somehow, get through this. He also knew that he had come within seconds of ending another person's life! He had never experienced such blind rage before. He now had some inkling of what was going on in the minds of the soldiers he had treated in Burma! His religious beliefs had taken a battering these last few months and he realised that this time he could not rely on the Army or Colonel Ronald Henderson to help him get over this!

As he wandered back to the house Chris doubted that life would ever be the same again. Where would he and Ronnie go? They must leave as quickly as they could. The Army would suspect that Henderson would make some sort of contact with them when they realised that the files had gone missing. The Army knew when to close ranks and they knew what to do to protect themselves. They were capable of these terrible acts on these poor unfortunate soldiers. Chris knew with absolute certainty that their lives were in mortal danger!!

As he approached the farmhouse Chris began to look around him. The farmhouse looked beautiful in the morning sun. The garden smelt amazing and as he looked into the greenhouses at all the various fruits, vegetables and flowers growing there Chris suddenly realised just exactly what he and Ronnie had achieved during the last 5 years. They had created their own little piece of heaven here on earth. Why should he let the Army take this away from them? Why should he and Ronnie flee like criminals?

The sounds of the other guests working filtered through to Chris's conscious mind. What would all the guests do if they just ran? He could not, he would not, be driven away!! He and Ronnie would find some way of solving this terrible problem. He did not know how but he also knew he would not give up without a damned good fight!

As Chris came into the kitchen the others looked anxiously towards the door. No-one knew quite what to say at first. Robert was the first to speak.

"Chris. How are you? We have all be so worried for you and Ronnie! Vanessa is with her now. I think you should go to her. She seems completely traumatised. We have tried talking to her but she doesn't seem to hear us."

Chris went straight past Robert without speaking and headed for their bedroom. Vanessa left, also without saying a word, and Chris stood over the bed and looked at his beautiful wife.

Ronnie was just lying there with her eyes wide open but it was obvious she was not seeing anything around her. She had retreated into her own mind and Chris did not know if he could reach her but he was going to try- My God! Was he going to try!

Chris spent the morning with Ronnie talking to her, holding her hand, soothing her tears and slowly, very slowly, she started to come back to him. He had never felt so grateful and so angry at the same time in his life. How had their lives unravelled in such a way? He would stay with Ronnie for as long as she needed him. He knew that the others were capable of looking after the day to day running of the farmhouse and quite frankly he was needed here so that he could support Ronnie. He had never seen her like this before and he was frightened. He could not live without her. She was everything to him. She needed him now more than she had ever done and he would not let her down – not now and not ever!

Pru and Laura had gone through the motions of making breakfast for everybody and neither made any comment when everyone just picked at the food. No-one had any appetite.

As they washed up Pru asked if anyone knew where Gordon was. She had not seen him come down last night and she had not heard him walking about this morning. Did anyone know where he might be?

Just as she said this they all heard Gordon coming down the drive in the Land Rover. The car had a very distinctive sound.

As Gordon came into the kitchen he knew something had gone on.

After it had been explained to him Gordon was as confused and concerned as everybody else but it had been decided that they would all show their support for Chris and Ronnie by ensuring that the work went on as normal. They obviously had a lot of things on their minds right now and no-one wanted to add to their burden by troubling them with minor worries.

And so it was that at 10 am   the house and gardens were deserted. Pru and Laura had been despatched to the flower greenhouses where they would attend to the flowers needed for the village and the town businesses. Gordon and Vanessa went to Thetford for supplies and Robert and Adam would tend the vegetable crops. Gordon and Vanessa did not say a word about them being sent off together. Now was not the time for things like that. Now was the time to show some solidarity and support for their hosts.

Upstairs in his room Henderson lay on the bed unblinking. He had lain there all night. Sleep had eluded him. As he listened to the sounds of the guests leaving he felt a terrible sense of regret. What had he done? Why did he not leave well alone? Chris and Ronnie did not need to know what was going on in the Army. He had betrayed them. He had acted out of pure self- interest.

 He had wanted to punish the Army for the way he had been treated and all he had succeeded in doing was destroying Chris and Ronnie!

Henderson got up and walked slowly down the stairs. He did not have any idea of what he would do now. What he did know was that he must try to repair, somehow, the damage he had caused for Chris and Ronnie.

He wandered around the house without really seeing it and he eventually came into the lounge where he had been last night. As he surveyed the damage to the room some of the events of last night came back to him. Chris had tried to strangle him and someone had dragged him away. He had no idea who that was but he was acutely aware that if that person had not done so then he Colonel Ronald Henderson would be dead by now!

He wandered into the rest of the house and even in his troubled state of mind he could see how beautiful the house was. The house had a wonderful calm feeling about it and as he continued exploring it came back to him just exactly what he had done! He had jeopardised everything that Chris and Ronnie had strived for. He would never forgive himself for what he had put them through!

As he went outside his mind went back into that dark tunnel and he slowly walked to the hire car, opened the door and sat contemplating his next move.

The journey to the village was done in absolute silence. Gordon and Vanessa had never spent any length of time together during their time at the farmhouse. They had agreed to be civil to one another but in the car the silence was oppressive!

"Gordon, I know that we got off on the wrong foot when we first got here but I think that maybe we need to talk don't you?"

Gordon did not reply at first and Vanessa groaned inwardly. The bloody man was not going to make this easy was he?

"Vanessa, I have an apology to make to you" said Gordon.

Vanessa held her breath. Gordon needed to apologise to her? What for? She had given as good as she had got. No apology was necessary as far as she was concerned and she said as much to Gordon.

"I was unfair to you when we first arrived. I made assumptions of you that were completely groundless and I am sorry. You reminded me so much of my daughter that I was not thinking straight."

"Gordon when we all arrived here we were different people. You had your demons and so did I. In view of what went on last night I think that there are more urgent things going on don't you?"

"What exactly went on last night? It seems almost unbelievable that Chris was strangling the life out of that man don't you think?"

As they continued with their day Gordon and Vanessa opened up to each other a little about their concerns for Chris and Ronnie, the situation they found themselves in and how much better they both felt for spending time at the farmhouse. They both agreed that if they had not come to Norfolk they could not bear thinking just which direction their lives would have taken. As they spoke they both realised that they had quite a lot in common after all. Their lives had taken an unexpected and unwelcome turn and they both had no idea how to get it back!

Gordon briefly explained about his estrangement from his children and how deeply it had affected him and he also admitted that he would never have had the courage to talk to his children about this before coming here but he had decided that he would write to his children and try to put into words just how he felt. He had never been more delighted than when he received a reply back from his daughter. He knew, also, that it would be a long and sometimes painful journey if they were ever going to have some sort of relationship together. He had realised, hopefully not too late, that he needed them more than he had ever thought and he hoped that they needed him to!

Vanessa listened intently to Gordon as he poured out his innermost thoughts. If only her Father had had the courage to do what Gordon was doing now.

She knew that her Father loved her. He just never showed it to her!

She had only ever wanted his unconditional love but she also knew that that would never happen. Her Father was the type of person who kept a stiff upper lip at all times and was consumed by appearances. God forbid that anyone might suspect that the life he had created for himself, his wife and his daughter was anything less than picture perfect! She had been a huge disappointment to her Father. She knew that without a shadow of a doubt. She had spent all her life trying so hard to get his approval. To no avail. When he was dying he had summoned her to his house. (She could never refer to it as home.) On his death bed he had wanted to say so many things to her, she was certain of that, but instead he had reminded her off all the times she had disappointed him. Her last memory of her Father was as she stormed out of his house vowing to never see him again as long as she lived if she had been that much of a disappointment to him!

At the reading of the Will she had sat impassively as the smaller bequests had been read out. He had made arrangements concerning most of his long serving staff. Typical she thought. Appearances needed to be kept up didn't they? Finally it had come to the remainder of his estate. He had left adequate provision for her Mother but the vast majority of his wealth had been left in trust to her!!

The Solicitor had handed her a hand written letter with instructions that she should read it only when she was alone. What was that all about?

When she read the letter all her pent up emotions came out and she howled and raged for a very long time. The letter was the most beautiful thing she had ever received. Her Father had told her just how proud he was of her, how much he loved her but not her choice of friends or lifestyle and he only wished that he had had the courage to say all the things he needed and wanted to say whilst he were alive.

Vanessa thought the tears would never stop coming. Even now all these years later she was consumed by a mixture of emotions. Why had the stupid bugger not said any of this when he was alive. If he wasn't already dead she would have killed him with her bare hands! She hated him and loved him and she had never really dealt with her feelings before. She had obliterated the pain with her hedonistic lifestyle which she knew he would not have approved of. How stupid people are! They should have the courage of their convictions and say what is on their minds! Easy enough to say thought Vanessa not so easy to do!

"Sorry Gordon I was miles away. What were you saying? Oh! Yes please I would love to go to the pub for lunch. My treat. And no arguing!"

And so it was that Gordon and Vanessa went into the pub in Soham Tarney and ordered two Ploughmen's.

Was it her imagination but did Mavis, the landlady, seem very flustered this lunchtime? And why was Gordon studying his shoes? Vanessa knew that something was going on and she was determined to find out exactly what that was!!

After lunch, which whilst not unpleasant was a trifle awkward, Gordon and Vanessa headed back to the Land Rover. They had a little time left before they needed to get back to the farmhouse. Both of them knew that they needed to get back but they were a little afraid of what they might find when they did get back!

"Gordon. Tell me it's none of my business if you want to, but are you and Mavis closer than you are letting on?

Gordon did not know where to look! Was he that transparent? Of all the people to ask him such a question it had to be Vanessa! Gordon took a deep breath and looked Vanessa straight in the eye.

"Actually, now you have mentioned it you are absolutely right. We have been getting to know each other a little better these past few weeks. I don't know how it may pan out but I feel more alive than I have done in ages!"

Vanessa's beaming smile put Gordon a little at ease. Perhaps it might not be a bad thing after all?

"Gordon I am so happy for you. I KNEW something was going on. You should have seen your faces when you first came into the pub. You did not know where to look either of you. That's what gave it away to me."

"I hope you won't go telling everyone about us please?" Gordon looked so embarrassed that Vanessa's heart melted slightly. Who was she to gossip about someone else's love life? She was in no position to judge! Had she not sought "love" with total strangers? Had she not done things that she was thoroughly ashamed of? Gordon was enjoying being alive for the first time in many months and she for one was not going to spoil his chances!

"Gordon, rest assured no-one from the house will find out about you two from me. You have my word; I am just so pleased that you look so happy!"

"Thanks hinny- that means a lot! Now I think it's about time we got back to the house and find out just exactly what is going on don't you?"

Vanessa and George headed back to the car both of them lost in their own thoughts. As the car pulled away from the car park Gordon glanced at Vanessa just as she looked at him. They both just smiled at each other. No words were spoken, none were needed, but a deeper degree of understanding and trust was developing between them and they were both delighted at the prospect of not fighting each other anymore.

Chapter 35.

Robert and Adam spent the morning digging, weeding etc. The physical labour helped to take their minds off the previous evening. However they both knew that they could not avoid talking about last night!

"Adam, what the hell went on last night? Do you know? Have you any ideas because I sure as hell don't!"

"All I know is that when I came down to see what all the noise was about Chris was strangling the life out of that other guy! Ronnie was just standing in the middle of the room not really registering what was going on if you ask me!"

"Vanessa said that when they took Ronnie to bed she did not seem aware that they were there! She just let them undress her and get her into bed without a single word! Vanessa was freaked out by that. Ronnie has always seemed so calm and collected don't you think? Whatever was said last night must have been devastating. Chris and Ronnie don't seem the type of people to react like that!"

"Robert I think that we should organise a meeting of everybody tonight in the lounge don't you? That way we can all decide what is the best thing to do. We need to carry on with all the farm jobs. We have orders expected out for the next few days- at least until the weekend."

Robert was again struck by the mature way that Adam thought things through. Who would have thought that of him thought Robert? Probably no-one in his entire life had stopped to find out if Adam had a brain or indeed any degree of intelligence! From the little he knew about him Robert was sure that Adam had had a difficult life. Society had labelled him as bad news and therefore not worthy of investing any amount of time or effort regarding him. He had been left on the scrap heap with countless others like him! The thought of this made Robert angry and also a little ashamed. Hadn't he done exactly the same thing when he had first met Adam a few short weeks ago? Robert had taken one look at Adam with his track suit, colourful trainers and "hoodie" and made the assumption that he was trouble!! How wrong could you be? Adam had proved himself to be a very sensible, sensitive person who , once he had let his guard down a little, had become someone that Robert found easy to talk to and easy to be with. Who would have thought such a thing was possible? They had little in common, they came from completely different backgrounds and yet they had one major thing in common after all. They had both been discouraged from living their lives the way they wanted to, they both were at a crossroads in their lives and they had both had the great fortune to have ended up her at "Haven's Retreat". Robert knew that the day he had arrived here had been the day he had been saved and he was certain that Adam felt the same.

As they continued toiling away for the rest of the day the friendship between them deepened. Adam admitted he had thought Robert was a snob and a wimp! (Thanks for your honesty Adam!)

 Pru was a geriatric old fool, Gordon was a miserable git, and Vanessa was a stuck up cow with more money than sense! Lauren came in for some praise though. Adam knew that she was basically O.K even though she was such a timid thing at first Adam could see that she was going to be good fun and anyway the youngsters had to gang together didn't they otherwise the "wrinklies "would take over! Robert had laughed out loud at this. Adam, the cheeky sod, had lumped him in with the "wrinklies"! When it came to Chris and Ronnie however Adam was more than a little reticent.

When Robert asked him what he first thought of them Adam said that he did not know who the hell they were, what they stood for or anything. He had never met anyone quite like them and did not know what to do. He had said to himself that he would give them a couple of days and if they weren't too weird he would stay. After he had discovered the library and admitted his lack of reading skills Adam had half expected to be ridiculed. After all that was what had happened to him his entire life, but when Ronnie and Chris had sat him down and explained what they would like to do to help him Adam had become a lifelong friend and advocate and nothing would stop him from helping them out in their hour of need!

After a few more hours of back breaking digging they had finally finished for the day and as they walked back to the farmhouse their thoughts turned back to the events of last night!

Robert knew that Adam was right. They needed this meeting and they needed to support Chris and Ronnie. Quite how they would achieve this he did not know but between them they could come up with a plan couldn't they?

Pru and Laura were in the greenhouse sorting out the best of the flowers to send to the Hotels and businesses in town. They worked in silence for some little while but when Pru saw Laura arching her back in discomfort Pru decided to take matters into her own hands(Not for the first time my dear thought Pru ruefully) and sat Laura down and gave her a cooling glass of water.

"Laura, how are you this morning? You seem very quiet and subdued. Are you feeling fine? Is it the baby?"

Laura closed her eyes slowly, took a deep breath and turned to face her best friend. The look of real concern on Pru's face touched Laura deeply. Here was a lady who was nearly old enough to be her great grandmother and yet she felt the strongest connection to her! She had never felt like this before. She had adored her Father. She had had a difficult relationship with her Mother. She had never really known her Aunties until after her parents had died. She had had no-one to confide in at all. And yet now looking at this amazing woman sitting before her with such obvious concern on her face Laura felt an incredible mixture of emotions. She should be talking to her parents about how she felt! She should be shopping for baby clothes at home in her old house with her Mother clucking away like a mother hen! She should not be pregnant with some stranger's child!! All these thoughts were whizzing around her head all the time that Laura often wondered how she got through each day! She needed to be calm. Her agitated state would not help her and the baby after all.

 She knew that her hormones were all over the place right now. She knew that she was going to have to find the strength, somehow, to get through this but she was scared. She was scared and frightened!

"Pru, I'm fine really. I just feel overwhelmed that's all. Last night scared me. I didn't know what to do. I just stood there frozen to the spot. What the hell is going on?"

"My Dear you must not worry your pretty little head about such things. You need to concentrate on you and the baby .We can sort something out I'm sure. Now, what's really troubling you? You can't fool me my dear I've been around too long to take what you have just said as the gospel truth, so out with it!"

Laura explained to Pru her worries for her future. Where would she live when the baby is born? She could not expect Chris and Ronnie to look after her could she? How would she manage for money? Where would the Council house her?

Pru listened attentively as Laura spoke. The poor girl was beside herself with worry! Pru knew then that what she had planned was absolutely the right thing to do. All she needed to do was convince Lauren that what she had planned for her was not charity (God forbid she thought that!) but was in fact the perfect solution for all concerned. And anyway it was all settled at her end so there would be no argument young lady when I finally tell you my plans!

"Laura, why did you react like you did last night? You seemed to disappear inside yourself. Why? I count you as a true friend. I hope you do to! Please let me help you if I can! What is really the matter my dear?"

Laura began to weep silently. Pru held her without words for several minutes and then slowly Laura explained that the violence she had witnessed last night brought back terrible memories of when she first left home and was "befriended" by that dreadful woman. Some of her "gentlemen callers" were vicious thugs who could not perform without getting violent with their girls. Laura had had more than one occasion when the Madam had had to send in the heavies to stop the violence getting out of hand! She had, luckily for her, not been subject to some of the awful things the other girls had had to deal with but, nevertheless, she had always found shouting and violent behaviour impossible to deal with and so she had found that she could not deal with last night's outburst!

As Pru listened she could not help but shudder. Men were bastards! She also knew, without a shadow of a doubt that she would telephone her Solicitor today and make sure that the lazy good for nothing was doing what she asked him to do. If he waffled on as he usually did about these things taking their time she would strangle him herself with her own bare hands the next time she went home!

"Laura, it's time for lunch, let's go back to the house and decide what we should cook for this evening. What do you say? We can decide together and after lunch you, young lady, are going to take a nap! Don't you look at me like that Madam! Mrs Prunella Okenden has spoken!!"

Laura took hold of Pru's hand and together they went slowly back into the farmhouse both of them nervous about what they might find but they were both relieved to discover that the house appeared deserted. Where were Chris and Ronnie? Never mind that now. They would surface when they were ready. Right now they had lunch to make and they had an evening menu to create! No time for shilly shallying there was work to be done!!

Chapter 35.

Chris stayed in their bedroom for 2 days. He only left Ronnie to use the bathroom. He had been touched to find that someone had left food for them both outside their door when he went to the bathroom. No-one had disturbed them and for that he was eternally grateful. Ronnie was still in a terrible state. She looked haunted and when she spoke it was still with the same level of disbelief. How could the Army do such a thing? They had both sat in bed the entire night and read every document that Henderson had brought with him. The evidence was damming and overwhelming. The Army was using mind bending techniques which contravened the Geneva Convention on Human Rights. There was absolutely no doubt in either of their minds. What sickened them the most was that they were implicated in the whole sordid affair! Their names and details were on file regarding the initial trials for Hypnosis and Regression Techniques and the implication of all the files was that Chris and Ronnie Gaskell were complicit and still active in its current state!

As dawn broke through to reveal another cloudless sky Chris and Ronnie had come to a joint decision regarding the files. They were to be destroyed! No evidence of their existence must be found here at the farmhouse. Chris knew, only too well, just what depths the Army would plunge to so that it could keep its own house in order! They were both now uncertain which Army or which country had been responsible for the mutilation and death of their friend whose body was dumped unceremoniously and publicly outside their apartment in Burma!

Chris and Ronnie also knew without a shadow of a doubt just how much trouble Henderson had brought to their door. The Army would stop at nothing to get those files back – even murder!

As they finished reading the final piece of paper Ronnie began to weep silently. Chris held her gently as she finally drifted off to a fitful sleep. She was exhausted, both physically and mentally, and she needed all her strength if they were to get through this! They would get through this Chris had no doubt, how hard it would be was impossible to say, but get through it they would!!

As Ronnie's breathing became deeper Chris knew that this was his opportunity to leave the bedroom and head for the office. He had always kept this room under lock and key. There was such sensitive material there that it was only prudent to do so. What he had to do next would be difficult but necessary. As he opened the door he took a deep breath, went in, and locked the door.

As Chris entered the office Henderson was walking around the gardens in a state of utter despair and anguish. He had not slept, eaten or washed since he had arrived. He was a soldier he admonished himself. This is how soldiers survived. He did not want to survive! He wanted to die! As these thoughts went around and around in his head Henderson found himself in a disused part of the farm. The land here was too steep to be of any real use to a market gardener like Chris and so it had been allowed to become overgrown and a haven for birds, butterflies and wild animals to roam free. Ronnie liked this part of the garden. She had told Chris to leave it well alone. Let nature take its course she had often said.

Colonel Ronald Henderson crept into the farthest corner of this wilderness where the tallest tree stood. He took the rope he had stolen from the barn and tied it to the tree. He slowly and deliberately climbed to the highest point and when he was there he carefully tied the noose of rope around his own neck, closed his eyes and jumped!

After Chris had been in the office for over an hour he emerged feeling slightly more in control of this horrendous situation than he had been. He showered, checked on Ronnie who was sleeping fitfully and went in search of Henderson. When he had looked through all the rooms he knew that he wasn't in the house. So where the hell was he? His hire car was still where he had parked it so where the devil was he? He has asked Pru and Lauren if they had seen him and he had ignored the looks that had passed between them. He knew that they must be worried about him and Ronnie but now was not the time for explanations that could come later. Now was the time for action and quickly!

Chris looked in the hire car, the door was unlocked, Henderson was probably not even aware of that thought Chris. Nothing in there of any interest! In fact there was not a single personal thing in there at all! Chris suddenly realised that he was exhausted. He desperately needed to sleep. He knew he must if he was to maintain his emotional as well as his physical strength for the battle ahead and so he very reluctantly went back to their bedroom, lay on the bad without undressing and was asleep in seconds!

As Chris climbed the stairs he was completely unaware that Pru and Lauren were watching him. He looked dreadful!

As they went back to work in the kitchen Pru's mind went back to the meeting they had had the night before.

Adam had said during the early evening meal that the meeting should be called and no-one had disagreed. After they had all gone over the previous nights experiences one more time they still had no idea what the hell was going on but they all agreed that it must be very serious indeed. They had unanimously decided to continue as normal with the farmhouse and under no circumstances was anyone else to know that they were any cause for concern. They knew the people from the village, and the businesses, were now quite used to the others delivering their orders. No-one would think to ask where Chris was. Ronnie was rarely seen in the village anyway so no difference there then.

Adam had really surprised everyone with his depth of insight regarding the situation. He had planned it all in his head before the meeting took place and everyone thought that his advice should be taken. How that young man changed from the "yobbo" he had appeared to be into this calm and collected young person Pru would never know but she knew that they would all look at Adam in a different light from now on make no mistake!

He and Robert had agreed to continue with most of the manual labour. Gordon had been assigned to do the maintenance work that; luckily, he and Chris had been talking about a few days ago. Vanessa would be the spokesperson for the rest of them. She would be the one going into the businesses and delivering the goods and it was agreed that if anyone could keep the secret she could!

 Lauren and Pru had been assigned to continue housekeeping etc which suited everyone as Pru had discovered a talent and enthusiasm for cooking which she was only too glad to pass on to Lauren!

This morning she had been shocked at Chris's appearance and she knew that they had all made the right decision to help out in any way they could. "Right old girl. What's for supper?" she said to herself as she took stock of the larder. She had decided to keep the food simple for without Chris and Ronnie's help around the farmhouse you could never be certain just how late it would be when all the days' jobs had been done.

Now that Gordon had fixed that temperamental "Aga" Pru had decided that she would slow roast a lovely beef stew with masses of fresh home grown vegetables and as a special treat she would make some dumplings to pop in the stew when she knew just what time people were ready to eat. She would make plenty she thought because everyone had developed the most amazing appetites since arriving at the farmhouse. They all looked healthy and happy. Let's hope it stays that way thought Pru as she set about making supper. How about a nice apple pie to go with the stew? Now Lauren could make a start on that thought Pru. She had made a really good job of it the last time she had tried.

"Laura my dear can you come over here I have something I need you to do for me if you don't mind?"

Another day was beginning at "Haven's Retreat" but how would this one end?

Only time would tell.

Chapter 36.

As the early evening sun began to cast its long shadows across the farmhouse all the guests began to converge in the kitchen. This room above all the others was the place where people gravitated to at the end of the day! It was such a homely, calming room that allowed the guests to begin to unwind at the end of a very difficult day!

Robert and Adam were the last to arrive and were grateful for the cooling glass of lemonade that was put before them.

"Thanks Pru, that's just what we needed eh Adam?" said Robert as he gulped his drink down in one go!

"Too right Pru me old girl!" laughed Adam as he quickly escaped around the table just before he got a clip around the ear from a smiling Pru.

"The youth of today have no manners or respect for their elders" laughed Pru good naturedly. The atmosphere was still a little fraught but she knew that they were all feeling the pressure right now and a bit of banter was no bad thing.

As the laughter died down thoughts returned, inevitably to last night. It was the right decision to carry on with the day to day running of the Farmhouse but when would Chris and Ronnie come back downstairs to reassure them all that everything was going to be alright?

Gordon spoke next.

"What about the other night? Who was that chap and where the hell has he disappeared to? Has anyone seen him today? I've been out side all day in the barn repairing some of the tools and I haven't seen hide or hair of him!"

"I didn't see him when I went out to the village first thing this morning." said Vanessa as she helped to lay the table for supper. "His hire car is still parked in the yard. I don't think it has moved since he got her do you?"

Robert was just about to reply when the kitchen door opened and Chris entered the room.

As Chris surveyed all the concerned faces looking at him he knew that what he was about to say to them all would have a profound effect on them all!

"Hi everyone, thanks for everything you have all done today both Ronnie and I are really grateful. I think though that you are all entitled to some sort of explanation don't you?"

"My dear man you do not have to explain a thing to us if you don't want to. Isn't that right everybody? As Pru spoke she was looking at everyone to make certain that she was speaking for everybody.

"Thank you Pru. That is really kind of you but I still think you deserve to know just what is going on because it will affect us all I'm afraid!" The look of shock and concern that crossed all of their faces saddened Chris deeply. Everything seemed to be going so well before Henderson turned up and look at it now!

"Ronnie will stay in her room for tonight but I would like to speak to everyone in the lounge after supper if that is o.k. with everyone? I hope you all don't mind but I will eat my supper in our room with Ronnie and I will see you in the lounge about 8 o'clock.

The meal could have been the most delicious gourmet experience in the entire world but no-one in the room would have noticed. As they collected the plates and cleared the table nobody spoke. The atmosphere at first had been one of enforced "bonhomie" but eventually silence has prevailed.

The antique Grandfather clock in the hall struck 8 and everyone looked at each other as they made their way into the lounge where they found Chris already there waiting for them.

Chris seemed to have aged over the last few days and was still looking very pre-occupied as he asked them all to take a seat.

During the next 2 hours Chris explained about the type of work that he and Ronnie had begun in their time in the Army. He also asked them to believe him when he said that he and Ronnie had had nothing to do with the way in which the Army was now abusing their skills! After he had explained about the methods currently being used by the British Army together with many other nations on soldiers he began to break down. With a supreme effort he shook himself and took a deep breath before he spoke again.

"I have explained in general terms what has happened and I hope you all appreciate the terrible shock it has been to both Ronnie and me?"

Pru was the first to speak. "My dear man, you have both been through a truly terrible time and I am sure that I speak for the whole group when I say that our thoughts are with you. I would also like to say, from a personal point of view, that I would be most willing to do anything I can to tell the Authorities that I believe you to be a decent couple who would not be a part of anything as heinous as this!"

Chris was about to reply when he was silenced by the sound of everyone else in the room speaking at once and all saying the same sort of thing! These people seated here in front of him were all offering their unconditional support!

"Thank you everybody I do appreciate it .Thank you. However I have not told you all the details yet."

After Chris had finished telling them some of the things he had read in the files Henderson had brought with him the silence in the room was palpable.

Gordon was the first to break the terrible silence.

"My God, I never thought I would say this but I am ashamed to call myself an Englishman! How could anyone do such a terrible thing? Have they no shame for God's sake?"

Robert stood up and looked around the room. "I cannot possibly know how you and Ronnie must be feeling but what I do know is, like Pru said, we must be able to do something to help you and Ronnie surely? After all you have been marvellous to all of us here in this room haven't they everybody? Adam spoke next. "I do not really understand everything that has been said tonight I must admit. It all seems so unreal like something from some disaster movie!

What I do know is that we all owe you and Ronnie an enormous amount and me for one am more than willing to do what I can to help repay you."

Laura, meanwhile, had not uttered a sound. As she stood up the room suddenly went quiet.

"Chris- how is Ronnie coping with all this? She must be devastated. I would do anything for both of you but I cannot think of anything we can do! Should I go and check on Ronnie for you? You have so much to deal with right now and it would make me feel more useful if you don't mind?"

Chris gave the slightest nod of his head but it was enough for Laura. As she made her way to the door she was not surprised, and secretly grateful, when Pru slipped her arm around her waist and they both went silently out of the room.

Vanessa took the opportunity to stand up and speak. "Everyone I would like to say something please! Where the hell is that weasel Henderson? How I see it is like this. Chris and Ronnie would never have had any dealings with this sort of thing. We all know that but we are not in a position to disprove anything. The only person who could help is the one person who has brought it all here to our doorstep so I suggest we all try to find this Henderson fellow and find out just what he proposes to do? Well don't just sit there get a move on!"

As everyone was galvanised into action downstairs things were also happening upstairs! Lauren and Pru had gently knocked on the bedroom door. When they had not had a reply Pru had tentatively opened the door to find the room empty. They had checked the en-suite bathroom and found that empty to. They had searched all the other rooms but Ronnie was not to be found upstairs. As they went down the stairs Chris met them at the bottom. They explained that they could not find Ronnie anywhere upstairs. Chris's face began to crumble in front of them as he struggled to control his emotions.

"Ronnie! Ronnie! Ronnie where are you?" The sound Chris was making as he began to search frantically around the rest of the farmhouse was the most wretched noise anyone in the room had ever heard!

After they had searched the entire house it was agreed that everyone should couple together and searched the grounds and gardens for Ronnie. The atmosphere among the group was one of panic, alarm and concern for Ronnie and Chris.

They had all seen the devastating affect the news had had on Chris but no-one had seen Ronnie for days and so were worried that her state of mind was in such a terrible way that anything could have happened to her!

Everyone spread out and they were all frantically shouting for Ronnie as the evening began to close itself around "Haven's Retreat". The evenings had always had such joy and happiness about them in the past. They had been filled with chat and laughter. Not tonight. Tonight the overall feeling was one of panic and despair. No-one had said it out loud but they were all concerned about Ronnie's state of mind and they all knew that they must find her! And find her soon!!

Ronnie, meanwhile, was oblivious to all the fuss she was causing. She was oblivious to everything at the moment.

She had heard the sounds of voices downstairs as she had finally woken from her troubled sleep. As she gathered her senses she had, once again, been overwhelmed by her thoughts. She had to get out of the house. She was being suffocated by the very house that had been her sanctuary and so she had slipped out whilst the others had been talking. She had wandered into the garden but had found no solace there. She eventually found herself wandering aimlessly around the grounds and was now heading towards the forest at the farthest end of their land. She had never really explored this part of the farm before. She had always considered this to be Chris's special place and so she had never ventured here- instead she had allowed it to remain Chris's special place.

How she needed Chris right now!

She knew that Chris was going to try to explain their situation to the others in the house and so she went towards the forest. If she couldn't have Chris right now at least she could try to be near him in his special place! The evening was casting long shadows amongst the trees but Ronnie did not appear to notice. As she went further into the forest she lost sight of the farmhouse and was now in another world. The forest seemed to envelope her and drew her ever inwards. The ground was uneven and Ronnie was unable to stay on her feet. She stumbled and fell headlong down a small embankment and found herself in a small glade. She had never seen this before and she had, temporarily, lost her bearings. Where was the house? Where exactly was she? As she struggled to her feet she looked around her. Standing alone in the centre of the glade was a really large tree. As she walked towards it she noticed something in the gloom. Her scream alerted the others who were searching for her! Ronnie had not realised she had screamed out loud. All she knew was that she was now looking at the body of Colonel Henderson as it hung, unmoving, from the tree. His body looked unreal. His eyes were open and his mouth was twisted in a grotesque imitation of a smile! She had seen bodies before and she knew, without a shadow of a doubt, that he was dead. Ronnie continued towards the body and began to scream and bellow with rage and shock.

When the others finally got to her they had to pull her physically away from Henderson's body as she pummelled it and swing it round and round as she screamed for answers.

"How could you?" "How could you do this to us?" "How dare you take your own life? You miserable man! You bastard!

Chris wrapped his arms gently around his distraught wife as he gently led her away from the awful scene in front of them.

Adam, Robert and Gordon were the first on the scene and all three of them stood in horrified fascination of the image in front of them. None of them had seen anything like it before and they did not want to witness anything like it again!

"Gordon, will you take Ronnie back to the house please? Can you make certain that the others don't see this please? When you have done that will you come back here and help us get his body down?"

Robert had spoken almost without thinking. He had taken a look at Chris and realised that he was in total shock and was, therefore, incapable of dealing with this right now!

Gordon did as he was asked without a single word being exchange. After Ronnie had been carried back to the house Robert looked at Adam. He had not said a word and he had not moved a muscle!

"Adam, are you o.k.? Adam! Adam listen to me – are you o.k.?" Adam seemed to jolt himself back to reality as he looked at Robert.

"What the hell do we do now?"

"We have to get his body down from there!"

"We can't do that. The police will need to see the scene surely?"

Chris was the next to speak. His voice seemed to come from a distant place. "We CANNOT have the police here! We must get his body down and then we must decide what to do with it!"

"What the bloody hell do you mean we cannot get the police involved? Are you crazy? I hate the police but we have to tell them don't we?"

Robert looked from Chris to Adam without speaking. He did not know what the hell was happening here. All he knew was that it was the most surreal thing he had ever experienced.

"Robert, Adam please believe me. We cannot get the police involved. It would be the end for Ronnie and me. We would be taken to court and charged with breaking the Geneva Convention. We could go to jail for years!!"

Gordon came back just as Chris finished speaking. "Right you two. What we need to do is exactly what Chris says. We owe him that at least don't you think?"

Without waiting for an answer Gordon started to climb the tree and move towards the smiling body of Colonel Henderson. Gordon had had the foresight to bring a large knife with him and he set about hacking away at the rope holding the body up. After what seemed like an eternity the rope began to fray and then a terrible thing began to happen!

As the pressure lessened on the rope Henderson seemed to be performing some kind of macabre dance. His body began to swing to and fro and his arms started to flail about. Adam was sick were he stood! Robert just looked on in horrified fascination and Chris just seemed to stare, unseeing, into space!

"For God's sake you lot help me out here will you?"

At the sound of Gordon's voice the others were galvanized into action. Robert and Adam grabbed hold of Henderson's torso to prevent it from moving in that terrible way and Gordon continued to cut the rope until with a final chop broke the last strands and the body of Colonel Henderson fell down to earth with a sickening thud. Robert and Adam were trapped underneath! Gordon grabbed Chris and shook him into action as they hauled the dead body off the two men. Gasping after their efforts all four men looked down at Henderson and all four thought the same thing. What the hell do we do?

Chapter 37.

At the farmhouse Ronnie had been sedated and was now sleeping fitfully in her room.

Vanessa was pacing the floor and looking out of the window to see where the men were.

Laura was sitting on the sofa and Pru was making soothing noises. All three women were in a state of complete shock. Gordon had explained, briefly, what they had discovered in the forest. He had asked them to stay where they were and to remain calm. Remain calm! How the hell were they supposed to stay calm for God's sake?

Vanessa spoke first.

"Pru will you be alright with Laura and Ronnie if I go outside to find out just what the hell is going on?"

"My Dear! Do you think that that is the right thing to do? I mean, it's going dark now isn't it and Gordon did seem most insistent that we stay here?"

"I know he said that Pru but I just can't just sit here doing nothing can I? What a mess! What the hell will happen now do you think?"

"I have no idea. What I do know is that this show of hysterics is not helping anyone at this moment-especially Laura!"

Vanessa looked at Laura who appeared to be in some discomfort. "Are you o.k. Laura? You have hardly said a word since we got back to the farmhouse! Are you in pain? Is it the baby? Oh my God it's the baby isn't it?"

"Vanessa. Sit down right this instant. You are not helping this situation at all!"

At the imperious tone of Pru's voice Vanessa sat down rather like a recalcitrant child.

"Thank you. Now we will have no more silly talk or silly behaviour! Do I make myself understood? Now Laura, my dear, how are you feeling? Are you in pain?"

As she spoke Pru continued to stroke Laura's hand and slowly but surely she began to visibly relax.

"I felt really strange when we first got back to the house but I feel much better now thanks."

"I think young lady that you should go to bed. Now don't look at me like! I doubt if any of us will get any sleep but you must at least try to relax. Now I am not taking no for an answer. I am going to make us all a milky drink, and you can change that look on your face Vanessa, I am taking charge here and you will respect your elders! Do I make myself clear? Well do I?"

As the three women went into the kitchen both Laura and Vanessa could not help but admire Pru. She was an indomitable person without a doubt. Right now that was what was needed.

Pru bustled around the kitchen organising the drinks. The "Aga" was now not the problem it had once been. (Thanks to Gordon- bless him!) The warmth in the kitchen was most welcome. Perhaps it was shock but all three ladies felt cold inside that night.

As everyone drank their drinks they all wondered the same thoughts. How had this happened to two such nice people? Why did Henderson come to spoil it? What drove him to suicide? How would their lives be affected by tonight's events?

The sound of the kitchen door opening focussed their minds on the events of the night. All four men came into the kitchen in an obvious state of shock. Without a word being spoken Pru poured them all a large shot of whisky and handed them all out. Chris downed his in one gulp. Robert and Gordon sipped theirs thoughtfully. Adam did not even pick his up.

Laura spoke in such a quiet voice that, at first, nobody heard her.

"Where is his body now? What have you done with his body? It's not here in the house is it? I couldn't bear that!"

"My dear, don't you worry about that. I am sure that in the morning this will not seem so frightful. Now, young lady, you are going to bed! I am not taking no for an answer so you and I will go upstairs right now! I hope everyone understands. We will all have plenty to talk about and to sort out in the morning. Goodnight. God bless!"

Chapter 38.

As the women went upstairs the others stood around not knowing quite what to do next!

Gordon broke the terrible silence.

"Chris, I think it is time to explain things don't you? I don't mean to add to your problems but we are all involved right now and I for one need to know just exactly what we are dealing with here!"

Chris nodded almost imperceptibly and walked out of the kitchen and into his study. The others followed silently behind him. When the door closed behind them Chris shuddered and sat down heavily at the desk. He started to explain everything!

When Chris had finished speaking the room remained totally quiet for an age. All the occupants were having difficulty dealing with what they had just been told! How the hell had this happened to Chris and Ronnie? What the hell were they to do now? All these thoughts and questions were whizzing around the minds of everybody in the room. Adam finally broke the dreadful silence.

"I know I'm the youngest here and I don't suppose anyone wants to hear what I have to say but I cannot keep quiet about this. I think that we should get rid of the body somewhere and pretend that Henderson never came here at all! Don't look at me like that Robert have you got a better idea? No! I didn't think so! So what other ideas has anyone got?"

"How the hell do we get rid of a dead body for God's sake?" Vanessa asked with a mixture of incredulity and admiration at the calm way Adam spoke.

"I don't know. I've never done it before but we can't sit here and do nothing can we?

Chris stood up and the room once again fell into total silence.

"I am a man of God as you all know but I cannot believe that it is his will that we all suffer for the sins of Henderson and the Army! I spent all last night wrestling with the very same thoughts Adam has just expressed and I believe that if we can do what Adam says I think I can convince the Army when they call, which they will, that nobody has seen Henderson and we don't know anything about his whereabouts. It would mean dragging you all further into our mess and I don't want to do that but I cannot think of any other solution to this problem. Can anyone else?"

Robert spoke next,

"Chris, I cannot begin to understand what you and Ronnie must be going through but what I can understand is the need to keep Henderson's visit a secret and I for one am willing to help in any way I can! There are so many unanswered questions though! Did he tell anyone where he was going? Did he steal the files which you now have Chris? Can you really convince the Army to stay away? What happens to you both after all this? Can you possibly continue as if nothing has happened?"

The next few hours proved to be a tremendous strain on everyone but at the end of it, just as dawn was breaking a plan had been agreed!

Would everyone have the courage to carry it out? Only time would tell!

Chapter 39.

As the dawn broke over the horizon the colours were truly breathtaking. All the colours of the rainbow were depicted in the shadows cast by the sun. The beautiful warm sun and its magic were lost on the people sitting at the kitchen table; No one seemed to notice the magic going on around them. They were all lost in their own private thoughts.

Pru jolted them back to reality as she came into the kitchen and startled them all!

"My goodness, you all look wretched! Now I am having no arguments about this but I am going to make everyone some breakfast and we are all going to do our best to at least eat some of it! Do I make myself clear? Do I? "As everyone nodded in exhausted defeat Mrs Prunella Okenden started her part in the day's events!

Upstairs, the smell of bacon cooking woke Laura. She had slept fitfully and the dull ache in the pit of her stomach was still gnawing away at her. As she went to the bathroom Laura began to do a quick calculation of her due date and gasped as she realised that she could have the baby any day now! She could not know exactly when she got caught, she had slept with men every day of her working life and so she could only hazard a guess as to when she might give birth! Please God, not now! Not now!

The pain became more insistent as she went downstairs. She stood in the hallway, forced a semblance of a smile on her face and went in!

"Laura, how are you my dear? Sit down and I will bring you a nice cup of tea! No thank you, I do not want nor need any help young lady – do as you are told will you?"

As Laura did as she was told she looked around at the others seated around the table. The atmosphere was very different today form other days. And no wonder! Everything had changed! Nothing would ever be the same for all these good people sat around this lovely farmhouse kitchen!

The pain took her breath away! She had not realised she had cried out until Vanessa came hurrying around to her!

"Laura are you o.k.? Is it the baby? Are you in pain?"

Everything happened at once. Her waters broke there and then as she sat at the table! She looked down in abject horror! Oh my God! She was having the baby! She was having her baby right now!

Within minutes Laura had been bundled back upstairs and told to have a shower whilst Prunella watched over her. Prunella had told her in no uncertain terms that today she, Mrs Prunella Okenden, was not going to take no for an answer. She was not to be embarrassed and she was to get a move on or else she would be having the baby in the farmyard surrounded by animals and God knows what!

And as much as Chris is a Christian man even he would have difficulty explaining another birth in a manger wouldn't he? The laughter seemed to break the terrible spell of gloom which had been hanging around and everyone seated around the table was, once more, galvanized into action!

It was decided that Vanessa was to drive Laura and Prunella into town where there was a maternity hospital and she was to come straight back here to help with all the other arrangements. It was also agreed to keep Laura and Pru in the dark about their plans! They had enough on their plates thinking about the baby without worrying about a dead body and what was going to be done with it! They all agreed that they would deal with the wrath of Pru at a later date!!

The men stood watching as the car disappeared into the distance. No-one was in a hurry to start the day!

Chris spoke." Look everyone are we sure we are doing the right thing? I cannot ask for your help like this. It isn't right or fair!"

"Chris, we went through all this last night! We are going to help you because we want to help you not because we have to!" Gordon's face spoke volumes and so with a muttered thank you Chris went upstairs to see how Ronnie was!

"Right Robert, you and Adam drive the car to where Henderson is and I will get the Land Rover as close as I can o.k.?"

It had been decided that Robert would drive the Land Rover to Bristol with Adam in the passenger seat. Gordon was to follow behind them in the hire car with Henderson in the boot! And after it had all been done the three of them would drive back to the farmhouse. It was going to be a really long day, they were all exhausted through lack of sleep but the adrenalin must have kicked in because right now all three of them were "hyper" as Adam would say!

Henderson's body was lying in the same grotesque position as they had left him last night!

Of course he would be thought Adam what else did he expect for Christ sake! Don't start Adam said to himself! He could still not quite believe that this was happening! How the bloody hell had they got themselves into all this?

"Adam. Are you o.k.? Only you look as white as a sheet! If you don't want to go through with this we will understand. Won't we Robert?"

Gordon looked genuinely concerned and Adam was only too quick to tell him that he was perfectly fine and let's get on with it shall we?

It took 20 minutes to maul Henderson's body into the boot of the hire car. They had had to put it into the Land Rover first as they couldn't get the hire car close enough and no-one wanted to drag the body up the sides of the glade thank you very much! The body weighed more than any of them had first thought and when it had finally been squashed into the boot and the lid had been forced shut everyone was sweating and exhausted!

All three men had worked in absolute silence. All three men needed to come to terms with what they proposed doing and all three men were scared to death if the truth be known!! As they drove the vehicles back to the farmhouse the enormity of what they were about to do hit all three of them! Please God; let us get away with this! Please God; don't let me be the one who cocks it up! Please God; let this day end soon! And so the most eventful day so far in the history of the house began to unfold!

Chapter 40.

As Chris walked into the farmhouse he stopped to look around him. This had been their home and their own personal "Haven" for over 5 years. They had had many happy times here and he did not want to give it up! Why should they? They had done nothing wrong!

At the door to their bedroom Chris wondered just how strong Ronnie could be because she needed to be stronger than she had ever been if they were to get through this together!

Ronnie was lying awake and staring into space as Chris entered the room. When she heard the door open she looked scared and frightened and bewildered! Chris had never seen her like this before and was at a complete loss as to what to do! They both stared at each other for a long time before Ronnie held out her hand towards Chris and beckoned him to her!

After the tears had all been spent and they had made passionate but gentle love both Chris and Ronnie felt better than they had done in days!

Chris had explained exactly what they others were doing that day and Ronnie had surprised them both by accepting unchallenged all the decisions that had been made in her absence. She had been in no position to help and, for the first time in her life, she was not in control of her own thoughts and destiny!

Ronnie was concerned about Lauren and Pru. She wanted to go to the hospital or at least ring to see how they were getting on but Chris assured her that Pru had promised faithfully that she would keep them fully informed about any progress.

For the rest of the day Chris and Ronnie had more important and urgent things to do!

They had to erase any trace of Henderson's visit. They had to ensure that there was no evidence of his presence anywhere in the house or grounds. The Army would not just take their word for it that they had not seen Henderson and just walk away with a cheery smile!

The office was the first port of call. Chris had spent hours poring over the files that were kept under strict security. He did not think that any connection could be made regarding their implication in the experiments being conducted by the Army but he was taking no chances and so Ronnie went over the files again just to make sure.

Chris went out to the glade where the body was found and spent a painstaking 2 hours going over the area in minute detail. No evidence must be found! No evidence would be found!

As he returned to the farmhouse he felt a little clearer in his own mind that they were doing the right thing and that with a bit of luck and an awful lot of praying, both now and for the rest of his life, maybe they could return to some semblance of normality! Whatever that was!!

As he walked to the office he was brought out of his reverie by the sound of the telephone ringing! Who was this? Was it the Army? Was it Pru? Was it one of the others? Only one way to find out!

Chris's hands shook for a very long time after he had put the telephone down! The Army had rung to ask if he had had any contact with retired Colonel Henderson recently.

They were most anxious to speak to him. No they could not divulge what they needed to speak to him about and why had he asked that? Chris had realised the instant that he had asked why that the Army's suspicions had been aroused. The Officer on the other end of the 'phone had been polite but evasive and had thanked him for his time and requested that should Colonel Henderson get in touch he should telephone him immediately!

Chris took several more deep breaths and slowly his breathing returned to something that passed as normal. He did not think that that was the end of the matter regarding the Army. He knew, without a doubt, that they would turn up at the farmhouse unannounced. They did not have much time left!

He hurried back into the office where Ronnie was shredding the last few pages of a file.

"That was the Army wasn't it? We need to move fast. Take these shredded files and burn them right now! I have nearly finished here and when I've done I am going to Henderson's room to make certain that nothing belonging to him is here in the house! Chris what are you waiting for? Hurry up my Darling our lives may depend on this and quite frankly I'm not ready to die just yet. Are you?"

Chris's face beamed at Ronnie. She was back! Ronnie was back and she was in charge!

Meanwhile at the hospital things were also happening at a pace. Laura had been rushed into the labour ward as soon as they had arrived and was in the initial stages of labour. The nurse in charge could not give them any real idea when baby was to be born but if Mum and Gran would take a seat in reception she would come to them when she had some more information.

Mum and Gran!

Vanessa had been horrified that the nurse had thought she was Laura's mother but Pru had seemed genuinely delighted at being referred to as Gran.

As Pru looked at Vanessa's appalled face she had begun to giggle. She then had a fit of the most uncontrollable giggles which started Vanessa off and before they knew it both women were laughing hysterically. Tears were streaming down their faces and they both left the reception and went and sat in the car until they had regained their composure. Both women also knew that amidst the tears of amusement there were tears of panic and hysteria!

During the journey to the Hospital, which only took 20 minutes, all the conversation had been about Laura but now sitting in the car park both women looked at each other willing the other one to speak first.

"Vanessa, we must talk. I know you need to get back to the farmhouse and I know that something has been planned regarding the awful events of the last few days. All I will say is that, whatever has been decided, you can count on my wholehearted support.

And I am certain that Laura fells the same way too! I do not wish to know what has been planned .All I do want to know is that everyone will remain sane and not do anything to stupid! Promise an old lady that will you?"

Vanessa promised that she and the others were going to be just fine and that she should concentrate on looking after herself and Laura!

As Vanessa pulled off the car park and headed back to the farmhouse Pru marvelled at just how her life had changed beyond all recognition. She had never felt more alive or more wanted even though the events of the last few days were awful she truly believed that they would all get through this together and come out of it as better people! Oh goodness gracious! Now she sounded like one of those awful programmes you see on the TV! She was turning into someone that she hardly recognized herself and yet she knew she was with true friends for the very first time in her long and eventful life and with that thought in her mind she walked back to the reception with as much of a jaunty step as her aged old hips would let her!

Laura was in pain. No Laura was in mortal agony!! What the hell was going on? She had never known such pain. Where the hell was that damned nurse anyway? She needed painkillers and she needed them now!!

As Laura waddled over to the bed to pull the communication cord a searing pain shot through her and she let out an almighty groan. Oh! Dear God when would it end? She had had enough now. She just wanted it to be over and quick! As the pain passed the nurse arrived with a young junior Doctor and between them they helped her back onto the bed and the Doctor said he would like to examine her if she had no objections? As Laura shuffled into position she felt strangely embarrassed! Why the hell she should be embarrassed she didn't know. After all she was hardly the innocent virgin was she? As she thought of her predicament she began to cry, just a few tears at first but then the flood gates opened and she was wailing like a banshee! What the hell was going on? She had never behaved like this before. She had never had a baby before either so why was she so tearful? As the Doctor completed his examination he told her that with a bit of luck she would be fully dilated within the next two or three hours and then baby would be here before she knew it! Two or three hours!! Dear God she could not stand another two or three minute's thank you very much! Laura opened her mouth to speak just as Pru entered the room. Pru smiled her most beautiful smile and began fussing around Laura like a mother hen and she soon forgot about her pain and began to relax under the watchful eye of Mrs Prunella Okenden.

Laura comforted herself in the knowledge that she was in the best place and she had her best friend with her so everything was going to be just fine. A few moments later when Laura had got her breath back and had stopped sweating after another horrendous pain had fought to rip her apart she was not so sure but she knew she could do nothing about it she would just have to grin and bear it my dear girl as her best friend kept telling her. This was the best friend who had never had a child of her own thank you very much Pru!

Laura mentally squared her shoulders and told herself that she could do this, she would be just fine and she would soon have a beautiful child to look after. Then, she thought, her problems would really begin!

If that young nurse said, once more, that she was doing just fine and that she should not worry about making all this noise Laura was personally going to strangle the life out of her with her bare hands! She was dying didn't anyone realise this? She was going to die right there and then if someone didn't do something about this horrendous pain. As these dark thoughts and other equally dark sentiments washed over Laura her knight in shining armour arrived and told her that she was now able to go down to the delivery room where they would look after her and she should have the baby within the next few minutes!

Justin James was born at 3.31 pm that afternoon weighing a healthy 7lb 10oz. Mother and baby were doing fine and Grandma Pru looked the happiest Grandma they had seen in a very long time!

As Pru went off in search of a 'phone Laura looked down at her new son and could not quite believe that he was here. She had thought the pain would never end but he was worth it. Oh! How he was worth it! Whatever life had in store for them both Laura knew she would lay down her life for the little man asleep in her arms. She would be the mother to him that her own mother had been incapable of being to Laura. She knew it would not be easy, God knows how she would manage, but she would do her best for him and never let him down. She had read about this surge of love that some new mum's experienced and she had, quite frankly, thought these women were stupid and not a little crazy! She now knew that they were neither stupid nor crazy!

When Pru came back from the telephone she was deeply touched by the scene in front of her. Justin was fast asleep in his cot beside Laura who was also fast asleep but with her hand outstretched and holding onto Justin's tiny little fingers as though her life depended on it which, thought Pru, was not that far from the truth. Pru sat down next to Laura and studied her sleeping face. She looked so young! How was she going to cope with life? Pru knew, with absolute clarity and certainty, that she had done the right thing by bequeathing her cottage in Hove to Laura and her little one! Oh! She knew that Laura would not want to accept such a generous gift. Pru had no doubt that she was an honourable person (despite her profession or rather because of her profession!) but she also knew the practicalities of bringing up a child on your own and so she had arranged with her Solicitor that Laura would only know of this bequest on Pru's death. In the mean time all Pru had to do was persuade Laura and Justin to come back with her to Hove and settle into a routine. That was the only stumbling block in Pru's plan. What if she could not persuade her to come and live with her? What if Laura insisted on going it alone? What if Laura hated the idea? What if? What if?

Pru mentally shook herself. No more talk like this Pru old girl. Think positively or else! She would persuade Lauren to do what she had planned if it was the last thing she ever did or her name was not Mrs Prunella Okenden doyen of the Brighton and Hove Women's Institute!

Chapter 41.

Vanessa drove back to the farmhouse on autopilot! She could not remember the journey at all! Which way had she driven back? As she turned off the road and along the track to the farmhouse the bumping and jostling of the car brought her back to reality!

There was a dead body! They had all agreed to move it.

They were all implicated in covering up a suicide and perverting the course of justice!

They could all go to prison!

As these thoughts crowded into the already overcrowded space left in her brain Vanessa knew, without a second's hesitation, that if the situation were ever to arise again she would do exactly the same thing in a heartbeat!

Vanessa strode purposefully into the kitchen shouting for Ronnie as she did so. Today was not a day for thinking - today was a day for action and she was ready for it, boy was she ready, so bring it on!

Vanessa and Ronnie spent the rest of the morning clearing any traces of Henderson, however faint or tenuous, from the farmhouse and the farmyard. They scrubbed the tyre marks from the dried mud in the yard. They checked in minute detail his room. They went over everything with a fine tooth comb. All the time they worked together neither woman spoke much except to ask what needed doing next or what had already been done etc.

In the kitchen making a drink Ronnie seemed pre-occupied and ill at ease. Vanessa spoke.

"Ronnie, don't look so worried. Everything will be fine I assure you! We are all adults here and we all agreed to help you and Chris out because we believe in you and we all know that you would not have had anything to do with the terrible atrocities the Army has carried out. We also know how easily the evidence could be misconstrued and used to hang you both out to dry whilst the Army gets off scot free with its reputation intact! My God! That is so unfair!"

It took several moments for Ronnie to compose herself before she answered in a quavering voice. "Vanessa, Chris and I will never be able to repay you and the others. We would never ask you to do something that could endanger you. I feel wretched that you are all so involved but what could we have done about it? We MUST get this right. We must let the Army think that we do not know the whereabouts of Henderson. If we can do that then maybe, just maybe, the Army will believe us and allow us to continue practicing here at the farmhouse. I don't want to go into details but we need the money the Army pays us in order to keep the farmhouse going! We cannot accept any more blood money from the Army and so we will be leaving here as soon as we can sell up! Oh! I'm sorry I've said too much already. Please don't look so worried. We will be fine. We still have each other and we can always start over again on a much smaller basis. We love each other more than ever and we will both be fine!"

Vanessa listened in silence. She had never heard Ronnie talk so openly and with such passion about their personal life and their expectations! She was completely taken aback. She had never thought of the long term consequences for Chris and Ronnie! Their lives had been turned upside down- no wonder Ronnie had been so distraught! What would they do now?

Throughout the rest of the day Ronnie and Vanessa worked hard. They talked a little more about the situation and wondered how the others were getting on in Bristol. When Pru telephoned to tell them the good news about Lauren both women felt their spirits raise slightly. A new life! The world carried on regardless. Pru suggested that she stay with Lauren for a little while longer as the poor girl was exhausted and besides Grandma Pru hadn't had a hold of little Justin James yet! Would it be alright if someone collected her from the hospital after visiting time tonight around about 8 o'clock if that was o.k.?

Vanessa said that would be fine. It was only after she had got off the telephone that she realised Pru had not mentioned anything about the events of the last few days. She did not ask where everyone was or what everyone was doing. Maybe she had just forgotten thought Vanessa what with everything that was going on at the hospital or more likely than not Pru was perfectly aware that something was going on and she did not need to know thank you very much! That old girl was something else thought Vanessa as she smiled at the memory of Pru sailing into the Hospital and demanding some immediate attention for this young thing who was about to give birth right here in the corridor if someone didn't get a move on!

When they had finished their coffees both women turned to look at each other at the same moment and held each other's gaze. Without a word passing between them they both walked towards each other and held on tightly.

"Right Vanessa, coughed Ronnie, I think we are almost done in here don't you?"

"Whatever you say Ronnie. So what's next to do?"

"I think you should go into town and take the orders for the rest of the week don't you? We don't want any suspicions being aroused do we? If the Army come, sorry WHEN the Army come, I would not put it past them to go and check in the village to ask if any strangers have been seen around the farmhouse. Oh Dear God! Did Henderson go into the village do you know? If he did maybe somebody will remember him. He did have a certain way about him didn't he! Oh what do we do then?"

"Ronnie, calm down, we will cross that bridge if and when we get to it won't we? Hark at me giving you advice! What the hell is that all about eh? Right I will go into town with my best smile painted on and show the world that everything is o.k. up at the farmhouse. I will take the usual orders if that is alright with you Ronnie but I don't think we should push for any extra business right now do you? We don't know how soon the others will be back yet do we?

And we don't want anything to go wrong just now do we? So I'll see you later. I have my mobile on me so get in touch if you need me won't you? I will be back around 6 o'clock and we can start to cook something for the three of us then if that's convenient. Laura will probably stay in hospital overnight and the men were staying out all night anyway weren't they? So I'll see you soon."

And with that Vanessa left and Ronnie was left alone in the house with her thoughts.

Meanwhile things were happening for the others.

After much heated discussion and eventual agreement Chris and Gordon were in the Land Rover (With Henderson's body) and Robert and Adam were in Henderson's hire car.

It had been agreed that Bristol was as good a place as any to dispose of Henderson's body and his hire car. There was no obvious connection to the farmhouse. Adam had been most insistent that he knew the perfect place to leave the body. He had grown up on the roughest, toughest council estate in Bristol. He was only too painfully aware of just how dangerous a place it was. They would drive all day to get there and then they would wait until the dead of night before dumping the hire car and torching it with Henderson's body inside! They had all eventually agreed to this after a lot of heavy persuasion on Adam's part. Did anyone have any better ideas then? Of course he realised that the Authorities would discover that Henderson was already dead when the car fire started! He knew that it might end up as a murder enquiry but so what! No-one would be able to pin this on anyone here in this car would they?

They would go into the part of the estate that the police did not even go into without full back up support and riot gear! They would set fire to the car and leave. The locals would not do a thing. They hated the police with a vengeance and a burning car was nothing new to them. It happens most nights on this part of the estate said Adam!

Adam smiled to himself as he remembered the looks on the faces of the others as he had said this! They had no idea just what sort of life he had escaped from and it would not do any of them any harm to have a little glimpse of what life could be like if you were born in the wrong place at the wrong time!

Chris had surprised Adam the most. He had wholeheartedly endorsed Adam's ideas. When he had voiced his approval the others had just stared at him for a long time.

Chris had also said that he believed that the army would get to know about Henderson's body being discovered because he would be in his Army uniform. (The thought of getting the body undressed and redressed into the uniform had made all the men queasy.) When the Army did find out about this they would do everything in their not inconsiderable powers to hush up the entire thing! They would not want any form of enquiry being undertaken. They had too much to lose didn't they! It was after Chris had said this that it was agreed to continue with Adam's plan. Chris knew more about how the Army worked and thought than any of the others didn't he! And if he felt it was going to be fine then the others would fall in with him!

As they made their way to Bristol all four men were lost in their own thoughts. When they eventually arrived in Bristol after hours on the motorway they were all exhausted but hyperactive at the same time!

Adam showed them somewhere where they could eat and told them that he was going to check up on one or two things and he would see them back here at the motel at 11pm.

No-one made any comment or put up any resistance to this suggestion. They were all too exhausted and nervous to put up a fight and so Adam left them and caught the bus into town!

As he walked anonymously around the city centre Adam was surprised that he did feel any connection with the city at all! Up until a few months ago this place had been his life. He had never ventured far from Bristol. He had never felt the need to before. He had honestly thought that his life would begin and end in Bristol and that he would prove all the Social Workers and the Authorities right by not amounting to much at all! He knew with absolute certainty and passion that he was going to prove all those bastards wrong. He was going to make something of himself.

When he walked past the bus station Adam remembered the fear and dread he had felt the last time he had been there. He had never felt so scared and alone he could now admit to himself. As he walked onto the bus that would take him back to the motel he did not look back at the city. Instead he looked forward to going back to Norfolk and his new life there! He had had regrets in his life before but he knew he was doing the right thing for himself for the first time in his short life and he felt good about it!

11.15p.m.

All four men walked silently to their vehicles and switched their engines on. Adam was in full control and all the others had a new found respect and admiration for the "hoodie" who had stood in front of them in the anonymous motel room a few minutes ago and described exactly what was about to happen. They were to follow his advice to the letter and no-one would get hurt! When he had said this all three of the men had looked at one another. Chris was used to this sort of thing because of his Army experience but the other two were out of their depth a little and so were more than a little grateful that Adam seemed so calm and in control!

As the cars went further onto the council estate it became obvious to everyone that they were entering another world! More and more of the streetlights were either not working or missing from the side of the road altogether!

Adam remained calm on the outside for the sake of the others in the car. Inside his head was a different thing altogether! He was frightened. He was back in his old hunting ground and he was not comfortable- he was not comfortable at all! What if he met someone from his past? What if he was recognized? What if? All these thoughts raced through his brain as he directed Chris towards the loneliest part of the estate. He knew that it was unlikely he would be recognised.

He knew it was unlikely that anyone would spend any time checking out the strange car in the area. Nevertheless he would be glad to be out of this place once and for all!

As they entered the darkest most remote area of the "ghetto" they found themselves in all the men focussed their attention on the job in hand. Apart from Chris the others had had no experience of this type of thing and they were all worried and concerned that they would all end up in prison for aiding and abetting a felony!

How the hell had this happened to them all?

What the bloody hell were they doing in the dead of night disposing of a dead body?

Did they really expect to get away with this?

What other options did they have?

As these thoughts troubled each man in differing ways Adam spoke. "Right Chris we are here! Switch off the engine and then we can discuss with the others just exactly what will happen next."

Robert and Gordon joined them in the Land Rover and all three men looked expectantly at Adam!

"O.k. Let's get on with this before we all lose our nerves right! You know what to do Robert don't you? Gordon, you and I will keep a look out and Chris and Robert will move the body into the hire car as we agreed. After that you and I will drive the hire car into that far corner and torch it! As soon as we know that it is burning we get out of here and join the others in the Land Rover and we get the hell out of here as soon as we can!"

Chris and Robert went to the back of the Land Rover and opened up the back. As they fumbled about in the dark Robert's hand touched Henderson's body. It took all of Robert's nerve not to run for his life! Chris noticed him shuddering and put an arm on his shoulder and gave him the briefest nod of encouragement.

Finally, after a great deal of pushing and shoving they managed to squash the body into the boot of the car. As they shut the boot down Robert flew to the bushes at the side of the road and was violently sick!

All four men then began to push the car into the corner. Gordon and Adam kept an eye out for any signs of activity. There was none! No-one it seemed came anywhere near this part of the estate and who could blame them thought Gordon. God! Was he scared? As they finished pushing the car all four of them were panting and gasping for air. It was not just the physical exertion that was making them gasp it was sheer terror to!

Adam put on the gloves he had got from the filling station they had called at on the journey down to Bristol. Thank God for filling stations providing these little touches. If only they knew just what their gesture meant to Adam and the others!

Adam began to pour petrol inside the car and all over the chassis. Gordon took one final look around them and then signalled for Adam to light the match! Robert and Chris, meanwhile, were back in the Land Rover but not a word had passed between them! They were both lost in their respective thoughts and concerns for the future. Adam moved slowly away from the hire car and continued to splash petrol along the ground taking care not to get any on his clothes! He did not want to go up in flames himself thank you very much!

Adam struck a match and with trembling hands lowered the flame towards the petrol on the floor. With a "whoosh" that startled Gordon and drew the attention of the others in the Land Rover the flame began its slow seductive dance towards the hire car and its gruesome contents! No going back now thought Adam.

Within seconds the flames were engulfing the outside of the car and soon they spread to the inside through the open passenger door. Everyone stared transfixed for several seconds until the first rumblings and sounds of breaking glass brought them all back to reality!

"Right Gordon let's get the f### out of here shall we?"

As they climbed back into the Land Rover the night was filled with a surreal orange glow as the car began to burn viciously.

Chris slammed the Land Rover into reverse and did a "u" turn in the road that sent a barrage of stones and debris flying into the air! No time now to worry about tyre prints thought Robert they needed to get out of here and fast!

As they left the estate behind the last memory for all of them was of the massive fireball that illuminated the sky behind them as the car exploded into an orgy of flame!

Without a word being spoken Chris drove the car out of the estate onto the bypass and straight home. Tonight was a night that no-one in the car or in the farmhouse would ever forget!

Chapter 42.

The sun was making another spectacular entrance into the world with a blaze of glorious techni-coloured hues bursting over the horizon. No-one in the car made any comment. It was doubtful if anyone in the car even noticed! They were almost home. Funny how they all thought, independently of each other, of the farmhouse as home!

As they turned into the courtyard they all relaxed a little and for the first time during the long journey home conversations started.

"Chris I don't know about you or the others but I am bloody knackered!" said Gordon. The others laughed and said that they all felt the same too and they couldn't wait to get in and have a cup of Pru's magical tea and some of her excellent bacon and eggs! With that pleasant thought whizzing around their heads it was a slightly more uplifted and trouble free party of shattered men that entered the kitchen and smelt the wonderful aromas emanating from the favourite room in the house- the kitchen!

Everyone was unusually animated around the dining table that morning! They all knew that today was not a normal day but they also knew that now was not the time for discussions about the last few days. Today was a day for catching up on all the things that had happened regarding Lauren and the baby! As Pru went into graphic detail of the horrors of childbirth that that poor girl had had to endure everyone laughed and teased each other about their new found responsibilities regarding the new arrival!

After they had all eaten a surprising amount of food the conversations turned to the itinerary for the rest of the day.

Vanessa had procured the orders for the village and it was agreed that today would be spent getting some semblance of normality back to the farmhouse. There was a lot to be done that day and so, despite their exhaustion everyone was secretly glad that they would all be incredibly busy for the rest of the day and there would be precious little time for thinking!

As everyone left to get on with their allotted duties Chris and Ronnie were left alone in the house together.

"How are you my Darling?" said Chris with obvious concern for Ronnie.

"I'm fine really Chris. Don't worry about me." Ronnie said. (Not quite as convincingly as she had hoped.)

"We need to talk. "

"I know my love- but not now eh! Later." Ronnie said with finality."We have masses to do and we don't have much time to do it all in do we?"

With that Chris sighed and nodded his agreement as they both went about their work duties. Time for talking later thought Chris.

Vanessa and Robert were hard at work sorting out the vegetable and flower orders to be taken into the village that morning. They worked in companionable silence for a little while until the silence became almost unbearable. Robert came up behind Vanessa and wound his arms gently around her waist and placed a gentle kiss on the back of her neck. Vanessa shuddered and melted into Robert as she turned to him with a strange look on her face.

"What is it Vanessa? Why are you looking at me like that?"

"I just can't believe the situations we have found ourselves in can you? All I do know is that, despite everything, I am so happy to have found you amongst all this"

Robert was astounded. He had wondered about the depths of feelings that Vanessa had for him and now here she was opening up her heart to him in the vegetable garden surrounded by potatoes , carrots etc! Hardly the stuff of romantic novels or movies was it? At that moment he did not care. He had fallen deeply in love with the beautiful woman standing in front of him and here she was smiling at him and telling him that, maybe, she felt the same!

Without another word Robert kissed Vanessa long and hard. That kiss was the defining moment in their relationship as far as he was concerned and he hoped that she understood the depths of his feelings for her as they finally parted gasping and giggling like two love struck teenagers!

They continued working all morning and kept exchanging long meaningful glances at each other. When all the orders had been arrange it was time for them to be delivered to the village. The Land Rover was fully laden and ready to go. Vanessa went inside to find Ronnie or Chris to tell them that they would both be going into the village together so that the orders could be delivered in double quick time and then they could both get back as quickly as they could. They both hoped that no-one would realise their ulterior motive in spending as much time together as they could!

As soon as Vanessa returned from speaking To Ronnie they both pled into the Land Rover and headed off to the village before anyone changed their minds!

Adam and Gordon were out in the fields digging and planting. It was back breaking work but neither of them was complaining. Gordon had relished the thought of hard physical labour this morning. He hoped that it would help to get rid of some of the nervous energy threatening to overwhelm him and he had been proved correct. At lunchtime he felt better and more alive than he had done for days. He enjoyed Adam's company far more than he had first thought he would do. That lad was a real surprise. Gordon had always prided himself on his ability to judge people. How wrong could he have been? Adam was intelligent and articulate. He was so enthusiastic about where his life was going to that his enthusiasm was infectious! Gordon realised that life was for living-especially after the events of the last few days!

 He hoped that he would, eventually, have a better relationship with his children and his new grandchild but meanwhile he was still alive and he was going to start living a little before it was too late!

He would always adore his beloved late wife but lately he had come to realise that although he might never get over the guilt he felt about the circumstance surrounding her death he was not the one who had died and he needed to live a little!" Was that selfish?" He wondered.

Maybe it was but the events of the last few days had taught him many things -not least that it was important to live your life as though each day was your last because one day it would be your last!

As they washed their hands before going in for lunch he knew that tonight he would go down to the local for a pint and he knew that he would flirt outrageously with Mavis the landlady! What harm could it do? And who knew where it might end? He had lived such a regimented life before he came here that now was the time to rid himself of the shackles he had bound himself with over the death of his wife and the trouble with his family. He felt excited and terrified in equal measure but My God! It felt good!

Adam had worked hard to all morning. He was shattered by the sheer physical work but he was also finally able to realise that he was free from all the restraints that living in Bristol had done to him. He was not thick! He was not stupid! He would show them all! No! He would not do anything to show them that he was not what they thought he was.

He would do it for himself!

He did not need to prove himself to anyone!

As that thought entered his head Adam smiled. He was doing something positive for himself for the first time in his life and he had not felt more alive and vibrant ever!

He could not wait to go back to Thetford and put his application in to go to College to learn all he could about the fascinating world of books and words! He loved words! They opened up a whole new world to him and he was thirsty and hungry for knowledge. He knew it would not be easy. He knew he would struggle at first but he also knew, without a shadow of a doubt, that he was doing the right thing for himself and he was raring to go!

Laura was shattered! Laura was in pain from childbirth! Laura was worried about the future!

Laura had never been happier!

She was the mother of a beautiful baby boy! Justin James – his name sounded so good to Lauren!

Justin James. She could not help saying it out loud and saying it to herself!

She was a mother. Oh My God!

As she lay on her bed at the hospital her thoughts turned, inevitably, to the future. She was not some naive new mum. She was wise beyond her years in many ways and yet she was still only a young single parent with no income and no real support mechanism in place.

She had had a visit from the Social Services Department only that morning. When the lady had introduced herself Laura had felt physically sick.

They were going to put her baby into care weren't they? They thought that she couldn't cope on her own didn't they?

After the Social Worker had left Laura felt a little more at ease. Jessica, her designated point of contact as she had referred to herself! , had spoken to her about all her options including adoption!

Laura had told Jessica in no uncertain terms that her beautiful baby Justin James would NEVER be put up for adoption as long as she still had breath in her body! Jessica had seemed both surprised and delighted at the vehemence behind Laura's statement and had been at pains to assure her that she would not be pressurised into any decision making and that if she decided to keep her baby then the local Authority would do what it could to help her. She must realise though that she was one of many single parents living in the area and funding was at an all time low!

Jessica promised to call at the farmhouse just as soon as Laura and Justin James had left the hospital and she could then help with any decisions that had been made!

Why did this not make Laura feel any better? Why did she feel that things were going to be taken out of her control?

Why did she feel like crying all the time? Where was Pru?

Right now she needed a true friend and Pru was nowhere to be seen!

Laura cried herself to sleep. When she woke she wondered just where she was at first and then the realisation dawned on her that she was in Hospital and she was a mum! She knew it would not be easy but she also knew that she had been through tougher times than this and survived!

Tomorrow was another day and with a bit of luck she would be out of here and heading home to the farmhouse. Home! Where was home? She had not had a real home for such a long time. She had had a lovely home with her lovely Dad but he was gone wasn't he? He would never know Justin James! He would never see him growing up would he?

Right! No more thoughts like that thank you! Laura mentally chastised herself for her "self pitying "thoughts. She was not a "whiner". She was a new mum with new responsibilities but right now all she wanted was a cuddle and a love from someone who would help her to cope! Just as the tears threatening to overwhelm her again a smiling face popped its head around the door and asked if it was alright to come in?

 Prunella Okenden was just who Laura needed to see right then and the tears changed from tears of despair to tears of joy and happiness! Pru wondered what the matter was and was Laura o.k. or was she in pain or was it little Justin James was he not well?

As she started to laugh and cry all at the same time Pru wondered, not for the first time, if having a child was worth all the stress and emotional trauma? Thank God she had never had a child she thought wistfully. She would never have made a good mother- would she? Too late now for all these silly thoughts old girl pull yourself together you silly old duffer! Justin James was beautiful! Justin James was going to be the most loved baby in the entire universe of that Pru was absolutely certain! He was adorable. His little fingers and toes were perfect. His little button nose was gorgeous! Good God woman! Get a grip will you! As Laura put him down after his feed Pru wondered if this was the right time for her to tell her about the plans she had put in motion regarding them all? When would be the right time for something like that thought Pru? Probably never- best just get on with it old girl and see how the fur might fly. Just as she was about to open her mouth in walks the Doctor on his rounds and Pru is asked to leave the room whilst Laura is examined! The cheek of that Doctor thought Pru does he not realise how important she is in the life of that young mother?

Anyway how the dickens is he qualified to be a Doctor he looks all of about 16 thought Pru as she leaves the room muttering under her breath! Well now wasn't the time obviously but soon the time would have to come and Pru was both excited and nervous in equal measure!

Ronnie was surprised to see Pru coming back into the waiting area so soon and it took all of Ronnie's not inconsiderable self control not to laugh at loud at Pru's indignation at being asked to leave the room by that young "whipper snapper" of a Doctor!

Ronnie had decided not to go straight into the room to see Laura as she was only too aware of the bond between the two women and she did not want to intrude. There would be plenty of time to be introduced to Justin James later. He was to be called Justin James and not just Justin thank you very much Pru had informed all the others at breakfast that morning. She and Laura had both agreed that Justin James was such a lovely sound that it would be unfair not to give him his full title at all times. Quite whether it was Laura's decision was debatable but Pru's obvious delight was infectious and no-one had dared to contradict her!

"Pru I'm sure the Doctor did not mean to dismiss you like that. I know that he must be busy with all the other patients here. Maybe, with a bit of luck, he will tell Laura that she can come home soon!

You know how busy Hospitals are these days. They need the beds .We might be able to take her and little Justin James home today what do you think eh?"

Pru was not so easily placated and her feathers were still a little ruffled when the nurse popped her head round and said that it was o.k. for them to go back in now as Doctor had finished with Laura!

"Finished indeed" muttered Pru as she bustled back into the side room where Laura was. Ronnie followed behind and was delighted to see Laura looking surprisingly well and smiling.

"Doctor says that I can go home as soon as I want to. Isn't that great? They just need to give him the once over and check that I am breast feeding him o.k. and then we can be off! Is that alright with you Ronnie? Do you have the time to wait? They have promised me faithfully that I should be no more than another hour. Will that be o.k.? Laura asked nervously.

" That will be just fine. Don't worry. We have all day if that is what it needs. Now let me have a look at this handsome young fellow I've heard so much about!"

As Ronnie gazed at Justin James and he gazed back at her Ronnie knew that the past few days were truly awful and the repercussions had not even started yet but she also knew that this little fellow being cradled in her arms was going to help everyone remember just what is important in this life!

What a responsibility young man! Thought Ronnie. I just hope you know just how important you are to all of us right now!

Justin James slept soundly in Ronnie's arms oblivious to everything around him. He looked contented and healthy. Long may he remain so thought Ronnie? She had never had the privilege of children herself but she hoped that Laura would prove to be a natural mother and that she would be able to lavish him with all the love and attention he needed .God knows it will be hard enough for her!

As she gazed into his peaceful face Ronnie felt an amazing rush of protective love engulf her, not only for the new life asleep in her arms but also for the young girl sitting beside her. Laura had had a difficult life up until now and Ronnie wanted to help her all she could, How could she help them both? How could anyone know what the future held for any of them after recent events?

As these thoughts troubled her Ronnie looked across at them both. Pru was fussing around Laura like the proverbial mother hen and Laura seemed to be enjoying the pampering and fussing. Maybe these two disparate people could actually make it work!

On the journey back to the farmhouse everyone talked about everything except the recent events! Time for long discussions later thought Ronnie as she turned the car into the driveway of the farmhouse and they all began to disembark from the car. It was just like a military operation mused Ronnie. Military! What an inappropriate choice of word thought Ronnie. It was the military that had gotten them all in this situation in the first place!

The rest of the day flew by. Everyone in the house seemed to have renewed energy and vigour. Chris realised it was probably the adrenalin kicking in and he hoped that when, inevitably, the euphoria died down that everyone was strong enough for the troubles ahead. Make no mistake thought Chris. Trouble was not going to be far away!

That evening the atmosphere in the farmhouse had changed. The farmhouse had always had the ability to capture people in its spell but tonight the aura surrounding all the occupants was one of calm serenity!

How could a house do this to people wondered Chris? He knew that both he and Ronnie had been transfixed by the house on their very first visit. Could the house be doing the same for all the others?

Don't be so stupid man! Thought Chris! It's just a house for goodness sake! What was the matter with him? Was he going soft?

The evening meal had been a roaring success. Pru had announced in her usual inimitable way that tonight the "boys" would be doing the cooking as the "girls" were busy with very important things! These being Lauren and the baby. Now, now everyone it is not the baby Pru reminded everyone it is Justin James!

The men folk did not dare suggest anything else and so they all dutifully worked together to produce a scrumptious meal of roast lamb and all the trimmings! It had been another gloriously hot day and it was not, perhaps, the most appropriate thing to be eating on such a balmy night but quite frankly no-one seemed to care!

Justin James had been fed and watered and was asleep in Laura's room. The baby monitor was installed in the dining room just behind Laura and Pru (of course) but he had settled down at least for the next few hours.

Laura seemed to be coping well and everyone breathed a sigh of relief at that.

Chris knew that the spell must be broken soon, but not just yet eh? Let's enjoy the evening a little longer.

Adam, meanwhile, had other ideas!

"Everybody, can I have your attention please? Thank you. I would just like to say a few words that I hope will not spoil the evening for everyone. These last few days have been a real roller coaster of emotions for everyone here and I think that we need to talk about the events of the last few days don't you?"

Gordon spoke next.

"Adam, I hope I speak for everyone when I say that without your help we would not have survived this ordeal but I do think that we should all enjoy this evening while we can. We will all speak tomorrow morning when we have all had a pleasant night enjoying each other's company. "

"Hear Hear!" Who might that be I wonder?

And so it was that everyone tried to relax and, despite the odds, a great time was had by all in the farmhouse that night. Laura bid them all a good night fairly soon after the meal finished. She could not drink as she was breast feeding Justin James and anyway she was shattered and so if nobody minded she would see them all in the morning!

Pru was about to go to her room at the same time but Vanessa asked her to stay downstairs for a little while longer and let Laura sort things out for herself! Everyone thought Pru would explode with righteous indignation but she surprised everyone, including herself, when she said that Vanessa was right and that she should let her do things for herself!

Vanessa wondered how she had had the courage to say such a thing to anyone and she knew that it was, in part, down to her experiences here at the farm but it was also because for the first time in her life she was truly happy and that was down to the handsome man sitting holding her hand secretly under the table!

Robert was holding her hand under the table and it was taking all her self control not to giggle out loud like a teenager and shout it out loud that she, Vanessa Floyd Wright was in love with the devastatingly handsome man seated to her left! Her grin must have been infectious because as she looked around her everyone else in the room seemed to be smiling their own secret smile!

Gordon was beaming like a Cheshire cat over something.

Adam was so animated in his manner and speech.

Pru was looking majestic and calm.

Ronnie looked at her most beautiful and serene.

Chris looked more relaxed and less ill at ease than he had done for a long time.

Robert!

Robert looked so handsome and so in love that it caught Vanessa's breath!

Was she worthy of him? Would she make him happy? Where would their lives together take them?

She did not know the answers to any of these questions. She did not have any answers to any questions right now but she did not care! She was blissfully happy and she hoped nothing would ever change.

The farmhouse kitchen positively glowed with the happy atmosphere created by everyone seated and it was very late that night when everyone said their final goodnights and" See you in the mornings!"

Chris and Ronnie cleared the debris of plates and empty glasses. A great deal of wine and spirits had been consumed that night with gay abandon but they both knew that it had been worth it. Everyone seemed to be in a better frame of mind to deal with whatever was going to be thrown at them. And they all knew that this was not over yet, in fact in many ways it was only just beginning!

Chapter 43.

The sound of a car entering the farmyard just after dawn the next morning did not wake Laura. She was feeding Justin James at her bedroom window seat. The early morning sunshine held a promise of another glorious day and Laura was going to take full advantage of it! Justin James had had a restless night and she hoped that he hadn't disturbed anyone else in the house! Laura had always loved the morning even as a little girl. There was something almost magical about early mornings before the rest of the world was up and about. She had always thought of this as her special time. She kidded herself as a child that she was the only person in the entire world and she could do anything she wanted to.

Laura looked across the farmyard with surprise and apprehension. Who was calling at this time of the morning? No-one usually came to the farmhouse anyway. Who could it be and what did they want?

The sound of the car did not wake Chris and Ronnie; however, it did disturb them! They knew who it was. Or more correctly they knew that it was the Army. They also knew that the Army would not be easily misled into thinking that Henderson had not been in contact with them. They also knew that the Army would talk to all of the others and they both hoped that everyone would have the necessary strength to deal with their questioning!

The cars crunched to a halt in the yard and several people got out of the car and walked purposefully into the kitchen. The door was never normally locked and this morning was no exception. By the time Chris and Ronnie had hurried downstairs their kitchen was overflowing with Army personnel!

Colonel John Burt stood impassively in the centre of the kitchen and looked around him. He had been to the farmhouse on several occasions and he had never really understood the nature of what went on in it. He was another career soldier who did not understand or appreciate the finer points of hypnosis or any of the other "therapies" that took place here. He was of the opinion that soldiers were real men and real men did not need cosseting. They needed to get a grip and get back to the job at hand which was fighting the enemy to the death if that is what it took! They knew this for God's sake when they signed up. Didn't they?

The other officers, less senior and in awe of Burt, stood silently to his side making certain that they were not the one who displeased Burt. A displeased Colonel Burt was not a pretty sight and they had all been on the wrong side of his infamous temper and no-one in the room was in any rush to repeat the experience thank you very much!

"Colonel Burt. This is a surprise! How can I help you so early in the morning? Do you want a tea or coffee perhaps?"

Chris did not salute Burt. He had no intention of bowing down to his superiority anymore! He was not in the Army and Colonel Burt held no authority over him anymore. So why was he sweating? Why was his hand shaking? Chris was glad that Colonel Burt did not attempt to shake his outstretched hand.

"We are not here for a social visit as I am sure you are perfectly aware! I think we need to get straight down to business don't you?"

"What business is that Colonel?" asked Chris with as much confidence in his voice as he could muster.

"Don't piss me off Gaskell. You know as well as I do the reason for my visit! Where the hell is Henderson?"

Chris was surprised at Burt.

He sounded annoyed and irritated but also worried and not a little frightened! What the hell had gone on in the Army since he and Ronnie had left?

"I'm sorry Colonel. I have no idea what you are talking about I assure you? If you mean Colonel Henderson then I cannot help you. I have not seen or heard of him since my wife and I came to live here in Norfolk. No, I tell a lie. We did speak to him a few times in the first few months of getting here regarding some of our initial visitors but I can assure you he has never been to the farmhouse! Why do you ask if I can be so bold?"

"Don't you take that tone with me you miserable little creep! We know Henderson must have been in touch with you. We also know that you and he go back a long way and must share some secrets regarding your Army careers that you might not want your darling wife to know about! Where is the lovely Veronica by the way? Still well and still beautiful I hope?"

Vanessa walked through the kitchen door. She looked amazing thought Chris. She had taken the time to dress and brush her hair. She looked in total control and not in the least nervous. How the hell does she do that? Wondered Chris not for the first time!

"Colonel Burt. We weren't expecting you. If we had known you were coming we would have organised a greeting party for you! As it is you'll just have to take us as you find us won't you?"

The venom behind the polite veneer was not lost on anyone in the room and Ronnie's status with the other Officers was significantly raised as they all stood open mouthed at the sight of this statuesque, beautiful intelligent woman smiling viciously at their boss!

"Still the same Veronica Gaskell I see!" smiled Colonel Burt with the same polite veneer.

There had never been any love lost between these two. Ronnie often wondered if Burt was responsible for the mutilation and torture of her best friend in Burma. She knew she would never be able to prove anything but the bitter resentment and hatred she felt for this odious man was coming to the surface with surprising speed.(Watch yourself Ronnie she thought. Do not let him get to you! Do not let him see how frightened you are! He will eat you alive for God's sake!)

"Please, gentlemen, take a seat either here in the kitchen or through into the lounge. Give us a few moments and we shall have some refreshments ready for you!"

"Like I said to Gaskell. We are not here for a social visit as I am sure you are both perfectly aware! We are here to speak with you about Henderson or as I suspect to speak with him in person! He is here isn't he? And don't bother to deny it. I will order the complete destruction of this entire farmhouse if I have to in order to find him! Do I make myself clear?"

"Perfectly Colonel Burt. You were always so clear with your instructions if I remember it right. And I do remember a great deal about our time serving with you in Burma Colonel!"

"Ronnie! Please take the other officers through to the lounge while I organize with Colonel Burt to talk in the study!"

A long moment passed as Chris and Ronnie exchanged looks. With a supreme effort Ronnie painted on her best hostess smile and turned to the other men crowding into her kitchen and asked them to follow her through if they didn't mind!

Chris walked towards the office and did not look back to see if Burt was following him. As he opened the door Burt pushed roughly passed him and scanned the room. Did he seriously think that Henderson was hiding in here? Burt was not his usual cruel efficient self thought Chris. Something was really bothering him and he did not know what it was just yet but he would do his best to find out!

"O.k. Gaskell. Cut the bloody crap. Where the f### is he? "

"Like I said just moments ago. I do not know where Henderson is! How would I? As far as I'm aware Colonel Henderson is still a serving officer in the British Army!"

"Don't you dare get smart with me? You ass hole. Where the hell is he? I will not be leaving here until I have spoken to him or found out exactly where he is! Do I make myself clear Gaskell?"

"Crystal clear Colonel Burt. I just hope you have the time to spare because, believe me, you are in for a long wait. A very long wait indeed!"

As the men continued to "discuss" Henderson with each other the rest of the household was beginning to rouse.

Lauren had decided to stay in her room and hope that Justin James would keep quiet! She did not really fully understand everything that had gone on. All she did know was that, right now, she was more than a little frightened!

Pru, meanwhile, was also preparing herself with the same steely determination that Ronnie had shown. She might be over 90 but, by God, she was not going to be intimidated by these thugs. Pru had been listening at the top of the stairs to the conversation between Burt and Ronnie. She had quickly picked up on the animosity between them both and so she had decided that she would do her utmost to show a united front. She took her time with her wardrobe and her toilette. She needed to create just the right air of confidence and grit.

She did not want them thinking that she was some little old biddy whom they could intimidate. It had been a very long time since she had been intimidated by the likes of these bully boys and she was determined that she would not be bullied at this time of her life!

Ronnie was just coming out of the lounge when Pru came down the stairs wearing the outfit she had worn when she travelled down here for the first time. Ronnie had almost forgotten just how smart and straight laced Pru had first appeared and she sent up a silent thank you to whoever was up there looking after her! Pru looked fabulous!

She looked like a school mistress who had swallowed a wasp! She looked as though she was a woman on a mission (which in many ways she was!).

Thank you mouthed Ronnie as she opened the door into the office and winked at Pru.

Mrs Prunella Okenden drew herself up to her full height and entered into the lion's den! God help the lions thought Pru. She was ready for battle if that is what it took.

"Gentlemen, my name is Mrs Prunella Okenden and I was just wondering what gives you the right to come barging in to my home at this ungodly hour disturbing my beauty sleep. I wish to speak to your Commanding Officer immediately! Chop chop young man. Don't keep me waiting!"

Colonel Burt was incandescent with rage! How dare some woman demand to see him immediately? Who the hell did she think she was anyway? Just wait until he got that soldier back to base. He would regret ever having disturbed Colonel John Burt. Oh! How he would regret it!

"Colonel Burt I presume? Thank you for taking the time to see me." Pru said in her most disarming way!

"I appreciate that you must have a job to do but I do object in the strongest possible way to being disturbed in such an ungentlemanly fashion at this ridiculous hour! Surely whatever it is you are here for could have waited until a more civilized hour?"

"Madam! Spluttered Colonel Burt, I do not need to explain myself to you or anyone else here! I am on official Army business with Mr Gaskell and I must respectfully ask you to leave!"

"Sir, I do not believe you know the meaning of respect let alone practice it! I will not be summarily dismissed in this fashion. I am not, thank heavens, one of your underlings and I thank you to keep a civil tongue in your head young man. I did not wish to have to say this, but say it I will.

I am a personal friend of the Chief of Staff of your regiment and believe me Sir Gerald Mainwaring or Gerry as I know him will be most displeased if I were to tell him of your disgraceful behaviour towards an elderly member of the public! Do I make myself clear young man? Well. Do I? Speak up my boy. Cat got your tongue eh?"

The young junior officer standing just behind Colonel Burt could not believe his eyes or ears! There was Colonel Burt who was the most frightening Officer in his regiment standing open mouthed and getting redder and redder in the face, never a good thing as he knew to his own misfortune, whilst this elderly lady tore a strip off him! Wow! Wait 'til he got back to barracks and told the others about this! They would never believe it!!

Chris found his voice at last.

"Pru, it's fine honestly. We are just going to have a chat regarding one of my old colleagues. Isn't that right Colonel? So! No need to worry. I'm sure that Ronnie would appreciate some help in the kitchen right now."

As Pru swept majestically out of the room she gave a surreptitious wink at Chris who nearly laughed out loud but just managed to contain him and covered his laughter with a fit of coughing!

That woman is truly amazing! Thought Chris, as he shut the door behind her and turned to face his old adversary once again. If he wanted a battle he could have a battle. Chris just hoped that they were all up to the challenge! Too late to worry about that right now though.

Adam, Robert and Gordon were all outside their bedrooms trying to listen to the conversations going on downstairs. Vanessa had joined them briefly but had then gone to Lauren's room to see if she could be of any help there. She also left strict instructions that- under no circumstances- was she to be left out of anything going on downstairs. If anything changed- anything at all- they were to come and fetch her immediately! Did they all understand?   Good. Then make sure they didn't forget. Right?

Adam broke the silence.

"What should we do now eh? Should we go down straight away or should we wait?"

"I think that we should go down straight away." said Robert decisively. "I think it might seem a bit suspicious if we look as though we are hiding away up here don't you think? After all we don't have a clue exactly who this Henderson character is. Do we?"

"Robert's right Adam." said Gordon quietly. "We need to go down straight away and show a united front. I'm sure Pru doesn't actually need our help but I'm sure she would be grateful for it don't you?"

And with that they went, as one, to fetch Vanessa, Laura and little Justin James.

Colonel Burt was more than a little surprised when he eventually came out of the office over an hour later to discover the farmhouse overrun with people! Who the bloody hell were these folks anyway? What the hell were they all doing here? Was that a baby in the corner? Dear God! This was going to be much more difficult than he had first imagined. His brief was to find Henderson as quickly as he could and ensure that he was taken back into the friendly bosom of the Army just as quickly as possible. For his own protection and comfort of course! His meeting with both Chris and Ronnie had been fruitless. Oh! He knew that they were both hiding something from him! He was absolutely certain of that. What he was not so certain of was what exactly was it they were hiding?

Colonel Burt was no fool. He knew a little about some of the work done here at the farmhouse but he had been completely unaware of the obvious sensitive nature of the work before he had been given the task of finding Henderson and finding him quickly!

Just what the hell went on here? He wondered.

Burt had been given 48 hours to find Henderson and bring him back. He had also been told that he was expected to complete the task as instructed or else there would be serious consequences not only for the Army as a whole but for him as a serving Officer with only a few more years before he could take his pension and retire! Burt recognized the not so subtle threat in that statement and he was a worried man. What if he did not find Henderson? What then? He needed the Army. It was his life. He had given his whole life to the Army and now they were threatening him with this! He needed the pension. He needed the status.

He was nothing without the Army. He would find Henderson if it was the last thing he ever did! As that thought struck home Colonel Burt shuddered involuntarily. Dear God! It might just be the last thing he ever did!!

Colonel Burt entered the kitchen to a cacophony of sounds. He drew himself up to his full height and, using his loudest Army voice, ordered silence!

What Burt got was not silence. What he got was Justin James screaming very loudly.

What he got was a group of VERY indignant people all talking at once and reminding him that there was a baby present thank you very much. And that, despite what he might think, they were not under his command and did not, therefore, have to obey his very rude request! (Which one of the houseguests said that I wonder?)

When, eventually, a degree of silence ensued Burt took stock of everyone in the room. As he stared at the others he was most surprised, and not a little disconcerted, to note that without exception all the houseguest were staring back at him. He was not used to being challenged in this subtle way and he was a little at a loss as to how to deal with it! During his Army career he had obeyed orders without question. He had given orders to be obeyed without question.

Now as he looked at the sea of faces before him he felt a little out of his depth.

He had interviewed Chris and Ronnie and he knew quite categorically that they were both hiding something! He could sense it with every fibre of his being. He knew this with utmost certainty but how the hell could he prove anything? He needed time to think! He needed time to revise his strategy! He needed time to…. ?

He had no time! He was under strict orders to bring Henderson back!

Colonel Burt mentally shook these thoughts and concerns away and focussed his attention on the disparate group of people he saw before him. He knew he had to find things out and fast.

 He made a decision.

"Ladies and Gentlemen I am sorry for creating such anger and distress and I do apologise to the young lady with the child for obviously upsetting the baby.

 I am here on urgent Army business and I will need to interview you all separately and so my Officers will remain with you at all times whilst I conduct individual interviews with all of you. You will be allowed to remain here in the farmhouse but you will not be allowed out into the fields or the village until my investigation is complete. Do I make myself clear?"

If Colonel Burt thought that the cacophony that greeted him earlier was loud he was ill prepared for the volume of sound that assailed his ears as he finished speaking! He was certain that the feisty old woman was going to physically attack him! The snooty posh sounding woman was screaming more abuse at him than a football hooligan! The Geordie chap was comforting the crying girl with the screaming baby and giving him looks enough to kill him on the spot. The bloke in his forties was shouting about this being inhuman and against the law and the thin, skinny "hoodie" was being held back by both Chris and Ronnie whilst he spat venomous words at all the Army personnel.

My God! Thought Burt! What had he unearthed? He knew that he was on the right track now because the vehemence of the attack belied their innocence! He could see that now. He smiled to himself and then he smiled his most cruel and sardonic smile as, slowly but surely, all the houseguests went quiet. When, finally, the noise subsides (apart from that wretched baby!)Burt stood up and signalled to one of his officers and left the room.

Right, thought Burt, if that's the way you want to play this then let battle commence!

Laura was ushered into the office first. It had been decided that she should be interviewed immediately as the baby needed to be fed and, as she was breast feeding, it seemed only polite and proper that she should have some privacy! (That bloody old woman is going to be trouble! Thought Burt!)

It became clear very quickly from his questioning of Laura that she would be of no help to his enquiry. She told him she had been in hospital for the last week due to complications before the birth.

"I can tell you all about it if you don't believe me?" said Laura flashing Burt one of her innocent smiles.

"That will not be necessary young lady thank you!" Burt had never been comfortable in the presence of women. He had been a "Man's man" all his life and he did not know the first thing about girls.

All he did know was that whenever he had tried to get himself a girlfriend it had always ended in a total disaster!

Colonel Burt was gay.

Colonel Burt did not believe, would not believe, that he was gay. He was a Soldier in Her Majesty's Army. He was all man. He was a fighter! He was not gay! HE WAS NOT GAY!

After Laura had left the office Burt called for Robert.

As he was interviewing Robert Burt had the distinct impression that he was watching someone who was well versed in what he was saying. It was almost as if Robert had had a script to remember. Burt discovered quite quickly that Robert was an actor by profession and this compounded his suspicions.

"So Mr Underwood let me see if I have got this right. You say that all of you have been working at the farm since the beginning of June this year and since that time there have been no visitors to the farmhouse at all apart from the postman? I find that very hard to believe Mr Underwood. No-one at all?"

"Colonel Burt it doesn't concern me that you find it hard to believe. You can believe what the hell you like for all I care! What concerns me is your attitude! Who the hell do you think you are coming in here and throwing your weight about. You might be used to doing that in the Army but we are not your soldiers. We are innocent civilians trying to get on with our lives and quite frankly the quicker we can all be interviewed the quicker you can be on your way, and the quicker life can get back to normal!"

"Mr Underwood I will tell you what I will tell all the others. I KNOW that you are all hiding something and, believe me; I am not leaving here until I find out just exactly what you are all hiding! Do I make myself abundantly clear?"

"Abundantly Colonel." And with that Robert stood up and left the room.

Burt was furious. How dare he leave until he had been told to? Who the hell do these people think they are?

Gordon was next and he gave an even harder time to Colonel Burt. Gordon wasted no time on pleasantries. He told Burt that he thought he was an arrogant bully who should sod off back under the stone from which he had just crawled!

How colonel Burt had not strangled him there and then with his bare hands he did not know but the interview with Gordon had lasted approximately 4 minutes!

Where had it all gone so wrong? How come he was not in charge here? How the hell was he going to find Henderson within the next 48 hours?

Vanessa strode purposefully into the room and Burt groaned inwardly. This interview was not going to end farcically like the others had he was certain of that and so Burt decided to change tack.

Colonel Burt smiled what he thought was his most enigmatic smile and approached Vanessa. Vanessa, meanwhile, wondered if the Colonel was feeling o.k. because he looked as though he was in pain and needed the toilet very quickly!

"My dear young lady, please take a seat. I do hope you have not been too inconvenienced by our sudden arrival? I am sure that this situation we find ourselves in can quickly be resolved to my satisfaction and my colleagues and I can leave you all in peace!"

"I must make one thing clear before we start Colonel Burt. I am not, nor ever will be as long as I have breath in my body, your dear young lady. I would rather die an agonising tortured death than be in the same room as you for any longer than is absolutely necessary! Do I make myself perfectly clear Colonel?"

It took a fraction of a second for Burt to fully comprehend just what had happened.

Vanessa had such a refined tone to her voice that, at first, it belied the vehemence behind the words. As Burt assimilated her statement the muscles at the side of his face began to twitch. His neck became redder and redder and Vanessa did actually think that he might just explode right there in front of her!

The interview proceeded to go downhill from there.

Vanessa's story bore an uncanny resemblance to what he had heard before but this only strengthened Burt's resolve to get to the bottom of this once and for all.

He called for Adam with a lot more confidence in his voice.

Adam's interview was an unmitigated disaster from the word go!

Adam was truculent, abusive, non-committal and all the other negative things Burt could think of.

Adam was his most disconcerting interviewee yet. Burt was not used to such levels of eye contact from people he "interviewed". Adam maintained complete eye contact throughout the entire 10 minutes he was with Burt. Burt found this unsettling and confusing to say the least. If his theory was right then Adam and all the others should be intimately examining either their shoes or the floor not staring challengingly at him!

As he watched Adam swagger out with that infuriating manner that all the youngsters have nowadays Burt thought, not for the first time; that a bit of National Service would not go amiss with the scumbag youth of today!

Mrs Prunella Okenden sailed into the office in her most regal manner.

Could this day get any worse thought Burt as he ushered her into a seat?

"I am quite capable of getting myself into a chair young man. Despite what you might think or hope I am not in my dotage yet!"

"Mrs Okenden I will not insult your intelligence by pretending that this interview will be an enjoyable experience for either of us. What I will say is, as I have to the others, I know without a shred of doubt that you have all colluded together to concoct this fairytale regarding your time here. What puzzles me, and makes me even more determined, is why you all feel the need to collude together in the first place?"

As he suspected the interview with Mrs Okenden did not reveal any further information but did reinforce his earlier suspicions that they had all agreed to say the same things to him. He KNEW they were all lying but he also knew that they were perfectly aware of his lack of authority over them. They were not under his command and he had no powers to force them to comply with his instructions.

Colonel Burt slumped into the chair with a resigned air and looked around the office he had commandeered from Gaskell.

It was furnished with an eye for function and not for comfort which surprised him a little. His first impressions of the house were ones of contentment and calm whereas this room exuded an air of melancholy and had a very definite feeling of doubt and uncertainty!

Stupid fool thought Burt , it's a room for God's sake. It cannot have a "feeling" about it! Pull yourself together man and get on with the job in hand !

As his eyes wandered around the room with its laden bookshelves his eye was caught by a gap in the otherwise pristine books. I wonder what book is missing from there - he wondered. He was just about to get up from the large armchair and investigate when the door opened and in walked Adam.

To say that Adam looked uncomfortable and ill at ease was an understatement of the highest magnitude! He positively squirmed with a strange mixture of embarrassment, annoyance and open hostility!

"So, young man. What are you doing sneaking about here then eh?" said Burt in what he hoped was his most authoritative voice. He needed to re-establish his, and the army's, authority if he was going to complete his mission in time and get out of here as quickly as he could. He never was able to fully understand or explain what he meant by this but he sensed that the house didn't like him here anymore than the people did! Now he really was being stupid!!

"I am not sneaking about , as you put it, I am merely returning a book that i borrowed from Chris and Ronnie! I hope that that meets with your approval......Sir?"

The open hostility and the challenge being thrown down at Burt by this young "thug" unsettled Burt even more and he vowed he would get out of here as quickly as he possibly could. He would not, however, be leaving empty handed! Oh no! He was now even more determined than at the start of this dreadful day to ensure that his Army career was not going to be jeopardised by these people!

When he returned triumphantly back to base with Henderson in tow he would be greeted as a returning hero and welcomed back into the Army with open arms. Back to the security of a routine, the security of rules and the security of knowing that the young soldiers under his command would never DARE to speak like this to him as this young layabout was doing!

"I am in charge from now on and this room is out of bounds to everyone, including the Gaskell's leave! DO I MAKE MYSELF CLEAR YOUNG MAN? Well do I?" Burt realised that he was shouting. He also realised that this cocky little piece of s### was smirking at him!

The menace in Burt's voice only served to heighten Adam's determination to ensure that the Army and this creep in particular would get nothing from him or from any of the other houseguests if he had anything to do with it!

Adam turned and, without a word, walked out of the room whistling. And left the door wide open!

Burt looked as though he might physically explode with righteous indignation right there and then. With a supreme effort he managed to stop himself from shouting out an order for that little s### to stand to attention and explain his blatant insubordination!!

Burt was breathing heavily as the telephone began to ring. As he listened to the voice on the other end barking out orders and threatening to personally deal with them all if they failed in this mission Burt felt the very real fear that this was not going to be his finest hour! In fact it could turn out to be one of his final hours in the Army if he didn't look out.

After he had replaced the receiver into its cradle Burt sat staring at it for several long minutes with his mind racing!

His commanding officer had just told him that a body had been found a few days ago. It was found in a burnt out car in a rough area of Bristol. The body had been burnt being recognition but a tiny scrap of material that had survived the inferno had been confirmed as coming from an Army uniform! The Coroner also confirmed that it was highly probable that the body had been moved from where the fatality had occurred. When Burt had asked how the Coroner had come to that conclusion he was aghast when told that the victim was already deceased BEFORE the petrol had exploded and turned the car into a raging inferno !

Burt was astounded to learn that the deceased had been strangled or hung before being placed in the boot! And, as the Coroner himself said, he had never known a dead man climb into the boot of a car and set fire to himself!!

As Burt was digesting this shocking information in another part of his brain a germ of an idea was beginning to grow.

The body had been found in a rough part of Bristol hadn't it?

A rough estate where lots of young men wear "hoodies", tracksuits and garish jewellery?

A rough estate were people talk with a particular accent and have no respect for authority?

Coincidence? No way thought Burt as the first flicker of a cruel, sardonic smile played at the corners of his thin hard mouth.

I've got you now, you little piece of s###! Now who's going to be so cocky when I've finished with them?

As Burt marched out of the office in search of Adam he did not notice that Laura was hiding outside the office door. Laura raced away in the opposite direction. She had to get to Adam first! She just had too!

Laura knew where to find Adam. She hoped with all of her heart that he would be hidden in the library. She had seen him go in there many times before and she had always respected his privacy. When Adam had admitted to them all about his reading difficulties Laura was even more determined to protect his privacy. But not any longer! She knew, instinctively, that he was in some sort of trouble and she also knew that she had to warn him that Burt was on the warpath looking for him.

Where the hell had he got to? Burt had been on the phone for less than five minutes and Adam had managed to disappear completely. He had ordered all his men to search the ground whilst he searched the house. During his search he had come across everyone in the house and been met with the same stony silence and open hostility. He knew that they were all hiding something. But what? What sort of hold did the Gaskell's have on these people? Why were they all sticking together? What did they have to hide? He knew a little of the type of work that went on in the farmhouse and , quite frankly, it scared him to death!

Messing with people's minds. Messing with people's emotions.

When, eventually , his men came back to say that Adam was not to be found anywhere Burt was at a loss as to what to do next when Adam walked into the kitchen with Laura who held his gaze with the same steely determination that that old biddy had shown!

Burt knew that the next few moments would be vital for the investigation. He had won every battle, however great or small, and he had no intention of letting this motley bunch defeat him. No Sir! No Sir indeed!

"Where the hell did you get to?" barked Burt.

"I went into the barn to help with the daily chores as I do every morning" smiled Adam benignly.

"So, you must have heard my Officers shouting for you? So why the bloody hell didn't you answer?"

"Language young man! You will not use foul language in the presence of ladies thank you very much!"(That bloody woman again! Thought Burt.)

Adam smiled at Pru and Burt wanted to smash his smug, arrogant face in right there and then. He would beat a confession out of him if that is what it took!

"I was listening to my i-pod with my earphones in. Sorry!" (Again that smug smile)

"Which part of Bristol do you come from?"

The question was asked deliberately out of the blue and Burt knew instantly that he was on the right track because Adam looked aghast and flustered for a while until he regained his composure.

"Pardon."

"You heard the question sonny."

"Oh! I'm sorry i didn't realise you were talking to me Officer. Well I live in the smartest part of town. Can't you tell by my cultured voice and my designer clothing? I am most hurt! Most hurt!"

The red mist was beginning to fall. Burt's fellow soldiers could see this. They had all been subject to his legendary verbal, and physical attacks.

One of the braver men stepped forward and spoke to Adam.

"Look lad, don't play silly buggers. Just answer the question eh?"

The telephone interrupted proceedings and Burt was furious, He had had the little sod. He knew he had him and now the little s### would have time to come up with some clever answer.

Ronnie entered the kitchen and, without a word or a glance at Burt, handed him the phone.

When Burt turned back to face the houseguests he had a look on his face that chilled everyone to the bone.

"That was my Commanding Officer. He informs me that I must go immediately to Bristol as there is something, or should I say someone, that might be very interesting and useful in my search for Henderson. The police have released a body into the loving care of the British Army!

The silence in the room was palpable but still nobody spoke! Colonel Burt spent an interminable time looking at all the houseguests before he smiled his cruel sardonic, sadistic smile as he saluted everyone in the room.

Ladies and Gentlemen I bid you good day!"

Burt marched to his car and, without a backward glance, drove away leaving behind a group of people who were now more terrified and frightened than they ever thought possible!

What would happen next?

Chapter 41.

As the sun rose by mid morning Laura was walking Justin James around the flower garden. He had had a good feed and was slowly losing the battle over sleep. He was such a contented baby thought Laura. I wish the rest of the house was a little more contented! She had not asked too many questions and she had received only sketchy half truths on the odd times she had probed a little deeper. She did not want to know all the details. It was enough to know that they were all in serious trouble!

Justin James finally admitted defeat and Laura breathed a sigh of relief. He would sleep for the next two hours if she was lucky. She needed time to herself but she also needed time to show her support for the others. The sun continued to bathe Laura in its pleasant warmth and before long she and Justin James were both fast asleep.

Meanwhile sleep was the last thing on the minds of the others who had gathered in the lounge after eating lunch in silence.

Vanessa and Robert had spent the morning working in the flower beds preparing the fresh flowers that were to be delivered the next day to the various businesses in the villages and town.

Adam and Gordon had into town on a flying visit just to ensure that their orders went out on time. It would not do to raise any sort of concern among the villagers. They did not need to know what the hell was going on up at the farmhouse!

As they all sat down together for the first time since the arrival of the odious Burt the atmosphere in the room was one of fevered excitement and fearful trepidation!

Chris was the first to speak.

"Thank you everyone for all that you have done for Ronnie and me this morning but this situation cannot be allowed to continue. Ronnie and I have put you all through enough already and we both want to say how much we appreciate everything you have done for us."

"Chris, stop there please." Said Gordon. "I know that I speak for everyone when I say that we all appreciate what you have done for us and none of us went into this with rose coloured glasses on. We made the decision to help you and we all stand by that decision. Don't we?"

Everyone murmured their approval of Gordon's speech and Adam was the next to stand up.

"That bastard Burt knows something I'm sure of that. What I am also certain of is that, despite what he thinks, he cannot prove a thing! All we need to do is to stay calm and stick to our stories. Is everyone o.k. with that?"

"I know that I speak for both myself and Vanessa when I say that we will do all we can to help you both. We are in this up to our necks anyway and that hateful man and the hateful Army will not get the better of us!" said Robert as he looked at Vanessa with such devotion that Pru had a lump in her throat!

"Hear! Hear! young man."

Pru had been unusually quiet at lunch but now the old sparkle was back in her eyes and you could have been forgiven for thinking that, despite everything, she was actually enjoying herself!

"Gordon and I had the chance for a chat during all the confusion when Adam went missing. By the way young man I must say that I for one thought you handled that overbearing bully very well!"

Pru's smile was one of such obvious delight that, despite the situation they found themselves in, they all agreed with her and they all smiled back at each other with total commitment for the future together.

Gordon spoke next. "I think we should all agree to continue with our stories. The Army cannot prove anything as Adam says. What can they do? They can't take us all into Army custody can they?"

Chris stood and faced his new found friends and co-conspirators.

"Ronnie and I have managed to destroy all the paper files with any slight connection to Henderson, however, we do not know if we have successfully deleted all the computer files. Neither of us are experts in computing and I am sure that, before long, they will send someone over who will hack into our systems and find something they can use against us!"

"We don't have time to worry about that now. We need to decide what we all do next." Vanessa had not uttered a sound during lunch. "How long before they identify Henderson's body do you think?"

"I think they will confirm it by his dental records either today or tomorrow. We don't know how long ago the body was discovered do we?" Ronnie stood and gazed at Chris. "They will be able to discover that he was dead before he was put in the car. What they cannot prove is how he got there in the first place."

"Well I think that what we should do is absolutely nothing! If we go around skulking in corners and whispering behind our hand then they will know we have something to hide. Don't you all agree?"

"Pru's right – as usual" smiled Robert. "What I think we should do is to try and act as normally as possible until Burt comes back, as I am sure he will, I know it's not going to be easy but what choice do we have?"

The afternoon sunshine was glorious and helped, in some small way, to lift everyone's spirits. The garden looked spectacular, the fruit and vegetables looked perfect and if anyone had happened to walk into the courtyard they could have been forgiven for thinking that they had stepped into heaven.

Or could it be hell?

The sound of Justin James crying had an effect on everyone at the farmhouse.

Gordon smiled to himself as he thought about his new, unborn, grandchild. He hoped he would have the opportunity to spoil the little one with tons of affection and a few presents too! He had not spoken to his family up North for a while, what with everything going on, and he felt this very real compulsion to contact them immediately. He decided that he would go into town this evening and renew his acquaintance with the delightful Mavis Riley landlady off the local hostelry!

What he needed right now was the company of a delightful woman. Someone he could flirt unashamedly with and someone who would flirt back! He was not much of a letter writer, even less of a wordsmith, but he knew that before he went out for the evening he would put pen to paper and write to both his children and tell them just how much he loved them and missed them and he would ask that they give him the chance to be the father and grandfather he needed to be! (I must be getting even softer in my old age you daft bugger said Gordon to himself.)He wondered whether his son and daughter would get together and come searching for him when they received their letters! He could just hear them now saying that Dad had finally lost the plot and he was obviously senile and needed looking after! He would take his time ensuring that the words were correct and that they both knew what they meant to him. He knew that if he got this wrong he could end up a lonely old man with a family that did not want to keep in touch! He had spoken to them once or twice since his arrival at "Haven's Retreat" but the atmosphere had been strained and unnatural for everyone. If he could just get the words right he was in with a chance! What it needed was a woman's touch. What it needed was his wife's touch. He would never stop loving his wife but he knew that he wanted to live. Did he have the courage to ask for Mavis' help in compiling the letter? What would she say? Where was their relationship going? - If you could call what they had a relationship. Don't be such a wimp! For God's sake! Be a man not a mouse!!!

Vanessa heard Justin James first. She and Robert were lying naked in bed together having disappeared like two naughty schoolchildren as soon as they could. They had given up pretending that they were just good friends. It had not fooled anyone.

As she lay staring at a still sleeping Robert she began to weep. Why was she crying? She had met a fabulous man. She was, in many ways, the happiest she had ever been. She knew that they could be in great danger still but she also knew that it was unlikely that the Army would be able to pin anything on them. So why was she crying? Even as she asked herself the question she knew the answer. She was jealous. She was jealous of Laura. She was jealous of Laura and Justin James.

 She wanted a child!

As she thought this she began to smile and weep and smile and weep until a very concerned and confused Robert woke up and tried to find out what the matter was. How could nothing be the matter? Why was she in tears and smiling if nothing was the matter? Robert had never really understood women and, after this little episode, he doubted that he ever would!

As he gently wiped away Vanessa's tears and reluctantly accepted the she was crying because she was happy it was Robert's turn to smile. He smiled as he watched her dressing hurriedly.

He smiled as he watched her telling him to stop grinning like a Cheshire cat and get a move on or else everyone in the house will know they have been doing! He had not smiled liked this in years. He doubted he had ever smiled like this in his entire life.

Robert Underwood was an out of work actor. He was an out of work failed actor. He had absolutely no idea what he was going to do for the rest of his life when they all finally left "Haven's Retreat" and he had never been happier! He wondered if he would ever stop grinning long enough to get himself dressed and downstairs in time for tea! Quite frankly he couldn't care less right now what anyone thought!!

Pru was only half asleep when she heard the crying! Who was crying? It was a baby's cry. For several moments Pru was at a loss. Where was she? Who was crying? As she slowly pulled herself together she remembered. She remembered the awful events of the past few days and she was frightened. She had not been feeling as well as she would have liked and, typically of her, she had not said a word to anyone! As she struggled out of bed she decided that she must get a grip of herself and pull herself together!!

She needed to telephone her Solicitor in Hove. She needed to know that her plans for the future were progressing. She knew that soon it would be time to leave this place and she did not want to leave here without knowing that everything was in order. She would ask Chris and Ronnie if she could use their telephone. She knew that they would not say no and she also knew that they would not ask awkward questions. She had to do this thing today. She had to do it immediately. She would feel better then surely?

Adam was in the Library. He had tried, without success, to read the classic novel he had begun before all the horrors of the last few days had taken place. As Justin James' crying became more and more insistent Adam realised that things had changed. They were no longer the same group of people that they had been only a matter of weeks ago. So much had changed that he knew, instinctively, that the time would come soon when they would all go their separate ways! He also knew that Colonel Henderson, Colonel Burt and the British Army had sullied this place for everyone. He hoped that the events of the last few days were behind them. Gone but not forgotten.

What would he do when he left? Would he be able to go to College as he hoped? Would he be locked away for the "crimes" he and the others had committed? (Don't even go there!)

Tomorrow, when he was in town delivering as normal, he would take the time to visit both the College and the local Housing Authority and check on his applications with both establishments. Nothing was going to get in the way of his future! Not if he could help it. As he left the Library he felt surprisingly optimistic! Maybe this was not the end of his new life. Maybe, just maybe, it was the beginning of his new life down in deepest darkest Norfolk!

Chris and Ronnie were in the office checking that no stone had been left unturned in their quest for the annihilation of Henderson and his cronies! Their lives were over here at "Haven's Retreat". They had not voiced this to each other. There had been no need. They both knew that they could not stay here now after everything that had happened. The place was never going to be the same again and whilst they had never walked away from anything in their lives before they both knew that it was over!!

Where would they go? What would they do with the rest of their lives? How would they survive with little or no income coming in? All these questions needed answers but not today. Today was about damage limitation. The Army would have only their suspicions. They would have no records or any minute detail linking them to Henderson

As Justin James' crying became ever more insistent Ronnie turned to look at Chris who was already staring at her and without a word needing to be spoken they embraced and held each other more tightly than they had ever done and together they looked around the office walked out and closed the door behind them! Tomorrow was another day!!

Chapter 45.

As the days past the atmosphere in the farmhouse began to return to some semblance of normality and routine. Justin James kept everyone on their toes with his demands. Everyone in the household assumed a role. Laura was a natural mother. She slipped seamlessly into her role and relished every moment. Pru was the doting grandmamma who was always on hand to offer advice however unwanted and unasked for it was! Justin James had numerous "aunties and uncles" all of whom delighted in looking after this happy, contented, soul. Adam was the one least comfortable in the routine that had begun. Adam needed to get away. Adam needed to stretch his wings and fly!!

The summer was beginning to turn inexorably to autumn and with it came the feeling that this incredible, exciting, frightening, exhilarating, life changing summer was at an end. No-one in the house seemed to want it to end. No-one voiced their concerns.

Every day, as he woke, Chris' thoughts turned to the Army and the events of the last few weeks. He had, surreptitiously at first, begun to browse the internet sites of the newspapers, radio and television stations surrounding Bristol. There had been a great deal of interest initially in the story. All the media had attempted to get the most salacious angle on the story. Everything from a cult murder of the military by a dissident group to a sex scandal involving Army personnel that was endemic in all aspects of military life! In the end all the Medias attentions had been fruitless and, eventually, the story had been relegated to a few lines in the more obscure parts of their publications until it had ceased to be high profile and another story of misery and degradation had taken centre stage!

After a few days of his surreptitious browsing Chris had admitted to everyone else his efforts and they had all agreed that if anything was going to happen then surely it would have happened by now?

Chris and Ronnie had agreed with this surmising in public. However they were not entirely convinced that it had, in fact, "gone away" as Pru put it. Both Ronnie and Chris doubted that the story was over.as far as they were concerned but they did not feel it wise or necessary to say as much to everyone in the farmhouse!

As the summer breathed its last the routine was comfortable and helpful to all who remained at "Haven's Retreat".

Gordon had gone to the pub that night, as he had said he was going to, and seemed more settled and at peace than he had done all the time he had been at the farmhouse. He had taken a lot of good natured ribbing from everyone when he had finally admitted his hopes and aspirations for his burgeoning relationship with the aforementioned Mavis Riley! He had blushed uncontrollably at first but now was stoic in his acceptance of the good natured and well meant teasing. He had received a reply to his letters from both his children within days of sending his initial letter. He had not fully discussed their contents but he had admitted that the tone of them had been one of tentative reconciliation.

He had also decided, but had not confided in anyone just yet, that he would remain in Norfolk as he felt more alive in the company of the delightful and beguiling Mavis than he had done in a very long time. He had explained some of this in his further letters to his estranged family and had arranged for them all to visit him in October when his children had some time owing from their respective jobs.

He would not admit, even to himself, how nervous he was a the prospect of meeting face to face with his erstwhile progeny. He knew it was going to be a difficult period of adjustment for everyone. He just hoped that they would see how happy he was and, given time, would come to accept that he wanted to start the next phase of his life here in Norfolk with the delightful and delicious Mavis Riley!!

Vanessa and Robert's relationship appeared to be running smoothly too. Vanessa and Gordon had long ago agreed to bury the hatchet regarding the unfortunate start they had had with their initial assumptions of each other.

Vanessa had not confided in Robert her desire to start a family. She felt that they needed to get to know each other better in the outside world, instead of this little cocoon they had created here at the farmhouse, and she hoped with every fibre of her being that once they got back to London things could only get better!!

Robert had also renewed a tentative relationship with both his mother and his brother. They had spoken briefly on the telephone where his mother had begun to demand where the devil had he been all summer and didn't he realise just how sensitive a creature she was. She had been out of her mind with worry all summer and so she hoped that once he came home and got all this silly nonsense out of his system she and his brother had arranged for him to have an interview at the call centre where his brother had gained a well deserved promotion. When, finally and exhaustingly, his mother had admitted defeat their relationship took a new direction. Instead of telling him what to do his mother was actually asking him what he intended to do with the rest of his life! Robert had been both astounded and wary of his mother at first but he had finally come to realise that she actually regarded him with more admiration for finally developing a backbone!! He had tentatively mentioned Vanessa's name in conversation and his mother, as he had expected she would, had latched onto this information like an "exocet" missile! He had managed to avoid agreeing to a date for his return into the loving bosom of his family but he knew he could not hold out for ever. When he had voiced his concerns to Vanessa she had been helpless with laughter! Not quite the reaction Robert had hoped for! When, finally, Vanessa had stopped giggling like an naughty schoolgirl, she had told him to step back and look at himself . Could he not see how he had changed? Could he not see what he had become? Was he not someone who had faced head on the British Army and the odious Colonel Burt and won? Surely he could handle his mother especially with his lover and girlfriend by his side to guide and support him? As the realisation dawned on Robert Underwood that Vanessa had described herself as his girlfriend and that she was willing to stand by him Robert's self esteem began to grow. So much so that everyone in the farmhouse remarked on it to each other. Everyone agreed that of all the people to arrive all those long weeks ago Robert had undergone a magnificent transformation and he should be proud of what he had achieved!

August ended as it had began in a blaze of glorious sunshine and azure skies. It was incredibly humid and Joseph James was finding it hard to cope with as was his exhausted mum!

 Laura had never known such complete and utter exhaustion! She was a natural Mother but she was still a girl in many ways and she was not coping with Justin James as well as she hoped. She confided her concerns to Ronnie who, in her usual efficient manner, organised for them both to see the local doctor. "Just to put your mind at rest dear!" said Pru giving Laura one of her best smiles.

The appointment was in town the next day and when Adam found this out he arranged for a lift into town in order that he could visit the local College to check up on his application for the new term which was starting in two weeks!

Adam was excited, nervous and daunted at the prospect of returning to education. He remembered all too well the horrors of his time at school! He had hated it with such a passion he wondered if he was doing the right thing in returning.

The next morning Chris took them all into town as he was making another delivery to the ebullient and difficult "Georges" at the French restaurant in town. Never a fun time at the best of times but Chris was determined that he "Georges" would not get the better of him this time and in a strange, perverse way Chris was looking forward to their meeting. The fruit and vegetables were of an excellent quality and not even "Georges" (real name Harry from Canterbury!) - could argue with that!

As Chris waved the two youngsters off and headed out to the restaurant he hoped that everything would turn out O.K for both of them. They had not had an easy start in life and they were both good kids they deserved a break!

Laura was laughing fit to burst as they left the Doctor's Surgery. Adam was helpless too. When they had gone into the Surgery the receptionist had assumed that Adam was Justin James' father and had wondered if he would like to go in to see the doctor with his "life partner" as she had referred to Laura. What had started Laura giggling she had later admitted was the look of abject horror written all over Adam's face. He had not known what to say and had, in fact, said that he was not the father thank you very much and he would not like to go in with Laura who was not his "life partner" and had never been thank you very much! The receptionist looked at Adam as though he was something nasty she had just trodden in and muttered something about the youth of today. Laura had found the whole thing hysterical and had continued to giggle to herself during Justin James' examination. The Doctor, who looked tired and irritable, had been efficiently professional when he told her that her exhaustion was only to be expected and that the child was suffering, as they all were, from the dreadful humidity. All she needed to do was to keep him as cool as she could and make sure he was not too de-hydrated!

Laura thought she had controlled her fit of the giggles until she saw the forlorn face of Adam. As soon as she clapped eyes on him the giggles had started in earnest and by the time they had staggered out of the Surgery they were helpless!

As they both brought their laughter under control the conversation had turned to the misunderstanding and Laura had been the first to broach the subject of Justin James' parentage.

Laura had been honest with Adam, to some degree, about her life before she came to "Haven's Retreat" and Adam had never appeared judgemental in any way. They both agreed that it was probably a perfectly reasonable assumption that two people of similar age wandering into the Surgery with a small child in tow would be "life partners". When Adam said "life partners" again they both collapse into hysteria again! "Bloody life partners" what the hell are they? Asked Adam as he wiped the tears away. "God save us from the oldies who think they know all the new and cool words." "Adam, she was only trying to be helpful." Exclaimed Laura as another laughing fit threatened to engulf them both again.

Right from their very first meeting both Laura and Adam, separately of course, had decided that they would always be good friends but there was never any chance of anything remotely romantic happening between them!

It had taken only a few days for the others to stop their teasing of the couple when it became obvious that they were more like brother and sister than boyfriend and girlfriend. "Boyfriend and girlfriend!" Adam had scoffed after Pru had first uttered that outdated saying. He had made fun of Pru behind her back until Laura had stepped in and defended her with vehemence. She reminded him that she was old and in her day that was what you called two people sleeping together!

The "romance", such as it was, never materialised and everyone in the house accepted their friendship for what it was. Just good friend. Friends for life without a doubt- but just good friends!

Laura took Justin James' to the local park whilst Adam went into College. When he caught up with her an hour later Laura remarked to herself that she had not seen him so animated and alive at the prospect of College and studying for a very long time and she hoped with all her heart that the events of the last few weeks were behind them all!

Chris had arrange to pick them up at 2p.m and so they had an hour to kill and so they decided to stay here in the park and feed the ducks and let Justin James enjoy the sunshine whilst they had their lunch. Laura joked that if anyone saw them together like this they would assume that they were a couple of youngsters who had got carried away and had had a child and were probably living in some grotty bedsit being paid for by the Social. "The youth of today." What were they like? As Laura looked across at Adam, whose face was a picture, she started to laugh and laugh and threw her arms around his neck and planted a smacker on his astonished lips.

When Adam began to kiss her back with a great deal of enthusiasm they both leapt apart as thought they had been electrocuted.

 Laura was the first too speak.

"What the hell just happened there Adam?"

"I honestly don't know. It just felt so right. I'm sorry I've made a complete fool of myself haven't I? Oh God! Why did I have to mess thing up eh?"

"Who said anything about you messing things up?" Laura said as she bent down to kiss him again."I can't promise you anything Adam, all I can do is say that I am as surprised as you how this has started. Surprised but not disappointed!"

As Adam realised what Laura might be saying he started to smile. Just a little smile played around the corners of his mouth and slowly, but surely, crept up his face until his whole countenance was beaming like the proverbial Cheshire cat!

Laura looked at Adam with trepidation. What the hell did she say that for? She had meant every word in the split second she had decided to utter the words but now she was terrified she had made a complete and utter fool of herself. As Adam's face contorted with a strange mix of emotions before her eyes Laura was convinced that she was about to be completely humiliated and she would lose one for her dearest friends into the bargain!

When Adam looked her in the eyes and she could see his smiling face her heart did a funny sort of jump right there and then and she wondered that maybe, just maybe, things might work out between them. Only time would tell. If anyone had indeed been watching the two of them as they fed the ducks in the park they would have been forgiven for assuming that they were indeed a young couple in the first flush of romance. Stranger things have happened at sea as the saying goes!!

Chapter 46.

As Chris pulled the Land Rover into the driveway of the farmhouse the good natured bantering between the three of them ceased in an instant!

As they all got quietly out of the car and walked towards the kitchen not a word passed between them.

Chris took a deep breath and opened the door.

Colonel John Burt was standing with his back to them as they entered the room and he took his time in turning round to face them all. Ronnie had a peculiar look on her face that Chris did not recognise. She looked worried, angry but the most troubling look on her face was one of defeat!

As he turned to look at them the expression on his face chilled them all.

 "Ah! Gaskell I was just telling your delightful wife that if you didn't arrive soon I might have to send out a search party! And that would never do would it?"

"What the hell do you want? You bastard." Chris had never liked this odious creep and he did not like him here in his house. Chris also realised that he was trembling as he said the words! (Don't let him see you tremble! You must not let him see that you are worried or that you have something to hide!)

"I want nothing from you. Yet." Said Burt as his gaze settled malevolently on Adam. "I need a quick chat with this young fellow if you don't mind? Young man I have with me a warrant for your arrest as a suspect in a homicide in Bristol. Although I am sure that you don't need me to tell you who the victim of the homicide is. Do I? You are to come with me right now and we are going for a little journey back to Bristol. You do remember Bristol don't you? The place where you were born and the place you were seen in only a few weeks ago? Ah I see that I have got all your attentions now haven't I? Why so guilty looking all of you if you have nothing to hide?"

Gordon, who had entered unseen into the kitchen, spoke first.

"You have no jurisdiction over this young man. He is not one of your unfortunate soldiers and so I suggest that if indeed he is needed for any sort of questioning, although I cannot think what he may have done, then you need to get the police here and issue a formal warrant from them! Do I make myself clear?" As he spoke the last few words Gordon began to move steadily toward Burt never once losing eye contact with him. When Gordon had finished speaking his face was less than an inch from Burt's.

When Colonel John Burt started to laugh he unnerved the entire company. The man was a maniac. He was a complete loony!

"I know why you are all so defensive I just cannot prove it yet. But prove it I will, mark my words. In the meantime I have already anticipated your reaction and I am pleased to tell you that I have indeed got a warrant for his arrest and it is in fact from the Police who are waiting outside in my car if things do get a little out of hand!

I assured him that the young man in question would volunteer himself if only to eliminate himself from our enquiries. After all if he is as innocent as he says he is what has he got to lose by accompanying me to Bristol?"

Adam looked around the sea of faces. Faces he had come to love and respect more than anyone in his entire life. Faces that showed dreadful concern for him. Faces that he could not bear to look at any longer. Adam drew himself up to his full height and, mustering every ounce of courage, looked Burt straight in the eyes as he replied.

"You know as well as I do that you have nothing on me. You cannot prove anything because there is nothing to prove. Nothing happened. If you want to waste valuable Army and Police resources taking me all the way to Bristol then be my guest.... Sir!" As he finished his speech Adam gave a salute. As his hand began to descend the salute turned into one of the two fingered variety. Everyone in the room laughed as Burt struggled to maintain any degree of composure and dignity. As the laughter rang around the room Burt lashed out at Adam who moved quickly out of his reach. The shouting and swearing that erupted with vehemence quickly brought the Police out of their car and within seconds the situation was once again under control. Only this time the Police Officer in charge made certain that everyone, especially Burt, knew who was now in charge of this situation. As the Officer read Adam his rights Laura began to cry and tremble. Pru, Vanessa and Robert came into the room just as Adam was being bundled into the car. They had been completely unaware that anything was going on as they had all been in various parts of the house or the outbuildings and had only realised something was amiss when they heard all the shouting!

Laura was inconsolable, Justin James was crying ,Pru just stood staring at the door where Adam had just left and Gordon, Chris and Ronnie were whispering together in the corner of the room!

Robert, meanwhile, had followed Adam out into the courtyard where he tried, unsuccessfully, to ascertain where they were taking him and how long would he be away and what exactly was he being charged with?

As the car turned around in the courtyard Adam's face was a mask of utter disbelief whilst Burt's was a study in divine retribution!

(I have you now you little shit. All I need from you now is a confession and I shall be back for the Gaskell's and not before time!)

As Robert watched the car speeding away he thought that for as long as he lived he would never be able to erase the image of that man's smiling, mocking and evil countenance. Robert shuddered involuntarily as he made his way slowly and dejectedly back into the farmhouse.

What the hell were they all going to do now? How the bloody hell were they going to get themselves out of this hole? They could all go to prison! Christ what a mess! What a bloody awful mess!!

Chapter 47.

The journey to Thetford Police station was interminable for Adam. His mind was racing in all sorts of crazy directions! One moment he was convinced that someone had seen him at Bristol and informed the police. The next moment he had convinced himself that no-one who lived on the estate where he had been had any time for the police or Authority in general! He could not have been seen and recognised surely?

As the car wound its way slowly through the traffic Adam made a conscious decision to avoid eye contact with Burt. Burt had insisted that he rode with Adam in the back of the car and the Officer in Charge had seen no obvious reason to deny his request, however, the Officer was feeling decidedly uncomfortable with the atmosphere in the car. Colonel Burt seemed to have an almost pathological desire for the demise of the young lad on his way to the Police station together with all the others at the farmhouse. Sergeant Benedict was far from convinced about the guilt of the young man sitting in complete silence in the back of his squad car. Benedict had been briefed on some of the details of the case but both he and his superiors had been told that this case was a matter of national security and therefore the Army would be conducting the cross examination of the young man in his care! What had the young lad done? He didn't look like your average master criminal but what did he know? All he did know was that he would be glad to get back to the relative quiet and calm of the local nick on a bust Saturday night! Not for him the bright lights and the inherent dangers of the big city thank you very much! All he did know was that he was glad he wasn't going to be on the receiving end of any interrogation by the psychopathic Army Officer sitting staring intently at his young victim. Why had he used the word victim? He was a suspect in a murder investigation! He was not a victim! Was he? Sergeant Benedict breathed an inward sigh of relief as the car turned into the secure car park of the Thetford Police station and he knew that in the next few minutes he could end his shift and go back to his wife and his three boisterous children. He never thought he would say that he mused but he was certain that his life, however hard, was infinitely preferable to either of the two men sitting tensely in his squad car!!

Adam was dumped unceremoniously into a police cell and told that someone would be along soon to talk to him. When Adam was left alone he looked at his surroundings and shuddered. Was this what his life had become? Was this how he would be spending the next twenty years of his life be like? Living like a caged animal with God knows who for company!

For the first time in many years Adam cried.

As Sergeant Benedict passed by the holding cell he heard, not for the first time and probably not for the last, the sounds of sobbing. Why did this particular lad's tears bother him so much? What was any of this to do with him? Pull yourself together man he said to himself. None of this is your problem, go home and do battle with your embittered wife and your ungrateful children. As the sound of Adam's sobbing decreased Sergeant Benedict squared his shoulders and headed home to resume his own battles. He must have done something really bad surely or why else was that crazy Colonel so hell bent on retribution?

The duty Solicitor assigned to Adam's case was efficient in his dealings with Adam but did not show any sympathy or understanding towards him.

He was here to do his job and he would do it to the best of his limited ability. Why had he decided that this was the career for him? Why didn't he just get a mundane nine to five job like the rest of his mates from school? How he hated his job!

After Adam had been advised of his right to remain silent Colonel Burt was allowed to interview Adam.

From the very beginning the duty Solicitor had his work cut out dealing with the ever increasing paranoia of Colonel Burt! After a particularly brutal round of questioning when Burt had almost struck his client the duty Solicitor had demanded, and received, a short respite in proceedings. As he re- read the notes he had hurriedly taken during the cross examination it became clear to everyone other that Burt that all the "evidence" he had against Adam was purely circumstantial and it would be impossible for any conviction to happen. What was the guy's problem? He had appeared almost manic in his desire to see Adam locked away for the rest of his life!

After two more hours of questioning the duty Solicitor informed Burt that unless he had concrete evidence to the contrary his client must be charged or released! As the duty Solicitor gathered up his papers and prepared to leave he could not get the image of Burt's contorted features out of his mind. That guy was deranged! He had spoken to the Sergeant just before he had clocked off for the day and they had both come to the same conclusion. This young lad might be guilty of some minor misdemeanour relating to drugs or stolen property or some such thing but there was no real evidence that this lad was linked in any way to the burnt out body of a soldier found in Bristol! O.K the lad was born in Bristol he had never denied that but was that sufficient reason for the brutal way he had been treated here in Thetford Police station? Neither the duty Solicitor or sergeant Benedict actually said it out loud but both of them wanted this young lad to be allowed his freedom. The evidence just did not add up and this Colonel Burt was such a maniac that even if the lad was a cold blooded murderer as was suggested by him there was a small part of both men who wanted him to walk just so that they could escape from Colonel Burt! British justice was, supposedly, the fairest in the world but right now it didn't seem like it to them. Never before had they secretly wished for someone to get off from a crime that had been committed but they would both make an exception in this case!!

Adam was released at 6.64p.m that night and the first thing he did was to get on his mobile 'phone and try to talk to Lauren. During his awful interrogation, where he had been more scared than at any time in his young life, his most pressing concern was getting back to Lauren and Justin James! As the interrogation dragged on Adam sensed the desperation in Burt and slowly and inexorably came to the conclusion that no matter what Burt thought and what Burt might suspect the evidence was so circumstantial that he would never be taken to court! As the realisation dawned that they might all have got away with the truly terrible thing they had all been a part of Adam's swagger began to return. He knew how much it riled Burt when he was a "Cocky little shit" as Burt called him on several occasions but Adam almost enjoyed the last few minutes of his ordeal when it became obvious that Burt had not enough evidence to charge him and so had no option but to let him go!!

The signal on his mobile was better here than at the farmhouse and he only hoped that Lauren's reception was just as good. How he needed to hear a friendly voice right now!

He spoke to Laura first, privately, and they both seemed tongue-tied but happy. He asked her if she would mind asking someone to pick him up and bring him home. Laura said she would get Chris on the 'phone and he could tell him where he needed to be fetched from. As he waited for Chris to come on the line Adam smiled to himself .Home! He had never really had a home before. He had lived in a house with his parents but he had never lived in a "home" before. It felt good just thinking these thoughts and so it was that a happy, smiling Adam crossed the road to get himself something to eat and did not see the Polish driver of an Articulated lorry run through a set of traffic lights.

As Chris put the 'phone to his ear the colour drained from his face. The sound of brakes squealing and the awful sound made by the lorry hitting Adam at 40m.p.h sickened him more than anything he had witnessed in the battlefield during his time in the Army.

He knew Adam was dead. He knew instinctively. He slumped to the floor and prayed like he had never prayed before!!

Chapter 48.

Wednesday 1st September 2010.

11 A.M.

Soham Tarney – Norfolk.

Wednesday 1st September 2010 was not a day to remember with any degree of affection. The grey overcast skies perfectly reflected the sombre mood felt by everyone as they gathered in the private function room of the local pub.

The last of the holiday makers were enjoying, or rather enduring, the best of the great British Summer!

The contrast from the gloriously sunny days of the previous summer was felt by everyone in the room.

This was the first time they had all been together since the dreadful events of the previous year.

As Gordon looked around the room he was glad that Mavis had added the feminine touches to the room. He would not have had the capacity to do the same.

Gordon had left the farmhouse the day after they had all driven to Bristol for the funeral.

God! What a day that had been!!

Adam's parents were bereft. They barely functioned during the whole terrible day. Adam's Aunty had had the unenviable task of formally identifying the body. Gordon remembered that Chris had pleaded with the authorities to do the identification himself. He had explained that, whilst he was not a relative, he knew who the lad was and he wanted to do this for his sake. He also explained that, as a former Padre in the Army, he was used to seeing terrible injuries on men. All this had proved to no avail. The Coroner patiently explained that whilst he sympathised with the situation his hands were tied. It was a legal requirement that a member of the family make the formal identification.

Chris met the Aunt at the train station and accompanied her into the room. Chris was grateful for the fact that Adam looked as though he was sleeping. The Coroner had confirmed that the victim had died instantaneously from the blow to the back of the head. He would not have felt a thing and from the reports of the eye witnesses the victim had probably never seen the lorry approaching! Chris sent up a silent prayer for the skill of the embalmer and undertakers. They had managed to swathe Adam's head in the shroud and so prevent anyone seeing the gaping hole in the back of his head where they had performed the autopsy. Chris had explained to both Gordon and Robert before the funeral but it had been decided that it would not be in the best interests of the ladies for them to know the true extent of Adam's injuries.

Gordon shuddered involuntarily as he recalled the first days back at the farmhouse after Adam had died. Laura seemed to shrink before their eyes as she went into full blown denial. She was cheery, she laughed and joked for three days until her resolve cracked and the crying started. Gordon knew how she felt in many ways. So many unanswered questions! So many regrets!

The terrible outpouring of grief from that young girl broke his heart. He heard her howling outside in the garden. He heard her crying herself to sleep night after night and he felt so impotent and useless!

Pru meanwhile had continued to astound him. That woman was a marvel. She took control of dealing with Justin James. She organised a rota for his feeds and his play time. She was an absolute trooper. Only after the funeral did she allow herself the luxury of tears. As she said to Gordon life was so unfair. Why had it not been her who had died? She had lived a full and long life. His was only just beginning! Pru could never and would never understand God. How could he allow this to happen? Pru spent many long moments with Chris over the first few days and, eventually, had to admit that whilst she did not have Chris' faith she had taken a great deal of comfort from speaking to him.

Vanessa and Robert took over the day to day deliveries from the farmhouse. Ronnie and Chris both agreed that, for the moment at least, they needed to stay at the farm and keep an eye on Lauren and the others.

After the funeral the life and light seemed to fade from them all and within three days of the funeral everyone was gone!

Gordon also recalled his feelings at that time. He had spoken at length to his son and daughter. He had told them how much he loved them. He told them how much he missed them and he told them that they must get on a train or a coach or in a car or even walk barefoot if necessary but they were to come down to Norfolk immediately and he was not taking no for an answer!

His children did as they were told and a very emotional meeting took place on the station platform as they all cried copious amounts of tears and nearly broke each other's ribs with the sheer force of their hugs! The euphoria had lasted longer than Gordon had expected. Slowly, however, questions were asked and some recriminations crept into the conversations. Gordon had been at pains to try to explain his actions but he knew it would take time and a great deal more talking between them all before things could get back to some degree of normality.

Gordon's children stayed at the local pub for a week and, at the end of those difficult but rewarding seven days, they all promised to keep in touch and try to see each other's point of view. Gordon had been worried that once his children got home things would slip back to what they had been before but to his intense joy and relief his kids had kept in touch and had even extended an invitation to come home and stay with them if he wanted to! Gordon had accepted in an instant and the experience had not been as difficult as he had imagined. They were still some way of from total peace and harmony but even his son had conceded that he had not seen his Dad so obviously happy in a very long time and wasn't it about time that he brought Mavis along with him on his next visit! At the memory of that conversation Gordon smiled to himself despite the sombre and sad reason for everyone gathering together.

Gordon had fallen in love!

No. Gordon had fallen hopelessly and deliriously in love!!

It all started at the time of the funeral. No –one had made any comments or teased him when he told them that he would be leaving the farmhouse and going to stay as a guest at the pub. They were all so caught up in dealing with their own grief and their own demons.

As he had stood in the foyer of the pub debating what to do Gordon almost laughed out loud. He had never been more grateful for the pep talk he gave himself that day. Don't be a bloody fool! Life is too short to mess about. Go in there and ask if she could put him up for a few days just until he sorted himself out.

Mavis had not asked questions. She was aware of the tragedy that had befallen the young lad staying at the farmhouse. Everyone in the tiny village knew about it. That was what happened here. She had welcomed Gordon with her usual good natured acceptance of other people's difficulties but she had secretly harboured a girlish pleasure in having a man about the house once again. She had also admitted to her best friend that she found Gordon very sexy and hoped that there was still life in the old dog yet!!

As the days turned to weeks and Gordon had still not moved out Mavis decided to take the bull by the horns and take their relationship to the next level. She and Betty, her only true confidante, had laughed fit to burst at Mavis' use of the modern parlance. Life and sex were not just for the young after all!

The seduction of Gordon by the voluptuous Mavis Riley had gone better than she had hoped. She had invited him to dine with her in her upstairs living quarters. It seemed such a shame that he had to sit night after night on a lonely table for one in the pub's dining room. Hadn't she a perfectly good apartment upstairs and, besides, she had not had anyone to cook for in ages and it would be her pleasure.

The next morning Mavis had watched a sleeping Gordon next to her and had smiled. He was a good man she knew that. She was a good woman too. To hell with the local gossip mongers. She knew she would be the subject of all their gossip for a few days until something juicier and more scandalous came along. And, just as she had predicted, that was exactly what had happened. Mavis Riley was held in great affection by her regulars and she could handle the good natured ribbing that she knew she would be on the receiving end of but could Gordon? Gordon rose to the challenge admirably. He had told her that he was worried for her. What would this do to her reputation and standing in the village? Mavis had roared with laughter. Her rich throaty laugh was one of the sexiest things about her according to Gordon and Mavis had said that her reputation could only improve when all the other single women knew she had bagged the best looking single man in the entire area!

As the months passed Gordon and Mavis became an unbeatable combination. Gordon found to his intense surprise that he thoroughly enjoyed the life as "mein host".

He was excellent at keeping a good cellar. He was an absolute godsend when it came to looking after all the little niggly jobs that Mavis had never got round to since she had been on her own.

Gordon had kept in touch with everyone from the farmhouse in the beginning but, as time went on, he found that he didn't need to be in constant touch any more. His new life here was enough for him now. As Gordon took once last look around the room before the others arrived he thanked God for giving him the courage to answer that advertisement in the newspaper.

Vanessa and Robert travelled from London the day before. They had decided that they would stay at a local hotel in Thetford that night which would allow them to travel the few miles back to Soham Tarney that morning.

As they dressed for the day Robert looked At Vanessa as she dried her hair in the mirror. God! She was gorgeous! Never a day went by when Robert did not thank his lucky stars for the way his life had turned out. He and Vanessa were to be married on New Year's Eve at the church in Richmond which was just a few miles away from their home. Robert had not realised just how wealthy Vanessa was! Her wealth had caused a few problems at first with their relationship until one night he and Vanessa had had an almighty row! Robert realised the next morning that it was his stupid male pride he was worried about. He told Vanessa that he was not comfortable being a kept man! God! That sounded so ridiculous now! Vanessa had cried Oh! How she had cried! After a few days of unbearable tension between them Robert had decided that this could not go on any longer. He loved her too much to see their relationship disintegrate like this. Vanessa listened patiently whilst Robert tried to explain how he felt. After he had finished Vanessa looked aghast. She said that she had had no idea he felt so strongly about this. She also went on to explain that she had never known love like she knew it with Robert. All the other people in her life had just accepted that she would be the one to foot the bill for everything. After all she had more than enough money. Didn't she?

As the dust settled on their first, and hopefully last, major row Vanessa came up with a plan. Robert had really enjoyed helping Adam learn to read and he had felt that this was the direction his life should take. Vanessa then said that, with his permission of course, she would like to invest some of her money in a business venture. Robert had had the good grace to listen as she outlined her plan and, despite himself, he thought the idea was wonderful.

Vanessa had suggested that she could be the backer behind starting a drama school for children in London. She suggested that Robert could start a Drama class as an after school project with the help of fully trained teaching and administrative staff of course. Robert could enrol at teacher training College in the mean time and become a fully fledged teacher if that is what he really wanted! Vanessa would be the silent partner who put up the original funding. Robert had said no to this idea immediately and so a compromise needed to be reached. Robert and Vanessa agreed that Vanessa's money would be a loan and not a gift. Robert and his staff would charge the parents an annual fee and would subsidise, wherever possible, children from less wealthy backgrounds. Under no circumstances was this to be charity as far as Robert was concerned.

He expected, and received, a written contract stipulating the terms of the loan and a repayment schedule. Only then did Robert agree to give it a go!

From the very beginning Robert's enthusiasm for the project knew no bounds. He had found a suitable building which had been converted to form a state of the art facility. He had organised the teaching staff and had run a very successful advertising campaign which had ensured that all the available places had been taken for the first term which was due to start next week!

At the thought of what was about to happen- Robert allowed himself a few moments of doubt. What the hell had he started? He knew that the teaching staff were good. He knew the admin. staff were good. Was he going to be any good? Only time would tell.

Vanessa had finished drying her hair and Robert was brought out of his reverie by the sound of Vanessa telling him to hurry up or they would both be late! As Robert and Vanessa left to travel to the pub both Pru and Laura were trying, desperately, to get ready!

Pru's health had not been great this last few months and the effort it had taken for her to travel to Norfolk was more than she cared to admit even to herself!

Pru just needed to get through this weekend and return to the comfort of her own home.

When they had left Norfolk for the last time just a year ago Pru had been in a state of nervous expectation as well as trepidation. What would Laura say about her plans? Would she go ahead with them? What would either of them do if Laura took offence at her suggestion that she and Justin James live with her in Hove just until she got herself sorted?

Laura had been astounded when Pru suggested it. She had been amazed at Pru's home in Hove. It was massive! There was plenty of room for them all to live their lives both together and apart as the need took them.

Laura had taken a great deal more persuading regarding the financial situation that Pru had set up. Pru told her that she had more money than she knew what to do with and she had no-one in the world to leave it to and she would be damned if the Government were to get any of it should she die without any relatives or beneficiaries! After much arguing and soul searching Laura had, very reluctantly, agreed to become Pru's housekeeper and companion. The generous salary afforded the post would ensure that Laura kept her pride and Pru got her own way!

As the days turned into weeks and then months it became clear to them both that they needed each other more than they would ever admit to! Laura was a natural mother and a true friend but, nevertheless, she found it difficult to accept her good fortune and, even now, was still uncomfortable with the arrangement.

The situation continued for several months until Pru's health began to deteriorate. Pru was admitted to hospital for tests and they confirmed what she had suspected for a long time.

Her heart was giving up and there was nothing that could be done for her because of her advanced age and all the other associated health risks with the elderly! When that young Doctor had said that to her Pru was incensed! How dare that young whippersnapper talk about her age like that? She might be over 90 but she was still young at heart thank you very much! As the news began to sink in Pru decided that she needed to have a heart to heart with Laura and sort this thing out once and for all!

Laura had sat for a long time staring into space after Pru had finished telling her what the Doctor had said. Pru began to wonder if the child had fully understood and was just about to ask her if she did in fact understand when she realised that the poor girl was in shock. The look of abject grief written all over her face had taken Pru's breath away and for several long moments neither woman could speak! Laura broke the silence first. "Why did you not tell me before how ill you were? How long have you been feeling like this? Surely there's something they can do? You can't die! You just can't!" As the words came tumbling out Pru could see the devastation written all over the young girls face! How Pru regretted not telling her sooner. She was not a child anymore – she was a young mother who had had a terrible life but had learnt how to cope wasn't she? Pru knew that she would be O.K when Pru was not around anymore but Laura could not, and would not, see this.

They had argued for the first time. Laura had told her that she was not a charity case and never would be and if Pru thought that then she did not know her at all. Perhaps it would be better if she and Justin James left?

Pru was horrified. How had this gone so horribly wrong? The poor child had misunderstood her intentions and now she had humiliated the one person in the world she held in the highest regard. What should she do? What could she do? Pru had spent the next few days persuading Laura to stay. Laura had eventually got over the shock news and took time to reflect. She loved Pru and she loved being here with her in Hove. She did not, however, like the idea that she was some poor soul in need of charity! In the end it was resolved by Pru's cleaning lady!

Marjorie had been cleaning for Pru on and off for over twenty years. She had been the cleaner both here in the house at Hove and in the residential home. Pru had, in her usual inimitable way, caused mayhem and offence at the home when she had told the management that she was unhappy with the cleanliness of her room there and she had arranged for her old cleaner to come in and give her room the once over to get it to the standards she expected which were higher than the present cleaners standards. When the dust finally settled on that particular argument Marjorie had become a regular part or Pru's life until she just vanished into thin air one day and headed off to Norfolk!!

Pru had contacted Marjorie prior to leaving Norfolk and heading back to Hove and she had instructed her Solicitors to organise a firm of professional cleaners, decorators, and electricians etc. to come to the large house in Hove and get it ready for her return! When they arrived back just over a year ago Marjorie had not said a word regarding Pru's guests. It was nothing to do with her or anyone else for that matter what Mrs. Prunella Okenden did with her life was it?

Marjorie liked Pru. Marjorie admired Pru. Marjorie secretly wished she was like Pru! So when she could see just what the situation was doing to both women she decided that now was as good a time as any to bang their heads together! Marjorie had arranged for Justin James to go and spend a few hours with her grandson who was just a few months older. That would ensure that the two of them had no distractions whilst they sorted themselves out! She would arrange for Pru to have her morning coffee as usual in the conservatory and she would make damned sure that Laura did not sneak off and avoid Pru like she had been doing for the last few days. Marjorie did not know the ins and outs of the situation all she did know was that both women were desperately unhappy and she for one was not going to sit back and do nothing! She would lock then in the room together if that is what it took!!

As it happened it was not necessary for anyone to be locked anywhere. As Marjorie left she took a quick peep into the conservatory and was relieved and delighted to see the two women hugging and weeping on each other's arms whilst both taking the blame for their stupidity, their pig headedness and their pride! As Marjorie quietly closed the front door behind her she permitted herself a wry smile! All these years working for a stubborn, opinionated woman like her friend Pru had finally paid off. She had turned the tables on Pru and she just hoped that she would be forgiven eventually. She knew that she would be in for a roasting when she came back to work the next day but she also knew that she would be fine. Hadn't Pru taught her everything she knew after all?

Laura took her time that day getting ready. She had been up very early that morning to ensure that Justin James was fed and dressed in order that she had the time to prepare herself.

She had chosen her outfit with great care. Today was about Adam. Adam who had been a true friend. Adam who had died too soon. As Laura looked at herself in the hotel bedroom mirror she reflected on her life so far. She had been a frightened girl then. Now as she surveyed her image reflected back at her she knew that she had changed. She was a mother to a fabulous little boy who would never know his father. She was more confident now than she had ever been. She also had a secret that she hoped to share with Adam. She knew, of course, that he was dead in the physical sense but he was very much alive in all their memories and she would find the time today to tell him her secret. She hoped he wouldn't mind. She knew he wouldn't mind.

Laura had registered Justin James' birth just 2 days after Adam's death and had, without anyone else's knowledge, put Adam's name down as the father of her baby! She hoped with all her heart that he would understand. He had known all about the circumstances of her pregnancy and, like the others, had not judged her harshly. She had spoken to him about the lack of father details on Justin James' birth certificate and Adam had joked that he would be glad to be registered as his father as long as she knew he was not in any position to keep up maintenance payments! She would tell him quietly that she would have been proud to have him as the registered father and she would tell Justin James all about the amazing friend she had met that glorious summer. Justin James would know that Adam was a very special part of their lives and he would never have to face the indignity and embarrassment of being a fatherless child! She and Pru had resolved their difference some little time ago and were now back to being best friends and confidantes.

Pru had told her that when she died she had left the house and a substantial trust fund for them both. Laura had looked at Pru when she had told her this and realised that the old lady really loved them both and, as she said, did not have anyone else who needed or deserved the money and security more than them. Anyway, she thought, Pru would probably out live them all. Wouldn't she?

Laura walked out of the hotel room and made her way purposefully across the hall to tell Pru to get a move on or they would both be late!

Pru, meanwhile, was sitting in quiet contemplation in her room. She knew that she did not have long for this world. Oh! The Doctor had told her she could last for quite a while yet but she was tired. Very tired! She had been determined to make this journey. She needed to see all the others one last time. She wanted, no needed, to know how everyone was. Were Robert and Vanessa still happy together? Had Gordon found peace with Mavis? Were Chris and Ronnie doing the right thing by going to the other side of the world and starting again? Pru knew that if she could just get through today, and get through she must, when her time came she would leave this earth with very few regrets which was something she should be proud of. How many people could say that about their lives she wondered?

The gentle tap on the door and Laura's smiling face peeping around it made Pru smile. She had found a true friend in Laura. She and the little one had made an old woman very happy at such a late stage in her life and for that she would be forever grateful. She just hoped that Lauren would not be too lonely once she had gone! Laura was young and pretty and deserved a better life than she had had so far. Maybe if God was listening he would answer one last prayer from a cantankerous old lady! You never know thought Pru. Stranger things have been known to happen!

The two women linked arms and painted a smile on their faces, held their heads high and went to celebrate the life of a very special young man!

Chris and Ronnie took one last look around the empty farmhouse. The removal people had taken all their things the previous day and all their worldly possession were , hopefully, heading for a cargo vessel bound for New Zealand !

As they walked holding hands through each of the empty rooms their thoughts were as one. They remembered the previous summer with all its conflicting emotions. They recalled all the previous summers they had spent at "Haven's Retreat" but none with the same intensity of emotions that recalling last year brought back to them.

In the weeks that followed the sudden departure of the others both Chris and Ronnie began to realise that whatever magic the house had once held for them had gone forever. What would they do with the rest of their lives they wondered separately? For the first time since they had met Chris and Ronnie were at a loss as to what to do for the best!

Chris had finally decided that both he and Ronnie should leave their home which, somehow, seemed tainted and dirty after last summer. When he eventually summoned up the courage to broach his feelings he had not been entirely surprised when Ronnie had said that at last he had got round to telling her what she had known for weeks!

 Chris had been very surprised, however, at Ronnie's next little revelation. She told him that she knew the day that Adam died was the beginning of the end for them here at "Haven's Retreat" and she also told him that she agreed that the farmhouse would never be the same for either of them again and she wanted them both to leave whilst the memories were not too tainted by resentment and frustration.

 With that in mind she had been looking around for somewhere else to live and she had found what she hoped would be the perfect spot! However, she had said, there was one possible problem. This fantastic new place was on the other side of the world!!

Chris thought that he could not love Ronnie anymore than he already did but on that day he realised that his love for her would never stop growing. He loved, adored, admired her with all his heart and so just 2 weeks after Adam's funeral they had packed suitcases and jetted off to New Zealand! They stayed for a month during which time they looked at properties to buy out there but had had no success. With just 3 days left of their holiday they were both feeling a little dejected and so had decided to go to the coast for a couple of days before heading back to England.

Picton is the gateway to the Sounds according to the brochures. As Chris and Ronnie disembarked from the ferry they both knew that this area was special. They could not, nor indeed needed to, put into words just what it was about this place that just felt right. Without a word passing between them they headed away from the tourist haunts and straight into town where they spent the entire 2 days looking at properties for sale. They found their ideal location at the end of their second day. The building was about the same size as "Haven's Retreat" but that was where the similarity ended. The view from the mountainside was breathtaking. The farm house itself was perfect. The rooms were just big enough. They had both decided, with that same unnerving ability to bypass mere words, that this was the place. They could live out here in comparative seclusion but still be close enough to civilization if they wanted to. The garden, or what would be the garden when Ronnie had finished it, would be perfect for their next adventure.

They could grow amazing vegetables and flowers for the local businesses and they could also grow herbs etc. to develop their idea of natural remedies for minor ailments.etc.

When Ronnie had tentatively spoken of her ideas to Chris she had wondered what his reaction would be. She was delighted when he was as enthusiastic as she was about it! Chris had eventually admitted to Ronnie that working with nature and spending time alone with her was just what he needed if he was ever going to regain his faith!!

Over the last year they had both been over to New Zealand several times to make absolutely certain that they were doing the right thing and each time they had to leave it became more and more difficult. The last time they had been there they had signed the papers to finally purchase their new home in Picton. Their new life was about to begin at their time of life! God moves in mysterious ways his wonders to perform thought Chris. Chris' faith had returned, slowly but surely, over the months following the tragedy that ended the summer. Ronnie had done her usual thing of keeping out of Chris' way as he wrestled with his conscience.

Ronnie did not share Chris' belief in God, however, she did pray to a greater being than herself in times of trouble so who's to say it wasn't God she was talking to after all? Chris and Ronnie had spent their last night at "Haven's Retreat" sleeping in the barn! All their furniture had gone and they were supposed to spend the night with Gordon and Mavis but had called to tell them a little white lie. Ronnie had been volunteered by Chris because, in his opinion, women were better liars than men! Chris had said that he was only joking as Ronnie was trying to remove his head from the rest of his body!

As they both collapsed with laughter they realised that that had been the most they had laughed in a year! Maybe time is the great healer after all said Chris. Ronnie had punched him playfully in the ribs and told him that time would need all the help it could get after she had finished with him! That night in the barn had reignited their love for each other and had restarted their uncanny ability to communicate without words. Both Chris and Ronnie had been worried that even their devotion to each other would not see them through this terrible time!

As they entered the kitchen they looked around and hugged each other tightly."Haven's Retreat" would always hold a special place in their hearts but now was the right time for them to leave and hand over the task of keeping the farmhouse alive to the next generation. The sound of a car pulling into the drive broke their reveries. The next generation had arrived!

Dr Gerald Carrington, his wife Elspeth and his two teenage children Thomas and Grace were to be the new owners of "Haven's Retreat". The farmhouse became theirs at noon and both Chris and Ronnie could not help but smile as they all piled out of their top of the range Audi amidst squeals of delight from Grace and grunting approval from Thomas.

Dr Gerald Carrington was a Cosmetic Surgeon at one of the top private hospitals in London and had fallen in love with the farmhouse when he had been surfing the net and saw the advertisement. After several conversations and a very brief trip by Gerry who admitted that, for the first time in his life, he had lied to his wife and told her that the conference he was attending in Norfolk was lasting one day longer than it really was! Gerry had fallen in love with the place instantly and he knew that Elspeth would feel the same.

He was so convinced of this that he arranged for a bank transfer of the deposit money within an hour of leaving the farmhouse that first day! Gerry had teased Elspeth all week by not telling her where they were going that weekend. It was a surprise and she must be patient!

When Elspeth saw the farmhouse she was enchanted by it and her enthusiasm for the purchase of said farmhouse knew no bounds and so it was just 8 weeks after seeing the property the Carrington's would be moving in. They had not quibbled about the asking price(both Chris and Ronnie were both staggered at just how much the farmhouse had been valued at!) they did not need a mortgage thank you very much- my husband is a very successful Doctor don't you know!

Elspeth had deliberately not allowed her precious children to see the place before they bought it. She was not wholly convinced that they would enjoy living out in the sticks.

She wasn't entirely sure herself if the truth be known but what a prize this place would be to show off to her friends. No- one else in their circle of friends could boast an 18th century farmhouse in their property portfolio could they? Besides they could still live in town if they wanted to. Hadn't she seen a delightful pied a terre in Chelsea which would be just divine!

After a brief conversation with the new owners and the exchanging of keys- both Chris and Ronnie climbed into their car. Without a backward glance, they headed off to the local pub to meet up with all their friends for the very last time in celebration of the life of their very dear friend Adam.

As the car pulled out of the farmhouse for the last time both Chris and Ronnie knew that this memorial would be the final time that they were all together and they both hoped that today would be a celebration of an unforgettable summer!

THE END........?

Printed in Great Britain
by Amazon.co.uk, Ltd.,
Marston Gate.